Heart Burn

THE FIRST FREAK HOUSE TRILOGY
#3

C.J. ARCHER

ISBN 978-0-9923761-0-9

Other books by C.J. Archer:

The Wrong Girl (The 1st Freak House Trilogy #1)

Playing With Fire (The 1st Freak House Trilogy #2)

The Medium (Emily Chambers Spirit Medium #1)

Possession (Emily Chambers Spirit Medium #2)

Evermore (Emily Chambers Spirit Medium #3)

Her Secret Desire (Lord Hawkesbury's Players #1)

Scandal's Mistress (Lord Hawkesbury's Players #2)

To Tempt The Devil (Lord Hawkesbury's Players #3)

Honor Bound (The Witchblade Chronicles #1)

Kiss Of Ash (The Witchblade Chronicles #2)

The Charmer (Assassins Guild #1)

The Rebel (Assassins Guild #2)

Redemption

Surrender

Courting His Countess

The Mercenary's Price

FOR

Samantha and Declan

My little shining lights.

CHAPTER 1

Frakingham House, Hertfordshire, December 1888

What young lady didn't love to attend balls? Particularly ones held in the glittering London residence of a nobleman?

This girl, that's who.

Ever since the invitation had come from our new friend, Mrs. Beaufort, I'd dreaded going. I'd never been to a ball, never attended a soiree, assembly or the theater. It's difficult to make your debut while locked in an attic. What made my anxiety worse was knowing that I didn't deserve to attend—I was a nobody with both feet firmly on the lowest rung of society's ladder. All the other guests would be so grand and important, like the Beauforts themselves. I kept sneaking peeks at the invitation to check whether it was a mistake, but there was my name in bold, sweeping strokes: Hannah Smith.

My friend, Sylvia Langley, was not so worried. She twirled around the entrance hall of Frakingham House, humming a tune she claimed was a waltz, but sounded more like a hive of angry bees. She'd tried teaching me the steps, but gave up after I stood on her toes for the fifth time. Dancing was not one of my talents.

I didn't mind sitting out while she practiced alone. I was too tired to put much effort into the activity, and it was pleasure enough watching Sylvia. She positively glowed with happiness, even when she'd tried to explain the etiquette of balls over and over to me. I simply couldn't remember half of the rules, but that was probably because my mind was elsewhere. One's pending death can be a distraction.

The heat inside me was slowly killing me, consuming my energy so that I was often exhausted and feverishly hot. Dancing certainly didn't help, which might explain why Sylvia didn't pressure me too much. I did wonder if she was in some sort of denial over my health as well as other horrible events that had occurred recently. She seemed too positive considering all that had passed in the last week.

Aside from learning that the compound injected into me as a baby was destroying me, two men had died on the estate, others injured and we'd killed not one but two demons. It was just like Sylvia to put all of that to the back of her mind and focus on something fun. She had a tendency to want her problems to magically disappear.

I couldn't blame her. I would have liked to forget it all too. Only I couldn't. Not when heat swirled through me like a fire and a madman named Reuben Tate wanted to abduct and experiment on me. He hadn't tried since the day we'd destroyed his demon assistant, Ham, but none of us at Frakingham assumed he'd given up. That's why I'd been confined to the house under the constant guard of Jack Langley. Jack had taken it upon himself to be my champion. I was rather pleased about it, to be honest. I liked being near him, talking to him, watching him.

It was *he* who'd been watching *me*, however. He stood in the arched doorway, one shoulder leaning against the frame, his arms crossed. He had the sort of face that made women look twice as he passed, and a physique built for power and speed.

The chiseled edges of his jaw and cheekbones were softened somewhat by the curved lips and dark lashes surrounding sea-green eyes. Usually those lips were set with determination, but now they smiled at me. Indeed, he looked relaxed, amused almost. He must have witnessed my attempts at dancing. How positively humiliating.

"How long have you been there?" I asked as he approached.

"Long enough to see how light you are on your feet."

"The bruises on Sylvia's toes would prove otherwise."

"She ought to keep them out of the way." He tilted his head to the side and frowned at his cousin. "What *is* she doing?"

"I'm dancing." Sylvia stopped in the center of the hall. Her full skirt swayed around her until it settled into perfect lines once more. Everything about Sylvia was perfect, from her golden hair and pretty face to her full bust and rim waist. She could be trying at times, and a little silly, but I enjoyed her company overall. "You are a philistine, Jack. Have you ever danced the waltz?"

"Have you ever seen me attend a ball?" he countered.

She tossed her blonde curls. "No."

"Well then, the conclusion would be that I've never danced the waltz. Which, I might add, you haven't either." He leaned closer to me, but we did not touch. We couldn't. We were both fire starters, and when our heat combined in passion, it became overwhelming. Intimacy led to sparks and a sensation within that I likened to my blood boiling. "I'm not sure she's the best teacher on the subject, Hannah."

"Better than you," Sylvia said, hand on hip.

I laughed. I enjoyed their teasing. It was never malicious. I knew they cared for one another as any true cousins would, despite it recently coming to light that they weren't related at all.

"If you've never been to a ball, Sylvia, how do you know all of these rules and dances?" I asked.

"I learned to waltz from a dancing master. As to the rules, the *Young Ladies Journal* has been a great source of information."

"You learned everything about balls from a periodical?" Jack scoffed.

"And my dancing master."

"I remember him. A small fellow with a false French accent."

"It was not false! Monsieur Bourgogne was from *Paris*," Sylvia said with a sniff.

"His accent was atrocious."

"Are you an expert on the French now? My my, haven't we come a long way from the gutters of London." She must have realized she'd spoken out of turn because she bit her lip.

Beside me, Jack seemed unfazed at the mention of his street urchin roots. He knew that it didn't bother me, and I was beginning to think it no longer bothered him like it used to. I liked that he'd accepted it as being a part of the man he'd become and not something that could be flicked off like an insect on the skin.

Sylvia signaled for him to join her. "I need a male partner."

"Perhaps Samuel can oblige," Jack said. "I'm busy."

"You are not. You're sitting there criticizing my dancing and poor Monsieur Bourgogne."

"Actually, I'm leaving."

"Oh?" I said. "Where are you going?"

"Into the village to see Mrs. Mott."

Mrs. Mott was the widow of the builder who'd recently died at the hands of a demon just outside the house. Although simply saying he died didn't convey the ghastliness of the situation. It would be more correct to say he was eaten. He and his colleagues had been working on the renovations to the house and uncovered a lost medieval dungeon from which the demon had emerged. Someone must have summoned it from the Otherworld, and since Mott had been closest to the dungeon and shown little fear or surprise, we assumed it had been him. He couldn't have done it without help, though. Not only did he bear us no grudge, but it was unlikely that he'd discovered how to summon a demon and gotten a hold of a cursed amulet himself. He must have had an associate, one with sound knowledge of demons.

Hopefully Mrs. Mott could tell us who. We'd decided to wait until the initial shock of his death had worn off before paying her a visit. We were in no hurry now that Jack had killed the demon. The amulet that had been used to summon it was also broken and useless, so it was unlikely Mott's accomplice would unleash another demon on us so soon.

The only urgency now was finding a cure for my condition. August Langley was working day and night. We'd hardly seen Sylvia's uncle or his assistant, Bollard, for days. Nor had we seen any sign of Reuben Tate, although I didn't think he'd given up trying to kidnap me. He was dying too, and dying people were desperate. I would know. I'd stood countless times outside Langley's door, trying to listen through the wood for any signs that the microbiologist was getting closer to discovering a cure. It took all my waning energy to not interrupt him every half hour.

"I'm coming with you," I said, standing.

Jack shook his head. "Stay here and rest."

"I need to get out of the house or I'll go mad."

"You *need* to rest."

Having a champion might be wonderful at times, but it could also be stifling. I adored Jack, and I knew he cared deeply for me, but my nerves were stretched to the limit. I supposed it was inevitable that I'd find confinement difficult after being released from the attic of Windamere Manor. I was like a jack-in-the-box toy. Once the lid opened and the jack released, stuffing him back inside the box wasn't the easiest of tasks.

"Jack," I said, trying for a gentle yet insistent voice similar to what I'd heard Samuel use when hypnotizing someone. "I need a distraction from..." I sighed and waved a hand at my body to get my point across.

He closed his eyes, and for a moment I worried that I'd taken it too far and only served to remind him of his troubles. I went to touch his arm, but withdrew my hand when it grew hot.

"Very well." He opened his eyes. They were filled with shadows that were there much too often of late. "You may come. Sylvia, I suppose you wish to come too as chaperone."

She gave an inelegant snort. "Don't be absurd. I've seen you two kissing in the lake. You're beyond worrying about appearances. Besides, it's cold outside."

I blushed to the tips of my ears. I should have guessed that she'd seen us. Jack and I had discovered we could touch each other in the freezing waters of the lake, although there was a limit to how...intimate we could get. Kissing was as far as we'd taken our relationship. I was well aware that propriety forbade even that, and I was surprised that Sylvia hadn't admonished us in her self-appointed role as my chaperone.

Then again, there were so few visitors to Frakingham that no one would see, and perhaps she thought a dying girl didn't have to follow the same rules as everybody else. It was certainly how I felt about the situation.

Jack winked at me. "We'll be all the poorer for your lack of company, Syl."

"Don't tease me, or I'll come just to spite you," she said. "Now wouldn't that put a dent in your plans to whisper sweet sentiments in Hannah's ear?"

He ignored her and turned to me. "Ready, Hannah?"

I rose just as Tommy the footman walked in carrying a vase of flowers with one hand. He set them down on the marble-topped table near the door and was about to walk out again when I spoke.

"Good morning, Tommy. How's your head?"

He touched the lump on his forehead. It had diminished in size, and the color wasn't quite so purple, but it still looked angry. He'd acquired the lump and a sore arm from Ham when he attempted to stop the demon from kidnapping me. "Much better, thank you, Miss Smith."

I rolled my eyes at him but did not tell him to call me Hannah like I used to do. I'd discovered that even though Tommy and Jack's friendship went back several years, he kept up a formal facade when he was in the presence of anyone else in the household. I'd tried on numerous occasions to get him to address me by my given name, but had failed every time.

"I have an idea," Jack said, a mischievous twinkle in his eyes. "Syl, why not practice your dancing with Tommy? You did say you needed a male partner."

"Don't be absurd." She screwed up her nose. "He's a servant." Sylvia might be sweet most of the time, but she was of the belief that servants and their employers shouldn't mix, nor should the staff have an opinion or a thought that didn't center around their duties. She and her uncle agreed on this.

"I'm quite sure that doesn't mean he can't dance," Jack said, brows raised at his friend in question.

"I can dance," Tommy said somewhat apologetically.

"The waltz?" Sylvia asked.

Tommy shook his head and rubbed his sore arm, as if that were the reason for his lack of dancing ability. Of course a man like Tommy wouldn't know how to waltz. Like Jack, he would never have had the opportunity to learn.

Sylvia tilted her chin, apparently oblivious to his discomfort. "Samuel will know how to dance with a lady."

"I'll fetch him," Tommy said quickly. He left before anyone could stop him.

Sylvia sucked in her lower lip and blinked after him.

"Do you have to be so cutting?" Jack scolded her. "He's protected you on more than one occasion. He deserves some respect."

Her blinking became more rapid and for a brief moment, I thought she was going to cry. Then the shadows passed from her eyes, and she thrust out that regal chin of hers even more. "He knows I appreciate his efforts in that regard."

"Does he?" Jack muttered.

"My opinion stands, however. He does not know how to waltz. Samuel does. I don't see how telling the truth can be construed as disrespectful."

"We'd better go," I said before Jack could berate her further and make the situation worse.

***

We traveled by coach to Harborough, driven by the new driver who'd replaced the deceased Olsen. Jack rode opposite me in the cabin, our knees close by not touching. We wore hats and gloves despite not needing them with our internal fires to keep us warm. It would have looked strange to the villagers to see us out in the depths of winter without them. We wanted to keep knowledge of our supernatural abilities confined to members of the household. It was bad enough that the Harborough residents called Frakingham 'Freak House' because of Langley's disability and Bollard's muteness. We didn't want to give them any more reasons to be wary of us. We'd managed to convince them that the recent deaths had been caused by wild dogs, but it had not lessened their distrust of us. Indeed, we'd found it difficult to get the servants to return to work until Jack had increased their salaries.

"Will you go swimming with me later?" he asked.

"I don't know if I should. We were spotted yesterday."

"Don't worry about Mrs. Moore," he said, referring to the housekeeper. "She's very discreet. That's why August likes her."

"Yes, but how long will it be until someone else sees? Someone less discreet."

Some of the good humor left his eyes, revealing the turbulence that I was more familiar with. "Are you...?" He swallowed. "Are you regretting our liaisons in the lake?"

"Not at all." I leaned forward. My fingers itched to touch him, but I held back. I would have to convince him with words. "I regret nothing. I know some consider our kisses shameful, but I do not. I look forward to meeting you in the lake more than anything."

8

His chest expanded with his deep breath. He stared back at me, his intense gaze seeing all the way through to my soul. The corners of his lips inched up in a small, relieved smile.

"I'm mindful of maintaining a sense of propriety," I said to fill the thick silence. "It's important to Sylvia and Langley. I don't want to give him any cause to send me away." Not only would I have nowhere to go, but I was dependent upon him to find a cure. I was dependent upon him for a great many things.

"He wouldn't do that," Jack said, but he nodded in understanding. I knew he wouldn't pressure me. "Hannah, if things were different, if you and I could touch, I would take you—"

"Don't, Jack. Please." I held up my hands for him to stop. "Not now."

Whether he was about to say he would take me as his wife or lover, I didn't want to know. Our future together could be wonderful. I knew that with deep certainty, but I had doubts as to whether I had a future at all. Making plans only saddened me, and I didn't want to spend what few weeks I had left wallowing in self-pity. I wanted to live my life as best as I could in the time I had left, and regret nothing when the end came.

"Perhaps we could go to the lake at night," I said, pushing my melancholy thoughts away.

He smiled, but it didn't reach his eyes. My dislike of discussing the future bothered him. Many times he'd wanted to make plans together, as if a cure was a certainty. But Langley had given us no such hope. I couldn't pretend, so I tried to ignore the future all together.

"I'd like that," he said. "Like it very much."

"Tonight then." I looked out the window and realized we'd slowed for the approach into Harborough. The shops along High Street came into view. Few people were out in the freezing cold. The small shops huddled together for warmth and company beneath the gray, cheerless sky. I scanned the area for Reuben Tate, but saw no sign of him.

Not that I expected to. He knew he could not abduct me while Jack was near. Tate was much too weak.

We turned a few corners and finally stopped outside a row of cottages with no front porches or yards. They were all joined together under a single roof, the brickwork a little crooked in places as if they'd been quickly laid. They seemed deserted, but perhaps that was because everybody was either elsewhere or inside. Younger children would be at school, husbands and older children at work and wives in the kitchen.

We knocked and waited. I was afraid Mrs. Mott wouldn't answer. She might be in a state of despair, or perhaps not home, although there was also the chance that she'd seen our arrival and wasn't answering. Some of the villagers avoided us at all costs, preferring to cross the muddy road than pass by the residents of Freak House.

Eventually the door opened, and I was relieved to see that she was neither terrified of us nor in the depths of despair. I'd been impressed by her composure at Mr. Mott's funeral. Her face had been stoic, her posture upright as she comforted her children. I did wonder if her lack of tears stemmed more from an acceptance of the hardship of her life rather than bravery.

The Motts were a part of that class that Sylvia did her best to ignore. They lived cheek by jowl in the cottages, wore ragged clothes, and scratched out a living in whatever way they could. I was suddenly very glad Jack had set Mrs. Mott up with an annuity until she remarried. Since her husband's death had occurred at Frakingham while he was employed to restore it, Jack felt somewhat responsible.

"Miss Smith! Mr. Langley! What a surprise." Mrs. Mott gave us a sad smile and opened the door wider. She was a tiny woman of indeterminate middle age. The bones in her face were sharp, the skin stretched tightly over cheeks and jaw. Small but pronounced wrinkles underscored her eyes. She seemed genuinely pleased to see us. Perhaps that was because Jack, as manager of August Langley's estate, was now her benefactor.

"Come in out of the cold before you catch your..." She swallowed, and her eyes dulled. "Well, come in."

She accepted the basket of pies, preserves and canned soup I'd brought with profuse thanks and led us to the front room. A fire burned in the grate, throwing out enough heat to make me feel like I was suffocating in the small parlor. A chair sat close to the hearth, a piece of brown woolen fabric on the seat and a sewing basket on the floor beside it. Mrs. Mott scooped up the fabric, but not before I saw it was a pair of men's trousers that she was shortening.

"Are your children at school, Mrs. Mott?" I'd seen the three children at the funeral, two lanky boys in their teens and a young girl. It had torn my heart as they'd watched their father's coffin descend into his grave. The girl and one of the boys had cried, but the older one did not. The modified trousers were probably for him, having belonged to his father.

"Aye, they are."

Jack and I sat in the only two other chairs in the bare room and Mrs. Mott sat in the one beside the fire. She self-consciously tucked her dark brown hair under her cap and smiled uncertainly at us.

"Would you like tea?" she asked.

"No thank you," Jack said. "This is a quick visit. We're sorry to disturb you at this time, but we wanted to express once again how sorry we are for your loss."

"Thank you." She blushed a little at Jack's sympathetic smile.

He didn't often show his gentler side, but when he did, I was reminded of just how charming he could be when he tried. With his dark good looks and bright green eyes, he was achingly handsome. It was no wonder Mrs. Mott blushed when all he did was give her his full attention.

"Do you have everything you need?" I asked her. "Is there anything we can do for you and your children?" I wasn't sure what to say. I'd already given her my sympathies on the loss of her husband at the funeral, but I still felt awkward sitting in her house mere days after his death. I wasn't sure of the etiquette for bereavement. Should I have brought flowers instead of the food? I wished I'd asked Sylvia before we left.

"That's kind of you, Miss Smith, and I thank you." She turned adoring eyes on Jack. "But Mr. Langley has already done so much for me and the children. I don't know where we'd be without his generosity."

"I'll pass your gratitude on to my uncle," Jack said.

Mrs. Mott's smile slipped a little, although mine broadened. I covered it discreetly with my hand. I knew the annuity had been all Jack's idea, and that he'd implemented it too. August was probably not even aware of it, although it was his money. It was just like Jack to downplay his own role and let someone else receive the gratitude.

"Right then," Mrs. Mott said. She rubbed her dry, cracked hands together and blew on them. "Sorry it's a mite cold in here. I'll add some more coal."

"Not on our account," I said. "We're warm enough."

"I insist," Mrs. Mott said, pouring coal from the scuttle onto the fire. "Don't know why I was savin' it anyway. We've got coal to last us through the winter and into spring. Mr. Mott saw to that just before he died." She set the scuttle back down and sat again.

That was something at least. I felt relieved knowing the family would be comfortable despite the icy temperatures.

"Mrs. Mott," Jack began, "we need to ask you something regarding your husband's recent behavior."

"Oh?"

"Was he acting any differently in the weeks before he died?"

Her bottom lip protruded as she thought. "In what way?"

"Did he become friendly with anyone new, for example? Anyone not from Harborough?"

She shook her head. "The only time he left the village was to work on Freak— I mean Frakin'ham House." She made an elaborate show of tucking her hair under her cap again, avoiding our gazes.

"How about new acquaintances *in* Harborough?" I asked.

"I couldn't say, Miss Smith. He might have met someone down at the Lion. That's the Red Lion, on High Street. Mr. Mott drank there twice a week, sometimes more. If he met anyone new, it would have been there."

I sighed, unable to hide my disappointment. We would have to traipse down to the Red Lion and ask more questions of the proprietor. It wasn't that I didn't want to. It was more that weariness was beginning to pull at me. Not that I would tell Jack. He would insist on returning home, and I didn't want to waste the opportunity of learning more.

"Thank you, Mrs. Mott," Jack said, rising. "You've been most helpful."

Mrs. Mott tucked her hair away again, although it looked neat enough to me. "It's good of you to visit me, Mr. Langley. You and Miss Smith. But, forgive me, why are you askin' about my husband's friends? Did he do somethin' wrong?"

"No," I said quickly. I didn't want her to know about the terrible thing her husband had unleashed up at the house. For one thing, she might think us mad, and for another, he probably didn't fully understand what he was doing. It was best that she remembered her husband fondly. What was done was done, and he'd paid a terrible price for his actions.

"Mr. Mott mentioned that he was doing some work for another builder," Jack said, lying through his teeth. "The plans sounded impressive, and I wanted to see them. I have an interest in architecture. That's all." He gave her a smile.

She smiled back, but it soon turned into a frown. "Well, that would explain the coal."

"Pardon?" Jack and I said together.

She waved a hand at the full coal scuttle. "He came home with sacks full of coal about two weeks ago. He shared it with our neighbors, and so pleased they were too. Another building job, you say?" Her frown disappeared, and she looked relieved. "Thank the lord. I don't mind tellin' you both now that I worried where the coal came from. Mr. Mott has always provided for this family, but I knew him well enough to know his work weren't always honest." She pressed a hand to her chest. "I am mighty relieved to hear you speak of another proper job. He must have been paid already."

"So you don't know who that employer may have been? Did Mr. Mott mention anything about another job to you?"

"I think I do recall somethin' like that." Her smile was quite false, and I didn't believe she'd suddenly remembered something important. Her reluctance to tell us earlier was understandable. If her husband had indeed gotten the coal by illegal means, she would have had to give it back. She might be an honest woman, but she was a widow with three children. Who could blame her for being cautious? At least now she was telling the truth.

"Oh?" I prompted. "Did Mr. Mott give you a name for the other builder?"

"Not a person's name," she said. "He just spoke of 'the Society.'"

Good lord. Surely not. The only society I knew was the Society For Supernatural Activity, a group that Langley and Tate had once belonged to. They had interests in all things paranormal and would certainly know how to summon demons.

"Does that mean anything to you?" Mrs. Mott asked.

"Not really," Jack said idly, without meeting Mrs. Mott's gaze. He had obviously made the same connection I did.

We said our goodbyes and thanked her. I waved at her from the carriage window and didn't turn to Jack until she was gone from view.

"Well," I said, settling back in the leather seat. "How do you think Mr. Mott came to be involved with the Society?"

Jack's finger skimmed across his top lip as he thought. "More importantly," he said, "*why* was the Society paying Mott to summon a demon onto Frakingham?"

CHAPTER 2

Jack insisted that I eat luncheon in my bedroom and nap afterward. I grumbled half-heartedly, but obliged. I awoke two hours later a little more refreshed. The internal heat still raged, however. I was always warm now, unless I took a dip in the ice-cold lake. Rest helped, but I refused to lie down any more than necessary. Time was too precious to waste it sleeping.

I found Sylvia downstairs in the drawing room. She was staring out the window, her lips plumped into a pout. I followed her gaze and saw Jack and Samuel standing off to the side, surveying the scaffolding frame that covered part of the house like an external skeleton. No work had been done on the renovations since the builders had run off in fear at the first sign of the demon a week earlier.

"Is something the matter?" I asked, standing beside her. "It's not falling down, is it?"

"Good lord, I hope not." She turned away with a sigh. "They're discussing what's to be done next. Jack is not having much luck enticing the builders back."

"Not even with extra wages?"

"Some, yes, but not enough. He and Samuel are considering whether to offer them more money or get others in from further away."

"People who aren't afraid of Freak House you mean," I said wryly. "He didn't tell me he was having difficulty finding builders."

"He's trying to spare you the mundane details of day-to-day life."

"I wish he wouldn't. There are so few things to focus on aside from…aside from Tate and the cure, that any detail, no matter how minute, is a welcome distraction."

She took my hand and squeezed it. "I'll be sure to tell you everything about my day from now on. Shall we start with what I ate for luncheon?"

"That's quite unnecessary," I said quickly. "Let's discuss your dancing practice instead. Was Samuel a capable dancer?"

"Oh yes. Not quite up to Monsieur Bourgogne's standard, but very good. I'm sure I improved. I wouldn't expect anything less from a gentleman though."

I refrained from rolling my eyes, but only just. "I'm sure he'll be very popular at the ball if that's the case. Indeed, if you have any interest in him at all, you may want to secure him before then." I watched her closely for any signs of infatuation.

She burst out laughing. "Don't be ridiculous. The man can hypnotize people with mere words. I want a husband I can wrap around *my* little finger, not the other way round, thank you."

I giggled, relieved. I was quite sure Samuel had no interest in Sylvia, but I was a little worried that she was beginning to like him in that way. He was, after all, very handsome and charming. Thank goodness I'd been wrong. They would have made a terribly unsuitable couple.

"It's nice that he's taking such an interest in the house," I said, watching the men. "He's certainly made himself at home here."

"Why wouldn't he?" She sat down with a flounce on the sofa, her skirts billowing before settling around her. "He's living here for free."

"I don't think money is an issue. His family is wealthy." His family also didn't know he was at Frakingham. He'd let that piece of news slip some time ago but never explained why he'd not told them. Nor was I completely satisfied with his explanation for being at the house at all. He'd claimed to be studying us as some sort of experiment on cognitive processes and behavior. Perhaps it was the truth. Perhaps it had nothing to do with his ability to hypnotize and more to do with his neuroscience interests. He had been a student of the subject before he'd left University College and come to Frakingham.

A more interesting question for me, however, was why was August Langley allowing him to stay?

"At least he and Jack seem to be getting along now," I said. Jack hadn't warmed to Samuel at first. Not until Samuel had risked his own life to save us. Since then, they'd become friends.

"He no longer sees Samuel as a rival." Sylvia pulled her sewing out of her basket and inspected her stitching.

"A rival? Over me?" I laughed. "He never was."

"Jack thought differently, believe me, particularly when Uncle continued to push you and Samuel together."

"At least he's stopped doing that."

Sylvia pressed her lips into a disapproving line. "He's been very busy and distracted. I wouldn't assume that he's given up entirely."

August Langley was full of mysteries, but his desire to keep Jack and I apart was the one that bothered me the most. Why didn't he want us to be together? The only explanation I could come up with was that I wasn't good enough for Jack. He might not be Langley's true nephew, but Langley certainly treated him as if he was. He also had a deep desire to be seen as an important man, hence the reason a mere microbiologist had settled his family in a magnificent house as soon as he could afford it. The daughter of working-class people would not figure into his grand plans for Jack.

There was no use dwelling on such knotty problems now. The future was too uncertain and Langley not very present of late anyway. Whatever his faults, he'd thrown himself into discovering a cure for me, and I was grateful beyond words. If he did find a cure and repaying him meant leaving Jack forever, I didn't know what I would choose to do.

I sat beside Sylvia and watched her stitching until I couldn't stand the tedium any longer. "I'm going out to see what Jack and Samuel have decided about the builders."

"Why bother?" she said heavily. "No matter where the builders come from, the house won't be finished for some time. We'll have to cancel."

"Cancel what?"

"The Christmas dinner party of course. The grand dining room is in the damaged wing, and we can't have guests rolling up to a house that resembles a spider's web." She set down her sewing and sniffed. "It's *so* ugly, and I'm terribly disappointed. It was to be our first dinner party here. My first as hostess."

She'd invited three other couples to dine with us two days before Christmas. I knew it was important to her, but I'd forgotten all about it, what with the chaotic events of the last two weeks. Clearly she hadn't.

I circled her shoulders with my arm and hugged her. "There'll be more opportunities in the new year. Next time we won't send out invitations until we know the house is absolutely finished. Besides, it's probably for the best with the Beauforts' ball taking place soon. We'll be much too distracted to give our full attention to the dinner."

Her face lifted at the mention of the ball. "At least that's something to look forward to. I cannot wait to go to London with you and Jack tomorrow."

"Tomorrow? But the ball isn't for another week."

Jack and Samuel walked in looking a little windblown from the wintry breeze. Samuel rubbed his hands and stood facing the fire. Jack smiled at me.

"You're awake," he said, coming to stand beside me. He rested his hand on the back of the sofa and crouched at my side. "How do you feel?"

"Fine," I said cheerfully. There was no point telling him I felt tired and hot. It would only make him melancholy with worry. "Sylvia says we're going to London tomorrow."

"Only if you're up to it. I need to go, and I can't leave you here." He was switching to his protector role again. I welcomed it. There was no knowing when Reuben Tate would attempt to take me again, and with his abilities, Jack was the best person to stop him. Besides, I didn't want to be too far away from him for long periods. I missed him.

"Why do you need to go to London at all?" I asked. "Has this got something to do with Mott's link to the Society For Supernatural Activity?"

He nodded. "I want to speak to someone about it, preferably a member. The Beauforts or Mr. Culvert may know of somebody."

The Beauforts and Mr. George Culvert were not only our friends, but also experts on demons and other supernatural phenomena. They didn't belong to the Society, but they were aware of it.

"Langley doesn't have any contacts anymore?" I asked.

"He claims not to." Jack stood. "Sylvia and Samuel insist on coming too."

"Wonderful. The more company, the better."

Samuel smiled, flashing his boyish dimples. They made him even more handsome, something that I suspected he knew. "I'd like to meet some members of this Society too. Someone may know something about my...talent for hypnosis."

"Oh? I had no idea you were curious about it." Indeed, he seemed as comfortable with his ability as Jack was with his fire starting. Samuel had hinted that in the past he'd used it for dishonorable reasons, but I was quite certain he now only hypnotized people when absolutely necessary. He was born with the ability to put someone in a trance with nothing more than his melodic voice and penetrating gaze. Other hypnotists needed to train in the art and required objects as focal points. Even then they weren't always successful.

"My curiosity was piqued when we learned that you were hypnotized by a member of the Society as a child," he told me. "Ever since then I've been curious about the man who did it. I think he must be like me and naturally gifted rather than learned in the art of hypnosis. It was certainly a powerful trance he put you in."

The hypnotist, a gentleman named Myer, had hypnotized me when I was in the care of Lord Wade. He had not only made me fall asleep when I emitted fire, but also forget the entire episode. The hypnosis had been lifted by my extreme anger, fueled by something August Langley had said.

"We'll have a grand time on Bond Street, Hannah," Sylvia said. Her eyes sparkled with enthusiasm. "We ought to look for ribbons and pins to dress our hair for the ball. And I need a new pair of gloves."

"There will be little time for shopping," Jack said.

"A 'little time' is long enough. Speaking of the ball, Mrs. Irwin is coming this afternoon for a final adjustment. Do try to be awake, Hannah."

Mrs. Irwin was the finest dressmaker in Haborough. Sylvia had wanted to commission a London *modiste* to make our ball gowns, but there'd been no time. Mrs. Irwin had to do.

"You may regret bringing the ladies," Samuel muttered to Jack.

Sylvia gave him a withering glare. I don't know how I could have thought she had an interest in him. The more I watched them together, the more I realized they behaved like brother and sister.

"The time for shopping will be very short," Jack said. "Particularly since Hannah shouldn't be exerting herself."

"Hannah is perfectly capable of inspecting ribbons," Sylvia retorted.

I arched my eyebrows at her. "Hannah is perfectly capable of speaking for herself. I'll go and pack now. Sylvia, will you help me?"

We were about to leave the drawing room when the rumble of wheels rolling down the corridor stopped us. We stood to each side of the doorway as August Langley entered in his wheelchair. A tray rested on his lap, upon which lay a white folded cloth. Bollard the mute servant brought the wheelchair to a stop near the fireplace. He stood stiffly behind his employer, his eyes blank as he stared straight ahead. Bollard was an expert on not revealing his thoughts. When I'd first met him, I'd been terrified of the tall, imposing man who couldn't talk. Now, he still made my heart skip when he silently turned a corner into my path, but I no longer feared him the way I used to.

"We're off to London," Sylvia announced, going to her uncle's side. "Isn't that marvelous?"

Langley narrowed his eyes at her. "Whose idea is that?"

"Mine," Jack said. He repeated his reasons for going.

Tommy entered before he'd finished. The footman balanced a silver salver on one gloved hand. It held a single letter from what I could see. His gaze was almost as blank as Bollard's, but he didn't ignore us like the mute. He looked at each of us in turn, finally settling on Sylvia standing nearby. I was sure she hadn't noticed, until her head tilted in what could only be described as defiance. What was going on between those two? I hoped she hadn't offended him again. She could be awful to poor Tommy sometimes.

"All of you are going?" Langley looked directly at me as he asked.

"Yes," I said. "Why should I miss out on all the fun?" The silence that followed was like a noose around my neck. The unspoken 'Because you need to rest' was as much a sentence as the fire that was killing me. If I had limited days left, I wanted to spend them with my friends. My loved ones. I looked to Jack.

He closed his eyes, but not before I saw the pain in them. "She's coming because I can't leave her here."

Langley nodded once, but did not seem convinced.

"Why are you so hesitant to let me go?" I spoke levelly, challenging him. Langley and I had not had the most harmonious relationship. Secrets and lies had damaged it from the start, some of which were mine, I was sorry to admit. In an odd way, our lack of affection for one another meant we could speak our minds. I think Langley even appreciated it.

"I'm at the testing phase," he said.

Sylvia gasped then covered her mouth with her hand.

Jack took a step toward Langley. "What sort of testing are you talking about?"

"Not the sort you're thinking of," Langley said.

Everybody, including me, exhaled. I had assumed that Langley was going to use me as a subject in the same way that Tate wanted to. Tate's plans involved injecting me with drugs he'd developed to see if any of them cured me of my fire starting. He gave no guarantees that they wouldn't kill me.

"I simply need some samples of Hannah's blood," Langley said.

Sylvia screwed up her face. "Do we have to discuss this here and now?"

"Will it hurt?" Jack asked.

"A mere pricking of her skin," Langley said. "It may sting for a moment, but that's all."

A sound of disgust gurgled from Sylvia's throat.

"And how is the blood removed from my body?" I asked.

Sylvia placed her hands on her stomach. She'd gone quite green. "Excuse me." She ran out of the room. Tommy set the salver down on a nearby table and slipped out after her.

"I'll use a syringe." Langley unfolded the thick white cloth on the tray in his lap, revealing a slender cylinder made of glass with bronze ends. I suddenly wanted to follow Sylvia.

"It looks worse than it feels," Samuel said, coming to my side.

I swallowed. "That's good because it looks rather barbaric."

"I've used them in my studies. If it makes you feel better, you may hold my hand while he does it."

I sat back down on the sofa and turned to Jack. He raked his hand through his hair, down the side of his face and over his jaw. I thought he would say something, but he didn't. The look he gave me said all the things I knew he wanted to say: *It should be me holding your hand.*

"Thank you, Samuel," I said, "but I'll be all right."

Samuel gave Jack a nod as if he knew what he was thinking. He stepped away from me.

"Stay near her, Gladstone," Langley ordered Samuel. "You'll need to catch her if she faints."

"I can assure you I'm not the fainting sort, Mr. Langley."

"All women are the fainting sort. It's part of your constitution."

I wanted to share my frustration with Jack, but he wasn't looking at me. He stood by the window, his arms crossed over his chest, his eyes downcast. I could just see one of his hands from where I sat on the sofa. It was clenched in a tight fist.

"Forward, Bollard," Langley intoned. The servant wheeled him toward me. "Roll up your sleeve, Hannah."

The sleeve on my dress was fitted from shoulder to elbow with a soft ruffle falling from elbow to wrist. I pushed it up as far as it would go.

"Present your arm, palm up."

I did and watched as he prepared the syringe. I was rather mesmerized by the process…until he stuck the needle into me.

"Ow!" It was more the shock of the needle pricking my skin than any real pain.

"Hannah?" Jack was suddenly by my side.

"It's quite all right." I gave him a smile which hopefully he thought was genuine. "It didn't hurt a bit."

"Then why did you say 'ow'?"

"A figure of speech."

He scowled, but the needle was already out. It was full of my blood.

"Do you feel faint?" Samuel asked, handing me his handkerchief. I pressed it to the drop of blood marking the spot where the needle had entered.

"Not in the least." No more than usual anyway.

Jack held the lace ruffled of my sleeve away from the spot. "Do you wish to lie down?"

"I've just gotten up!"

"Nevertheless, you should stay seated for a few minutes," Langley said. "Bollard."

The servant seemed to need no instructions. He took the handles of the wheelchair and began pushing Langley out of the room.

"Wait," I called after them. Bollard stopped and swiveled the chair so Langley could see me. "What happens now?"

"Now I perform some tests on this." Langley indicated the syringe on the tray in his lap.

"How long will that take?"

"It depends on the results."

I gritted my teeth and tried again. "Are you making progress?"

"Somewhat."

"What does that mean?"

"It means I've made some progress."

The man was being evasive just to vex me. I was certain of it. "How much? Do you think you're on the path to finding a cure?"

"Hannah, be patient."

"*Patient!*" The word exploded from my lips. "How can I be patient at a time like this? In case you haven't noticed, I'm *dying*, Mr. Langley."

"Calm down," he snapped.

Samuel's hand rested on my shoulder. I shrugged it off. "I apologize if my hysteria bothers you, but I find it difficult to maintain composure when my life may end in a matter of days." Hot blood thumped through my veins like a raging torrent. My hands suddenly felt like they were on fire and before I could stop it, a spark shot from my fingertip.

Samuel stamped it out before it could burn the rug. My temper dampened instantly. I didn't want to set fire to the house. I'd already done that once, and the consequences were still visible. Besides, it made me sweat in uncomfortable places and weaken further. I flapped my hand near my face until Jack fetched the latest copy of the *Young Ladies Journal* and took over the flapping for me.

"It isn't a matter of days," Langley said with a sigh. "You'll have a few weeks yet, I'm sure."

"*How* can you be sure? For all we know, Tate may already be dead. I won't be far behind, will I?" I couldn't control the words. They flowed out of me, propelled by frustration and anxiety.

"We can't know that," Langley said quietly.

"Precisely! We can't know anything." I stood, unsure what I wanted to do. Perhaps shake him until the formula for a cure fell out of his head, or simply get the point across that I was desperate, in case he couldn't tell from the high pitch of my voice.

But all I did was sit back down on the sofa again as dizziness swamped me.

"Hannah." Jack's voice, close to my ear, rumbled low and deep in his chest. It soothed me somewhat. "Breathe." I closed my eyes and drew air into my lungs several times before the dizziness faded.

"Put your head down," Samuel said, pressing his cool hand to the back of my neck and forcing me to lean forward.

I obeyed even though the position felt awkward, particularly with the tight waist of my gown restricting movement. Thank goodness I'd eschewed corsets of late.

"Forgive me," I muttered into my skirt. "I shouldn't have spoken like that. I appreciate everything you're doing for me, Mr. Langley."

"He's gone, Hannah." Jack sounded almost apologetic. "It's all right. He knows you're upset. He won't take it to heart."

"Is that because he doesn't have a heart?" I couldn't resist the jest. Then I burst into tears.

"Hannah," he murmured. He didn't say anything else, nor did he have to. His solid presence was enough. It was reassuring having him by my side, taking care of me, worrying about me. It made me feel like I was the most precious thing in the world.

My breathing finally calmed and the heat and dizziness subsided. I sat up and noticed that Samuel had left too. Jack and I were alone on the sofa together. He gave me an uncertain smile.

"I'll fetch you something to drink," he said.

"I'm all right. Stay with me a few moments." We sat side by side without speaking. Although I wasn't looking at him, I could feel his gaze on me. He was probably worried that I was going to faint.

"I forgot to ask Langley if he needs me to stay here instead of going to London," I said, breaking the silence. "He might want to perform more tests."

"I'll ask him, but I'm sure he doesn't. He would have said so."

"I know. But I'd like to be certain. I wouldn't want to delay his work."

"I'll remain too if you're staying. I'm not going anywhere without you."

"Thank you, Jack. You're wonderful."

He blushed, which I found adorably sweet. "Do me a favor and tell Sylvia that. It'll irritate her no end to hear it."

I laughed. "Speaking of Sylvia, I'd better see if she's all right."

We walked together and parted company outside Langley's door. Jack knocked and went in while I continued along the corridor to Sylvia's room. I was about to put fist to wood when the door opened. Tommy stood there, gawping at me. He looked quite horrified to have been caught in a place he certainly should not have been.

"Tommy!" I was so surprised to see him that I stared back, lost for words.

"I, uh…Miss Smith. I was just…" He shut his mouth and swallowed heavily. Clearly I wasn't the only one lost for words.

The door widened and Sylvia appeared. Her face was flushed, and her eyes sparkled like sapphires. "I was feeling unwell, and Tommy came to see if I needed anything." She pressed the back of her hand to her forehead, and avoided my gaze. "Thank you for the offer of tea, Tommy, but I'm quite all right now." She opened the door wider. "You may go."

"Um…"

"*Go!*"

He slipped past me. I stared after him as he walked down the corridor. I wanted to see if he looked back, but Sylvia dragged me into the room. She shut the door and leaned back against it.

"Sylvia? Are you quite all right? You look—" I was going to say unwell, but that wasn't quite true. "Troubled. What was Tommy really doing here?"

She pushed off from the door and threw herself on her bed. She reclined on her side and tucked her slippered feet up. "I told you. He followed me here to see if I needed anything."

Since when did that require him entering her bedroom *and* shutting the door? I found the whole situation utterly confounding. She wouldn't allow anything of an intimate nature to happen, not with a servant. The very thought would be abhorrent to her. Yet that was how it appeared. Very curious.

"But Sylvia—"

"I don't want to discuss it any further," she bit off. "Let's talk about other things. *Better* things. Like London and the ball. I cannot wait to dance with a *real* gentlemen."

"Samuel is a real gentleman. You've danced with him in practice."

She sighed and rubbed her forehead. "Yes, of course he is. I meant real, *normal* gentlemen. Ones who don't mesmerize women."

"Samuel is a hypnotist not a mesmerist, and he's equally capable of hypnotizing men as well as women. Any mesmerizing of ladies is purely due to his charming nature."

She was no longer listening. Her gaze had grown distant, unfocused. She lay back against the pillows and sighed deeply.

"Jack has gone to ask your uncle if I need to stay at Frakingham for more tests," I said. "Shall we wait until we have his answer or start packing?"

"Hmmm. Yes. I'll join you in a moment."

I gave a little shake of my head and left her. So much for Sylvia being the open book of the household. It would appear she was as capable of being as mysterious as anyone.

***

Nightfall came early in December. It gave Jack and me the opportunity to walk to the lake together before dinner without being seen. Not that I cared, but I knew Sylvia did. I told Jack about her strange response to being discovered with Tommy in her room. I thought he might be outraged. As her cousin, he had every right to be. But he seemed curious about their secret meetings when I told him.

"Do you think they're having a dalliance?"

"Sylvia and Tommy?" He laughed, his breath a frosty puff in the freezing air. "I doubt it. I can't imagine Tommy wanting to be in the company of someone who looks down on him as much as she does. Sylvia can't stand him unless he's saving her life or bringing her tea."

"You're right. It is absurd." I dismissed the idea. Whatever they were doing, it was not what Jack and I did when we were in the lake together. "So what did Langley say?"

"He won't need any more blood from you for a few days. He said we should go to London."

"Oh? Does that mean he's had a breakthrough with the tests he performed today?"

"I don't know." His voice was thin, drawn out. "You know what he's like. He gives nothing away."

We reached the lake's edge and shed our shoes on a grassy patch. The mist hadn't had the chance to burn off during the day, and it became thicker now that the air had turned even colder. It clung to the inky lake surface like a spectral blanket in the moonlight.

I set my pack of dry clothes down, and Jack did the same with his pack. I already wore my bathing costume beneath my coat. Sylvia had helped me fashion one from an old shift and pair of men's trousers. It was quite a hideous outfit, hence the coat I'd thrown around me to hide it, but it was more practical in the water than skirts. Jack wore shirt and trousers, held up with suspenders.

Clouds passed across the moon, but I could still make out his silhouette. He held his hand out toward the lake and bowed. "Your bath awaits, Miss Smith."

"Why, thank you, sir. Shall we?"

My toes squelched in the mud that soon gave way to pebbles. The icy water soothed my skin, deliciously soothing. I stood still for a moment and sighed with contentment. It made me realize how hot and uncomfortable I'd been in the house.

As soon as we were hip-deep, Jack touched my elbow. Heat flared, but there were no sparks. He guided me in further, holding me in case I slipped on the rocks. As soon as the water reached his waist and my breasts, he drew me close.

He kissed me without words or warning. It was a tender kiss, filled with longing and sadness that made my heart ache. I pressed my hands to the back of his head, keeping him there, right where I wanted him. My nipples peaked beneath my damp shift and brushed against his hard body. He sucked air between his teeth, and I knew he wanted to touch me there, as I wanted to touch him. But we couldn't. From previous experiments, we knew deeper intimacy would cause my heat to reach unbearable levels. The risk was too great, which was why we'd decided to keep our clothes on. Even Jack's shirt was a necessity. The sight of his broad shoulders and muscles was enough to set my fever rising.

"I've missed you," he said, stopping the kiss before the heat became too much. He did not pull away entirely. We'd found that we could hold one another for a long time. It wasn't enough for either of us to be completely satisfied, but it was better than nothing.

"We were in the lake only last night," I said, smiling against his lips.

"Too long ago. I want to be with you all the time, and not just here." He kissed me lightly and retreated a little. I wished I could see his eyes, but it was too dark to see more than their shine. I did know he was watching me. "I want to lie in your arms, Hannah, and feel your skin against mine. I want to make you mine in every way."

"I am yours," I said, breathless. "Always."

He kissed me again, harder. All our frustrations and sorrow poured out of us in that kiss. I couldn't get enough of him, nor he of me. I wanted him closer, wanted all of him, in the most carnal way possible. It was wrong—my thoughts were not at all appropriate for a pure young lady—yet I didn't care. All I could think about was claiming Jack and being claimed by him.

A surge of heat suddenly blasted from my hands. Jack's body jerked with the shock and he fell back. Water splashed in my eyes. I blinked and rubbed them. When my vision cleared, Jack was nowhere to be seen.

CHAPTER 3

"Jack?" I called out. No answer. No splashes. "Jack!" I stepped forward, reaching under the inky black water, searching.

Nothing.

I took another step, another. Surely the blast hadn't propelled him so far away from me. Oh God, where was he? My heart pounded in my chest. My throat tightened. I tried to scream his name, but it came out as a sob.

My hands dug through the water, feeling around. But there was only the endless, empty lake.

I slipped on a rock and slid under the surface, but did not stop searching. He had to be here somewhere, unconscious. The alternative was too horrible.

Combustion.

I paddled as best as I could, using feet and arms to feel for him. The lake's icy fingers wrapped around my chest and squeezed. I'd never felt colder.

I touched something. Hair! A head and body too! I grabbed him by the shoulders and hauled him up. I listened for breathing, but it was difficult to hear anything over my own ragged breaths. "Jack? Jack?" I thumped his back in the hope that would clear his airways, but in truth, I didn't know what to do.

Finally, after what seemed an age, he spluttered. A cough wracked him. Coughing was good. I wrapped my arm around his waist and supported him until it subsided. There were no sparks this time. We needed desire for that, and I was simply too relieved to have any passionate thoughts.

"I'm fine," he said eventually, his voice rough. "You?"

I nodded, too choked with tears to speak. I didn't know if he saw it in the dark, but he didn't ask again.

"What happened?" he asked after my tears subsided.

"An enormous spark shot from me. Jack, we need to be more careful. I don't think we can do this anymore."

"Don't say that, Hannah."

"It's too dangerous. You were under water a long time. I couldn't find you. What if next time...?"

He brushed his knuckles lightly down my cheek then pulled away from me entirely. "Very well. We'll be more careful." He swore and punched the water. "I hate this."

"He'll find a cure. Don't worry."

The shine returned to his eyes. They sparkled like stars in the darkness. "We have to believe it," he said without much conviction.

We waded out of the lake and dressed. I didn't try to hide myself from him. For one thing, it was dark, and for another, I wasn't ashamed to show my body to Jack. One day, when Langley cured me, I would allow Jack to look all he wanted. And touch.

***

Jack, Sylvia, Samuel and I left for London the following morning and arrived at Claridges after sunset. The grand hotel provided a good base, being close to both the Beauforts and Culverts.

We sent word to the Beauforts upon our arrival and received a response the following morning in the form of Emily and Jacob Beaufort themselves, and George Culvert too.

"Are you sure you wish to speak with someone from the Society?" Mrs. Beaufort asked.

All seven of us sat in the hotel's drawing room, surrounded by rich, tapestried decor that was a little dated, but nonetheless opulent. Heavy brocade curtains were tied back from the large windows, but the amount of light that filtered through was miserly. No less than three liveried footmen had asked if we needed anything, but we'd waved them all away. We did not wish to be disturbed.

"Why?" Jack hedged.

"Is the Society to be feared?" Sylvia asked. "Only...I don't think we ought to seek anyone out who may wish to do us harm."

"That's the thing," Mr. Beaufort said. "We don't know what the members are like."

"We haven't heard much about them in recent years," Mrs. Beaufort explained. She looked so delicate next to her husband, but I knew from the stories about her past that she was courageous. Her pretty face was currently marred by a deep frown that cut across her brow as she leaned forward a little. "Until now."

Mr. Culvert, the demonologist, nodded. "You say the Widow Mott mentioned the Society? Are you sure?"

"We're sure," Jack said. "It's possible it's not the Society For Supernatural Activity at all, but some other society. Only I doubt it."

"It seems unlikely," Mrs. Beaufort agreed, "given the nature of what the deceased man did." She glanced at her husband and he frowned back. They seemed to communicate to each other without words, but I didn't suspect there was anything supernatural in their methods, merely a deep understanding of one another.

"Are you able to help us?" I asked. "Do you know where we can find a member of the Society?"

"I'm afraid not," Mrs. Beaufort said. "None of us have maintained a connection to it. The only man we knew who belonged died some years ago." She swallowed heavily and glanced once more at her husband.

He placed his hand over hers. "He wasn't the nicest of men, but that doesn't mean everyone in the Society is a bad apple."

"I'm sorry we can't help you," Mr. Culvert said. "Your trip to London has been wasted."

"There's one more thing." Jack pulled the small knife out of his jacket pocket, the one that had turned the demons to dust, a knife that shouldn't have been able to harm them at all. Only blades forged in the Otherworld could kill a demon. Jack's blade, his only link to his parents, was a deep mystery. He handed it to Mr. Culvert. "What can you tell me about this?"

"Ah!" Mr. Culvert turned over the knife and studied the carvings in the wooden handle. "Is this the one?"

We'd written to them about the demise of the demons, but this was the first opportunity to show them the knife. Mr. Culvert handed it to Mr. Beaufort. "It looks normal enough to me. Jacob?"

Mr. Beaufort inspected the blade and shrugged. "And to me." He passed it to his wife.

She rubbed her thumb over the handle. "The pattern is beautiful, and a little unusual. It came from your parents, you say?"

Jack nodded. "You can't tell me anything about it?"

"I'm afraid not," Mr. Culvert said. "I've never actually seen a blade that can kill demons before, neither in real life nor in any of my texts. I'm sorry, Mr. Langley. It would seem your journey has been doubly wasted."

"Not at all!" Sylvia brightened. "I, for one, am glad we won't be meeting anyone from this Society anyway. If they were involved in the summoning of that creature, it's a very bad idea to meet them at all. At least now we can shop in peace and without fear."

"There may be another way to look at this," Samuel said.

Sylvia groaned.

Samuel had said very little since the Beauforts arrived. He sat in a burgundy leather armchair a little to one side, looking relaxed. It was a charade, however. I knew him to be very interested in the conversation. "We know one gentleman who used to belong to the Society years ago. Perhaps he still does. His name is Myer. He hypnotized Hannah when she was a small child."

"Hypnotized a child?" Mrs. Beaufort stared wide-eyed at me. "I'm not sure you should seek him out then."

"Agreed," Mr. Beaufort said. "Hypnotists shouldn't be trusted. You never know if you're being put under their spell or not."

Jack pressed his lips together in an attempt to hide his smile. Samuel cleared his throat. "Thank you for your opinion," he said crisply. I don't know why he didn't just tell them he was a hypnotist. Perhaps he didn't want them to look at him differently or with fear. I could understand that, in a way. "So, do you know of any Myers?"

"Everett Myer," Mr. Beaufort said. "He's a member of my club. Seems like a nice fellow, but I don't know him well. We mix in different circles. He's a very wealthy man."

"What line of trade?"

"Banking. He's a major shareholder of Hatfield and Harrington, one of the oldest banks in the country."

Jack whistled. "Hatfield and Harrington!"

"Myer's wife is a Hatfield. She was an only child and her parents died a few years ago. She inherited everything."

"Edith is her name," Mrs. Beaufort added. "She's a quiet lady and doesn't socialize overmuch. She dresses rather plainly too, which is odd considering her wealth. It's almost as if she's embarrassed to flaunt her affluence."

"What is a shareholder?" I asked. My education in financial matters had been lacking, I realized.

"It means he owns only a part of the bank, a share of it, albeit a large share," Jack explained. "The bank is a joint-stock company. August is a shareholder too, in a minor capacity."

"Myer's share gives him great influence, but not complete control," Mr. Beaufort said.

"Are they young or old?" Samuel asked. "The man who hypnotized Hannah must be twenty years older than her at least."

"He would be about the right age," Mr. Beaufort said.

"Do you know where we can find him?"

"They live in Mayfair I believe, but I couldn't tell you where precisely. I've never been to their house."

"Nor I," Mrs. Beaufort said. "Edith Myer isn't one for holding parties. She's quite the recluse. Is Mr. Myer like that?" she asked her husband.

"Not at all. He's very amiable and popular with most of the gentlemen." Mr. Beaufort's blue eyes flashed wickedly in his wife's direction. It was quite unexpected, and I warmed to him even more. He wasn't the stuffy gentleman he first appeared to be. "Some would call him charming. You would like him, my dear."

"Would I, indeed? Then pray I don't meet him. I'm quite sure I have enough charming men in my life."

Mr. Beaufort laughed. "Are you referring to me?"

"Actually, I was referring to our son. He charms me every day."

He grinned. I couldn't help smiling too. I did so enjoy the way they joked with one another.

"We need to find Myer," Samuel said. He seemed the only one unaffected by the Beauforts' display of family contentment. He was a hound on the scent of a fox. Now that he'd caught a whiff, he could think of nothing else.

"Come with me to the club," Mr. Beaufort offered. "If he's not there, it'll only take a few minutes to learn where he lives."

"What are you going to say to him when you meet him?" Mrs. Beaufort asked.

Jack shrugged one shoulder. "We'll think of something on the way."

"If nothing else, we can discuss Hannah's hypnosis with him," Samuel said. "That's the one thing we can be sure he was involved in."

Sylvia shot me a worried glance. "I'm not sure Hannah should go."

"You do look a little unwell, Miss Smith," Mrs. Beaufort said, frowning. "Perhaps you should rest."

"I'll stay with you. I don't particularly wish to meet this Myer gentleman anyway." Sylvia shuddered. "I don't want to succumb to his hypnosis."

"Good lord." Samuel threw his hands up in frustration. "Just because he's a hypnotist doesn't mean he's unethical."

"He hypnotized a child!" Sylvia cried.

"That was years ago. Perhaps he learned his lesson and has changed. Everyone deserves a second chance." This last part came out as a mutter.

"Of course they do." I tried to catch his gaze, but he didn't look at me. He didn't look at anyone, but stared down at the vibrant Oriental rug under his feet. "I'm sorry, Sylvia, but I won't be staying here with you. I feel quite well enough to go, and I wish to speak to Mr. Myer too."

"Well I'm staying here for the day," Sylvia said with a click of her tongue.

"Why not come with me?" Mrs. Beaufort asked.

I could have kissed her. Sylvia's smile lit up her face and assuaged my guilt at leaving her.

Sylvia positively bounced in her seat. "Shall we go shopping?"

"If you wish. We'll luncheon at home with the children, if that's all right with you. Afterward, I'll take you wherever you wish to go."

Sylvia clapped her hands. "Are you sure you don't want to join us, Hannah?"

"Quite sure. It sounds even more tiring than meeting Mr. Myer."

Both Mr. and Mrs. Beaufort frowned at me again. They would have guessed from the look of me that I was unwell, but manners forbade them from asking outright.

The three of them waited for us in the foyer as we retrieved our hats, coats and gloves from our rooms. While our carriages were being brought around, Mrs. Beaufort invited us to dine with them that evening. "George and Adelaide will be there, and Cara too."

"It sounds wonderful," I said, hoping I'd have time for a nap before then.

***

Mrs. Beaufort, Mr. Culvert and Sylvia took the Beaufort coach while Jack, Samuel, Mr. Beaufort and I climbed into ours. The drive to St. James' Street was short. Women weren't allowed in White's gentleman's club, so I waited in the coach. Jack remained too, most likely to keep an eye on me, although that wasn't the reason he gave.

"A place that doesn't accept female members sounds dull," he said with a devilish grin.

"We women are indeed great conversationalists," I said. "You only have to listen to Sylvia to agree."

He laughed. "If all women were like Sylvia, then I might see the point of a gentleman's club. But I wouldn't want to belong to something that doesn't admit the likes of you, Hannah."

His rich, masculine voice made me blush furiously again, and it took a moment for the heat in my face to subside. It wasn't until Jack lowered the window and let in the cold air that I cooled down.

"What if Mr. Myer is there?" I asked, taking a more serious approach. "You should be inside to question him."

"They'll fetch me if necessary. Here they are now."

Samuel climbed back in the cabin while Mr. Beaufort gave the driver an address.

"Are you not coming with us?" I asked him through the window.

"I have business to attend to in the city."

"Can we drive you there?" Jack asked.

"Thank you, but I'll catch an omnibus." He urged the driver onward and gave us a wave. "See you tonight," he called out as we rolled away.

I leaned back in the leather seat and regarded Samuel, sitting beside Jack. "The manager gave you Mr. Myer's address?" I asked him. "Just like that?"

"There was no 'just like that' about it. Beaufort claims he doesn't go to White's often, but he's clearly an important figure there. The manager couldn't get the address fast enough."

It wasn't far to Myer's house in Mayfair. Samuel acted as tour guide along the way, pointing out the houses belonging to various noble families. I was surprised that he knew where they lived, and wondered if he'd been inside. The driver stopped in front of a tall townhouse that commanded a view over pretty Berkeley Square. We alighted and climbed the steps to the gleaming black door.

"Mr. Myer is not available," said the footman who answered Jack's knock.

We met his response with silence. He had not said Myer wasn't home, simply that he wasn't *available*. Etiquette dictated that we couldn't question him further.

"I'll leave my card," Jack said.

"Wait." Samuel held up his hand. Oh God, he wasn't going to hypnotize the poor footman, was he? "Tell Mr. Myer that Hannah Smith wishes to speak to him. If he doesn't remember her, then please inform him that she was the ward of Lord Wade. I'm sure he'll become available shortly."

The footman's mouth opened and shut and opened again. "I, I…" Poor man. I couldn't blame him for his indecision. He probably didn't get confrontational visitors very often.

"It's all right, Adamson," said a woman standing high up on the curved staircase. She descended toward us, her dove-gray skirts fluttering with each step. "I'll entertain my husband's visitors while you fetch him."

Adamson bowed. "Yes, madam."

"I am Mrs. Myer. Please, come in." She was tall, with gray streaks through her dark hair and sagging jowls. She wasn't at all feminine in appearance, being broad of shoulder and solid in girth. Her face was wide too, and flat, as if invisible fingers had grabbed her by the ears and pulled back. Her lackluster eyes matched her dress in color and plainness. She smiled at us, but it was polite and impersonal.

"Mrs. Myer," Samuel said with a smooth bow. When he straightened, I could see from his smile that he had slipped into charming mode. Mrs. Myer's lips tightened at the corners, and her eyes widened. She looked quite startled all of a sudden. Perhaps she wasn't used to being charmed. "I'm Samuel Gladstone, and these are my friends Jack Langley and Hannah Smith."

She continued to stare at him. I admit that he was a handsome man and had a compelling way about him, but her scrutiny continued for a remarkably long tome considering he hadn't hypnotized her.

Samuel shifted his stance and cleared his throat. I'm sure he was used to being the object of female observation, but even he must have felt a little uncomfortable with her interest.

"Thank you for asking your footman to fetch Mr. Myer," Jack said.

She tore her gaze away from Samuel and turned it on me. "Your announcement intrigued me," she said. "You are Hannah Smith, the ward of Lord Wade?"

I nodded. "Do you know him? Have you heard of me?"

"I've not heard of you, but I do know Lord Wade. I haven't seen him for many years. How is he?"

"He's, uh, well." I had no idea if he was or not, but I'd learned that it was the standard answer for a polite social call. "You seemed quite intrigued when Samuel mentioned my name," I went on. "Are you sure you've never heard it before?" Perhaps she'd known the other Hannah Smith, the one I'd been named after. That woman had been a friend of Lord Wade's or perhaps his lover. Langley hadn't given us any details, if indeed he'd known any. As always, he'd been evasive.

"I was curious simply because I didn't know Lord Wade had a ward," Mrs. Myer conceded. "But as I said, we have not seen him for many years."

"We?" Samuel prompted. "Neither you nor your husband have been in contact with Lord Wade recently?"

She glanced over her shoulder at the staircase, but it was empty. There was no sign of her husband. "I don't believe Everett has seen his lordship for some time, but you'd have to ask him. Come into the drawing room and wait for him. There's no telling how long he'll be. My husband does not usually rise before noon, you see."

"Oh?" Jack said. "He doesn't work at the offices of Hatfield and Harrington during the week."

Mrs. Myer smiled tightly. "My husband's presence isn't required at the bank, and he prefers to stay away anyway. The arrangement suits everybody."

She walked ahead of us. Behind her back, Jack and I exchanged glances. I understood what he was saying without words: Mr. and Mrs. Myer were not a couple on happy marital terms. Samuel didn't join in with our silent discussion. He seemed pre-occupied, even worried. I couldn't think why. Mrs. Myer might not be the easiest lady to talk to, but she *was* talking. She'd also known Wade around the time her husband hypnotized me. She might know more than she realized. I wanted to find out as much from her as I could before Myer arrived.

The drawing room was large but spartan compared with Frakingham's. A single framed daguerreotype of an elderly couple occupied a round table in the center of the room, and empty vases decorated other surfaces. Two paintings of the same country house in different seasons hung on a wall, and a portrait of the same man from the daguerreotype took pride of place above the mantelpiece. Most drawing rooms saw tables cluttered with sketches, paintings, figurines and stuffed animals, but the Myers had none of that. It must have been used rarely, or perhaps Mrs. Myer preferred minimal clutter.

A small fire warmed the room, and I removed my coat. Mrs. Myer did not offer to hang it up.

"Would you mind telling me what Lord Wade has to do with my husband?" she asked, sitting on one of the dark green leather armchairs.

"We'll wait and speak to him directly," Jack said. "Will he be long?"

Her lips pressed into a thin line. "Let's hope not."

Silence blanketed us, and I shifted uncomfortably as Mrs. Myer's gaze flicked between Samuel and myself. It was as if she couldn't decide which of us was more interesting. Yet she didn't ask questions. I'd found that strangers usually liked to pinpoint where we were from, who we were connected to, that sort of thing. It was a way of categorizing us, I supposed, and helped determine how we should be treated. Mrs. Myer asked us nothing. It was refreshing in a way, yet disconcerting at the same time. I wasn't sure how to react.

It appeared it drove Samuel to distraction too. His fingers drummed on his knee and his foot tapped on the rug. He avoided Mrs. Myer's scrutiny by staring at the door, as if he could conjure her husband by sheer force of will. What was wrong with him? Why was he so agitated?

Finally, a man joined us, thank God. His entrance broke the tension in the room. Samuel sprang off the sofa as if something had bitten him. He thrust out his hand in greeting. "Mr. Everett Myer?"

"Yes," the man said, smiling.

"My name is Samuel Gladstone."

Myer shook his hand. He was as tall as his wife, but more slender with long, fine fingers. He had very little hair on the top of his head, most of it having migrated southward to his side whiskers and eyebrows. He wasn't a handsome man, but pleasant enough to look at with his gentle smile and soft hazel eyes. He introduced himself to each of us, bowing when he came to me in a most gracious manner.

To Jack he said, "Langley? Are you a relation to August Langley of Frakingham?"

"He's my uncle," Jack said. "You know him?"

"We've met. I hear his estate is an ancient one with ruins of an old abbey on it. I have a passing interest in archaeology," he explained.

"It is indeed old."

"Please forgive my footman's brusqueness earlier. I'd given him instructions not to disturb me while I finished some business matters."

Mrs. Myer's cough didn't quite cover her derisive snort, which I think was her intention.

"Ah, Edith dear," he said with a sigh in his voice. "You're here." Had he not seen her when he walked in? Or was that his way of reluctantly acknowledging a wife he didn't like?

Her glare was so cool it could have soothed my hot skin if it had been directed at me. "Of course I'm here. I couldn't allow your guests to languish in the hall."

Myer's fingers stretched at his sides. He turned to us, but the gentleness had gone, replaced by a frosty glint in his eyes. "Shall we adjourn to my study?"

"No need for that," Mrs. Myer said before anyone could answer. "Stay here where it's more comfortable. I'll have Adamson serve tea."

"We wouldn't want to bore you with business matters, dear."

"It wouldn't be a bore. I would very much enjoy hearing what these young people have to say. Besides, I do believe they're not here to discuss business at all. Mr. Gladstone seems to have a familiarity about him. If you look into his eyes, perhaps you can see it too, Everett. Go on, look."

Myer did not look, merely shook his head at her. There was a sort of tug-of-war happening between them, but I wasn't sure of the rules or who was winning.

"Edith, dear," he said, standing in front of his wife, blocking my view. "Perhaps you ought to retire. You did say earlier that you had a sore throat." His voice was like honey warmed by sunshine. It made my head hum and my eyes droop. It was compelling and eerily familiar.

A sharp shock in my shoulder jolted me out of my stupor. Jack glared at me and shook his head. I frowned back, and he showed me his finger. It was red. He had touched me, firing a spark between us. Whatever for?

Then it struck me. I was being sucked into a trance by Everett Myer's voice. He was hypnotizing his wife! I swallowed my gasp and blinked back at Jack. He gave me a reassuring smile. Now that Myer had stopped, I was in no danger of succumbing, yet I still couldn't quite believe what had happened.

So it was true. Myer *was* a hypnotist, and a powerful one at that. One who didn't need a swaying object or very much time if his wife's vacant look was anything to go by. Like Samuel.

I tried to catch Samuel's eye, but he didn't notice. He was staring at the Myers, his brow deeply furrowed and anger vibrating off him.

"I think I'm getting a sore throat," Mrs. Myer said, staring at her husband with adoring eyes.

"Perhaps you should retire to your room to rest," Myer said. "I'll see you later, my dear." He held out his hand and she took it. "Say goodbye to our guests, Edith."

"Goodbye," she said, and left the room.

I watched her go in stunned silence. There were a million questions I wanted to ask, but I couldn't get my tongue to work. I was utterly speechless.

"That was low, Myer," Samuel said, his jaw hardly moving.

"Agreed." Fury edged Jack's voice like sharp flint.

Myer sat in the seat his wife had vacated and crossed his legs. He didn't seem to care what opinion we had of him. "She'll suffer no ill effects. I'm very sorry you had to witness that. She's a stubborn woman and needs a little husbandly guidance from time to time."

"Don't you dare try to justify it," Samuel growled. "Not to me and especially not to yourself. What you did was despicable."

Myer seemed taken aback by the outburst. He frowned at Samuel and gave a single shake of his head. "It's nothing more than what you yourself have done, Mr. Gladstone."

I gasped. "You know what Samuel is?"

"I do now. I admit that I didn't suspect a thing at first, although Edith did. Perhaps her experience with me has led her to see the same quality in others. You two gentlemen are immune, it seems. Although *you* look quite pale, Miss Smith. It is Hannah Smith, isn't it?"

It took me a few moments to recover. Myer seemed quite unconcerned by the fact that he'd just hypnotized his wife and equally unconcerned that we knew it. I hadn't feared him before, but that may have been a mistake. If someone from the Society had paid Mott to summon the demon, there was no reason why it couldn't have been Myer himself.

"I am Hannah Smith."

"Just now you said that I know what *Samuel* is," he went on. "Which would imply he is the only one of the three of you who is like me." His gaze focused on Jack. "That begs the question, why are *you* not touched by my little parlor trick, Mr. Langley?"

"It's no parlor trick," Jack said. "It's a despicable practice." He stood and approached Myer. Myer smiled. If it weren't for the vein pulsing above his collar, I would have thought him unafraid. "Nobody deserves to be hypnotized against their will."

"Calm down, Mr. Langley. Don't pretend you haven't been a party to Mr. Gladstone's own hypnotizing on occasion."

A lump weighed heavily in my chest. We had indeed witnessed Samuel hypnotize a woman, but only to find out where her sister lived. She'd been Reuben Tate's housekeeper and our only link to finding him. Surely Myer didn't know that. How could he?

"Enough games," Jack snapped. "We know who you are. We know you hypnotized Hannah when she was a child."

"Is that what this visit is about?"

"Yes and no."

"Which is it, Mr. Langley? Yes or no?"

"Mr. Myer," I said before Jack's temper could make matters worse, "are you a member of the Society For Supernatural Activity?"

"That's not the question I thought you were going to ask," he said with a laugh. The tension left his shoulders, and his eyes brightened. "I am a member. I am also the Grand Master."

"Grand Master?" Jack said. "So you give the orders?"

"Orders to do what, Mr. Langley?"

"To summon demons."

CHAPTER 4

Myer's eyebrows drew together to form a bushy hedge. He pressed himself into his seat and held up his hands, warding Jack off. "Mr. Langley...I...I don't know what to say to that. Demons? What in God's name are you implying?"

I rubbed my temple where it felt like a small hammer was tapping away at my skull. I was hot, tired and my patience had worn thin shortly after walking through the door. The Myers were an exhausting couple. "Don't play the innocent with us," I said to him. "We know you're aware of the existence of demons, just as you are aware that the power of hypnosis isn't necessarily a learned gift. So, does Mr. Langley need to ask you the question again?"

Myer's nostrils flared. I half expected him to try to hypnotize me as he'd done his wife, but he did something more unexpected instead. He smiled. "I like your spirit, Miss Smith. You are correct. I do know about demons, but I didn't want to be tricked into admitting anything. There are some people in this country who would commit members of the Society to asylums simply for stating they believe in demons and other paranormal things. It's a natural tendency of mine to be cautious."

"Of course. I'm sorry, Mr. Myer, I hope you can forgive me." He *had* taken a risk, and it was only fair that I acknowledge that. It didn't mean I trusted him.

Myer clasped his hands together and rubbed one thumb along the other. "Let me assure you that I have never summoned a demon, nor have I given the orders to anyone else in the Society to do so."

"Why should we believe you?" Samuel asked. For someone usually so amenable, he was behaving rather aggressively toward Myer. I thought he would have liked to meet someone like himself. Myer may have hypnotized his wife in front of us, but it wasn't like Samuel had never done it. He'd hinted that he'd committed numerous sins with his talent in the past that he was now ashamed of.

"Because it's the truth, Mr. Gladstone," Myer said. "There's no way I can prove it, so you'll just have to have faith and trust me." He turned to Jack. "You'd better tell me why you've come here accusing me of such a despicable thing."

Jack returned to the sofa and explained about the demon that had tormented us for several days until we'd managed to kill it.

"Kill it?" Myer echoed, frowning. "You mean sent it back."

Jack leveled his gaze on Myer's. "It's gone. That's all that matters."

Myer's thumb rubbed faster. "Of course. I'm glad it's no longer here. Very glad. A demon running loose is an extremely dangerous thing."

"You have experience with demons?"

"Not personally. I'm no demonologist. Others in our organization have more knowledge of these matters than I do. I leave the demon hunting to them."

"Do you know of anyone who might summon one?" Jack asked.

"Of course not. Why would they do such a thing?"

"To do harm," Samuel said. "Revenge. Greed. Jealousy. Why does anyone do anything evil, Mr. Myer?"

Myer's thumbs stilled. "A good question, Mr. Gladstone. Let me assure you, the members of the Society are carefully selected. They have an interest in the supernatural, but from a curiosity and scientific perspective only. We don't allow loose cannons."

"How fortunate that you're able to see into a person's mind and know what they're thinking."

Myer tilted his head to the side and regarded Samuel through narrowed eyes. He stared for so long that *I* felt uncomfortable for Samuel. Remarkably, he didn't look away. He met the other man's scrutiny without blinking. "You know I can't do that," Myer said. "My talent doesn't stretch so far. Does yours?"

"No."

A log in the fireplace shifted as the low flames ate through it. The movement broke the standoff between the two men, and they both looked away. I couldn't determine what had just transpired, and I didn't try too hard to think it through. My head hurt enough.

"Why do you think a member of Society summoned the demon?" Myer asked.

"We're not certain," Jack said. "It's one option we're considering among others." He explained about Mott and how his widow mentioned he'd met with someone from a 'Society.'

Myer unclasped his hands. "That's flimsy evidence at best."

"We're aware of that," Samuel said through a clenched jaw.

"And what are your other options?"

"We don't have to discuss them with you."

"Samuel," I said gently.

He tore his gaze away from Myer and raised his brows at me. "You wish to tell him...everything? Are you sure?"

"It's quite all right." I tried to smile, but it probably wasn't very convincing if his worried frown was anything to go by. Beside me, Jack shifted a little closer, but he didn't try to counsel me against speaking. I wasn't sure I wanted to talk about it, but it was necessary. Myer had a long history with Lord Wade and the Society, and that meant he probably knew Reuben Tate. It also meant he was aware of unnatural phenomena. He might be shocked by my revelations, but he wouldn't call me mad.

I told him everything, beginning with how Tate had summoned a demon and used the creature to try to abduct me. I went on to explain why Tate wanted me and that led to my fire starting and failing health.

"Miss Smith, I..." He approached and squatted beside me. He took my hand and cradled it loosely in his own. Whatever unethical things he'd done with his hypnosis, I was certain that the sympathy in his eyes was genuine. "I don't know what to say except that I'll help in any way I can."

"There's nothing you can do," I said, forcing myself to smile for him. I saw no point in wallowing in his pity. "Unless you know of a cure."

"I'm afraid not."

"Do not pretend that you're shocked," Jack snapped.

Whatever had upset him? Did he not like Myer touching me? Did he think Myer was trying to hypnotize me?

Myer let go of my hand and returned to his chair. "Mr. Langley, I can assure you I am very shocked."

"You knew she could start fires," Samuel said. "We know you hypnotized her as a child at Lord Wade's request."

"Yes. Well. That's true. It improved her immeasurably."

"*Improved* her?" Jack snarled. "She was a child!"

"Her ability frightened her, Mr. Langley. Have you ever witnessed a terrified two year-old? No? Let me tell you, it's not an easy thing to calm one. After I put the narcolepsy and memory block in place through hypnosis, she forgot her temper and slept through the worst of it before she could do too much damage. I labeled it a success, as did Lord Wade."

"I label it inhuman. What you did was unforgiveable and a gross abuse of your power." Jack's voice was as cold and sharp as a shard of glass.

Myer clasped his hands in his lap again. The knuckles went white. "Don't judge me, Mr. Langley. You weren't there. Lord Wade and I did what we thought best. Mr. Gladstone, I hope *you* understand at least."

Samuel looked down at the floor and didn't answer.

"Miss Smith?"

"I don't think we should dredge up the past," I said. "What's done is done."

Jack closed his eyes and breathed deeply. He gave a single nod. "Let's discuss the present and how you can help us now, Myer."

"I'm not sure that I can," he said. "If Tate summoned one demon, it stands to reason that he summoned the other by the same means."

"One doesn't automatically equate to the other," Samuel said, looking up. His eyes were clear and bright. Where earlier he'd been angry with Myer for hypnotizing without consent, I was beginning to think he saw the likeness to himself now.

"Whether Tate did it or not, it doesn't matter," I said. "We don't know where he is."

"Do you?" Jack asked our host.

Myer shook his head. "I haven't seen Reuben Tate or August Langley for many years. Not since they let their membership lapse."

"What were they like?" I asked. "Others have said they were brilliant."

"They were. They had a fiery partnership though." He winced. "My apologies, I should have chosen a better word."

"That's quite all right." I removed my gloves to cool my hands. They'd grown progressively hotter. My head ached too, and my skin prickled. I needed to escape the room soon and get into the fresh, cool air. I didn't want to faint in the Myers' drawing room.

"Tate and Langley argued like a poorly matched married couple," Myer said. "But when they set aside their differences and worked together, they produced marvelous things. I wasn't surprised when I heard that one of their cures sold for a substantial amount of money. It was a shame they went their separate ways after that. A great shame."

"What exactly did they do for the Society?"

"Nothing in an official capacity. Studying the supernatural was a hobby of theirs. Their investigations into the scientific basis for unexplained phenomena helped us determine who was fraudulent and who was genuine, particularly in the area of spirit mediums and hypnosis."

"Hypnosis!" Samuel said. "So Langley has been aware of people with natural hypnotic abilities for some time?"

"Oh yes. He even studied me. He declared me genuine. Has he done the same for you, Mr. Gladstone?"

"He hasn't studied me."

Myer laughed. "Don't be so sure about that."

Samuel pouted and looked as if he would ask another question, so I got in first. "Do you know why they stopped being friends?"

"Why not ask Langley himself?" This he said to Jack.

"We have," Jack said. "Now we're asking you, Mr. Myer."

Myer's Adam's apple bobbed furiously. "I don't know. I never knew them well."

"Do you know of anyone else in the Society who can start fires?" I asked.

"You're the only one I've met, Miss Smith. And Tate as it turns out, although that's news to me."

Nobody told him about Jack, nor would we. Myer did not need to know all our secrets.

"Do we have any more questions for Mr. Myer?" I asked Jack. Talking had taxed me. All I wanted to do was get cool and sleep.

Jack must have understood. "We'll go," he said, rising.

"Wait," Myer said. "I have a question for you, Mr. Langley. Why didn't you feel something when I hypnotized my wife? Mr. Gladstone is immune, and I could see that Miss Smith was affected by my voice, but not you. Why?"

Jack lifted one shoulder. "I don't know. Have you never met anyone who wasn't affected?"

"No. Never. Have you, Mr. Gladstone?"

Samuel smiled, and I was relieved to see it was his usual charming one, dimples and all. He'd been out of sorts ever since our arrival. "Only Langley here."

One corner of Jack's mouth lifted in a cocky smile. It was pure arrogance, yet I loved it. I suspected he enjoyed keeping his secret from Myer just as much as I did.

"Any idea as to why?" Myer asked.

"None whatsoever." Samuel stood and held out his hand to me. "Let me help you, Hannah. You look worn out."

I was glad for his strong, steady arm to lean on, and equally glad to see that it didn't bother Jack. His old jealousy hadn't surfaced for some days. I attributed it to their newfound friendship since Samuel had fought the demons alongside Jack. Our lake trysts probably helped reassure him too.

He carried my coat over his arm, and I still held my gloves. I glanced up the staircase as we entered the entrance hall, but there was no sign of Mrs. Myer. I thanked Mr. Myer for his assistance.

"I feel as if I haven't helped at all," he said with an apologetic shrug.

"You may still be able to," Jack said quietly so as not to be overheard by the hovering footman. "If you think of anyone in the Society who may have a connection to Harborough or Frakingham, send word to us there immediately. Speak of this to no one. Hannah's condition is not something you can discuss with others."

"Nor is Samuel's," I added.

"I understand," Myer said. "Trust me. I'm used to secrets of that nature." He signaled for Adamson the footman to open the door. "Mr. Gladstone," he suddenly said, "would you like to dine with me tonight at White's?"

I felt a ripple travel up Samuel's arm. Surprise, perhaps? "I don't see why not," he said. "We have other plans, but I'm sure my company won't be missed."

Myer grinned. "Excellent! I think we'll have a great deal to discuss."

We made our way down to the coach and climbed in. I sat on the bench seat and yawned. "Samuel, you *will* be missed at dinner. Are you sure you want to meet with Myer on your own?"

He shrugged. "Why not? Are you worried about me, Hannah?"

"A little."

"He can't hypnotize me."

"I know, but…" I clicked my tongue. I couldn't explain it, but I had an uneasy feeling in my chest. "I'm not sure I trust him."

"I know I don't," Jack said. "Be careful, Gladstone."

"I will. I don't trust him either. The man hypnotized his own wife right in front of us with no thought how it would affect anyone else." He held up his hands when I opened my mouth to speak. "I know I'm not exactly a paragon of ethical behavior in that department, but I amended my ways before the age of twenty at least. Myer should know better."

Jack pulled out a cushion from the compartment beneath the seat. "Rest until we're back at the hotel, Hannah."

"But I want to talk some more about Myer."

He shook the cushion at me. "Rest, please."

His plea and the lines of worry radiating from his eyes had me reaching for the cushion. I placed it behind my head and closed my eyes. It was blessedly soothing and I instantly relaxed.

"Sorry, Gladstone," I heard Jack say through my sleepy state.

I wondered why he was apologizing, then a blast of cool air washed over my face, cooling me down. Jack had opened the window.

"Not at all," Samuel said. "Pass me Hannah's coat since she doesn't need it."

***

I slept for the rest of the afternoon in my room at Claridges and awoke when Sylvia returned from her outing with Mrs. Beaufort. She helped me dress in a light, summery gown for the evening. I'd decided that the Beauforts and Culverts already knew that I suffered from the heat, so there was no reason to hide it.

Dinner at the Beauforts was an intimate affair with Mrs. Beaufort's young aunt, Cara Moreau there, and Mr. Beaufort's sister, Adelaide Culvert and her husband George too. She was pregnant with their second child, but in good health and spirits. A remarkably pretty woman, she reminded me of Sylvia. Both were fair and rosy-cheeked with a regal tilt to their chins, although Mrs. Culvert's manner of speaking was more measured. Sylvia could learn a thing or two about tact from her.

"I'm quite relieved that Samuel didn't join us," Sylvia said to the group as we sat down to dinner. "Now we can talk frankly about him and Myer."

"Syl," Jack warned.

"Gladstone *and* Myer?" Mrs. Beaufort asked.

Her husband held up his hand for silence, and we all fell to watching the servants, waiting for them to leave so we could talk freely. The footmen brought in a series of dishes and served while the butler poured wine. Once they'd finished, Mr. Beaufort dismissed them, and they departed without a backward glance. Either they were well trained or were used to the informality of their employers.

"Now may I ask why you mentioned Mr. Gladstone in the same breath as Myer?" asked Mrs. Beaufort. "Is he a hypnotist too?"

I felt a twinge of guilt at discussing Samuel and his ability without him present, but it was too late to dismiss her question now. His secret had been revealed and I doubted the Beauforts would allow us to avoid answering.

Jack told them about Samuel's hypnosis. He was met with raised eyebrows, but not derision or disbelief. Very little seemed to surprise this family.

"So how did the meeting with Myer go?" Sylvia asked. "Is he a natural hypnotist like Samuel?"

"He certainly is," Jack muttered.

"You sound disapproving," Mrs. Beaufort said. "Yet you accept Mr. Gladstone's ability."

"He doesn't hypnotize people for amusement or because they disagree with him." I noticed how he didn't say 'against their will.' It would have been a lie. "Myer hypnotized his wife in front of us."

All the ladies gasped. "Good lord!" Mrs. Culvert said, a hand at her throat.

"Despicable man," Mrs. Beaufort muttered. "Utterly without morals, it would seem."

"Did you fall under his spell, Hannah?" Sylvia asked.

"Jack made sure that I didn't."

"Needless to say, the meeting didn't get off to a promising start," Jack said.

"*Why* did he hypnotize his wife?" Mr. Culvert asked. "Did he give you a reason?"

"Does he need a reason?" his wife retorted.

He waved his fork about. "If she were being particularly difficult, for example, or—"

"George!"

He lowered his fork and pushed his glasses up his nose. "Of course, it's a terrible business. Absolutely despicable. He should never have done it. But...what was she like, Miss Smith?"

"I found her to be very odd," I said.

"See!"

Mrs. Culvert glared at her husband. "George, oddity is not a reason to hypnotize anyone."

"No. Of course not. I find the situation interesting, that's all. I'm trying to understand it from Mr. Myer's point of view."

"Perhaps you ought to try to understand from his wife's. Imagine living with someone who can hypnotize you whenever he likes and feels no guilt in doing so."

"Indeed," he said, nodding. "I see what you mean. Poor Mrs. Myer. It's no wonder she's odd."

I exchanged smirks with Miss Moreau sitting across from me.

"Now that George is enlightened, please go on, Miss Smith," Mrs. Beaufort said.

I told them how Everett Myer had ordered his wife out of the room and how he'd been curious as to why none of us had been affected. "Samuel and Jack are immune, but I was succumbing to his voice until Jack poked me. We told Mr. Myer that Samuel was like him, although he'd already guessed. His wife had too."

"She did seem very curious about him," Jack said, frowning into his wine glass. "It was as if she could tell just by looking into his eyes what he was. She wasn't afraid, though. What do you think, Hannah?"

"You're right, she wasn't afraid of Samuel. Perhaps disturbed by him, even a little angry. It grew worse when Samuel tried to charm her with a few smiles and compliments."

Sylvia laughed. "Do you mean the charmer failed to charm a lady? How I'm going to tease him about that."

"He was most put out by it. I've never seen him so out of sorts. He wasn't at all like himself."

Jack nodded. "He told me later that Mrs. Myer unsettled him. She seemed to know instantly what he was capable of and disturbed by it."

"I can see why," Mrs. Beaufort said. "With a husband who hypnotizes her without warning, perhaps she expected Samuel to do the same."

"She was used to it, you mean," Mr. Beaufort said. "That's why she wasn't afraid. She was used to being hypnotized, yet doesn't like it, naturally."

"How awful for her," Miss Moreau said quietly. "The poor woman."

We ate in silence for a few moments, the weight of Mrs. Myer's situation dampening further conversation until Mr. Beaufort spoke.

"Did Myer offer any suggestions as to which Society member may have summoned the demon?" he asked.

"None," Jack said. He told them everything Myer had claimed, and there the conversation ended.

Mr. Beaufort rang for the servants to clear away our main course dishes and bring in the next. As jelly and blancmange were served, Mrs. Beaufort declared that she would invite the Myers to the ball.

"Are you mad?" her sister-in-law said. "After all we've heard tonight?"

Mrs. Beaufort smiled mischievously as she sliced into her jelly. "Not mad, merely intrigued. Besides, I'm sure Mr. Langley and Miss Smith would find it useful to study the man further."

"Not to mention Samuel," I added.

"This way, we can all help. What do you think, Jacob?"

"I think you've got a penchant for causing trouble." He raised his glass to his wife and winked at her. "If you think the Myers ought to come to the ball, then who am I to disagree?"

***

The journey home to Frakingham was long and tiring, partly because of my illness, and partly because we argued with Samuel much of the way.

"I'm going to return to London," he declared before we'd even left the city behind. "Myer wishes to study me and I him."

"What!" Jack exploded. "Are you mad?"

Samuel crossed his arms and raised his eyebrows. Jack swore.

"Language," Sylvia scolded. "There are ladies present."

"You can't live with Myer," Jack said. "He's a disreputable cur with no concern for his own wife! Bloody hell, Gladstone, I thought you better than that."

"Have you quite finished?" Samuel huffed. "For one thing, I'm not going to live with him. I'll rent rooms nearby. Secondly, I may be able to talk some sense into him and make him see that he can't go hypnotizing his wife whenever she disagrees with him. Thirdly, I'll never get this chance again. He and I both believe there are no others of our kind. I have to study him to understand more about this talent, and he wishes to study me. I would expect you, of all people, to see my point, Jack."

"I do see your point, I just don't agree with it. You were perfectly content to live at Frakingham until you met Myer. He didn't hypnotize you, did he?"

Samuel rolled his eyes. "Hannah, talk some sense into this obstinate fool who thinks I should be at August Langley's beck and call."

"I don't think that," Jack said before I could answer. "This has nothing to do with August and everything to do with your reckless willingness to allow someone of dubious character to poke around inside your mind."

Samuel smirked, but there was no humor in it. "Ah, so you're worried about me. Nice to know you care, Langley."

"Shut it, Gladstone, I can't stand the sight of you."

We all knew that wasn't true, not anymore. Samuel laughed and slapped Jack's shoulder. Jack grunted and appealed to me for help.

"Jack *is* worried about you, Samuel," I said. "As am I."

"And me," Sylvia piped up. "I don't think Myer should be trusted."

"I'm very aware of his capabilities." Samuel skimmed his hand over his blond hair, ruffling it. "I am also aware that he can't hypnotize me. I'll be safe."

I don't think he quite understood our concerns. Myer's morals were questionable. Samuel's had been once too, although it seemed he'd left that behind him. But what if

Myer led Samuel back down that path? Was Samuel strong enough to resist?

He leaned across the gap between us and touched my hand. "Have faith, Hannah," he murmured. "I've changed." It would seem he did understand after all.

"We trust you," I said. "Don't we, Jack?"

Jack grunted again, which may have been agreement or not.

"You can't tell me what to do, Langley," Samuel said. "Nor can August. I'm free to come and go from Frakingham as I please."

"But you *belong* at Frakingham," Sylvia whined.

"Why? Because I should be at Freak House with the other freaks?"

"You're not as freakish as these two," she pointed out. Her sigh echoed around the cabin. "Samuel, when will you come home again?"

Home. Frakingham *was* home, and not just to Jack and Sylvia anymore, but to me and, I'd thought, Samuel too. Of all of us, however, he had fewer ties to the estate. He had a family somewhere and could return to University College to finish his studies or to Dr. Werner's practice if he wished. It pained me to admit it, but he didn't need Freak House or us.

He looked down at his hands in his lap and shrugged. "I have to do this."

We tried several more times to talk him out of it, sometimes in subtle ways, and other times more obviously. But he was determined to go, and we hadn't changed his mind by the time we reached the large iron gates of Frakingham. He declared he would return to London with us for the ball and remain there for an indeterminate length of time.

"I'll tell Langley now," he said, grim-faced. "Wish me luck."

Sylvia pouted. "I will not." She climbed out of the coach and stormed off toward the front steps. I followed her, but could not keep up. She bent her head against the strong wind and, not looking where she was going, barreled into Tommy coming to greet us.

"Steady, Miss Langley," he said, catching her by the elbows. He did not let her go immediately, but held her. He smiled and it was clear to anyone who looked that he was happy to see her. "Are you all right?"

She wrenched herself free. "No, I am not. Watch where you're going, Tommy! Honestly," she muttered, striding away. "What is wrong with the men in this house?"

"Sylvia?" said August Langley, appearing in the doorway. Bollard stood behind him, not meeting anyone's gaze. I'd not seen them arrive. "Is something wrong?" Langley glanced past his niece to me. The raw concern in his eyes alarmed me, but it vanished just as quickly. He focused on Sylvia as she approached him.

"Samuel's leaving!" she cried, taking her uncle's hand. "Tell him he can't go."

"Thank you, Sylvia," Samuel ground out, joining us on the steps. "I'm returning to London for a while, sir. I'm going to study Myer, and he me."

Langley stilled. "Are you mad?"

Samuel smirked. "Are you sure you're not related to Jack after all? You're sounding very much alike lately."

Langley clasped the arms of his wheelchair, turning his knuckles white. "Inside. Now."

Bollard wheeled him backward. Samuel took my arm while Jack remained behind to help Tommy with the luggage. I knew they'd want to exchange news. It's what they always did after a lengthy separation.

We followed Langley and Sylvia into the drawing room. The wheels of the chair rolled over the uncarpeted floor like an ominous rumble of distant thunder. "Go to your room and rest, Hannah," he ordered me before I'd even set foot in the drawing room.

"I'll stay here if you don't mind."

"I do mind. Go. You too, Sylvia."

I was about to protest when Sylvia grabbed my hand and steered me away. She pulled me to the end of the corridor where I finally resisted. I slipped my hand free of hers.

"What do you make of that?" I said.

"He's furious," she whispered.

"Whatever for? Samuel's a free man. He can do as he pleases. I don't like the way your uncle thinks he can dictate to everyone."

"It's his house."

"Yes, but he's so...vehement. Why?"

"I don't know, and it's best not to ask."

I glanced over my shoulder in the direction I'd come from. "I don't plan on asking. I'm going to eavesdrop."

"Hannah! You can't."

She went to take my hand again, but I evaded her. "Don't stop me, Sylvia. You wouldn't want me to become angry?"

Her eyes widened, and she quickly shook her head. One point to me. It would have taken a lot more to get me mad and spit fire from my fingers, but I wasn't going to tell her that. I felt a little guilty for tricking her, but not overmuch. She gave me no other option.

I tiptoed down the corridor and listened at the dining room door. Langley was speaking.

"You cannot go." His voice was calmer, but no less commanding.

"Why not?" Samuel asked.

"I forbid it."

"That didn't answer my question. Why?"

"Isn't it obvious? Hannah needs you."

I straightened. Me? What did I have to do with the matter?

It would seem Samuel was equally baffled. There was a moment's silence before he said, "Hannah has Jack to take care of her."

"I don't *want* Jack to take care of her," Langley said. "They cannot be together."

"It's a little late for that."

"It's never too late. I may have been busy, but I know what they've been doing. Bollard has kept me informed. I'll be putting an end to their rendezvous in the lake now that they're back. I should have done it earlier."

"I...I don't think that's a good idea. They have strong wills of their own. How will you stop them, for one thing?"

"Simple. I'll give them no choice. I'll tell them I'll put an end to looking for Hannah's cure."

CHAPTER 5

My stomach heaved and bile rose to my throat. I pressed back against the wall, near the open door. *Breathe, Hannah.* I tried to comprehend what I'd heard. Tried to understand how Langley could be so cruel.

I failed.

I thought he'd changed. I thought he *wanted* to cure me, that he considered me part of his family now. Recent signs had pointed to him caring.

I was wrong.

He cared nothing for me. Nothing at all. Only his own reputation, and what he thought was best for Jack. And I was *not* best for him.

"You must see that it's necessary," Langley was saying. "I need you to take Jack's place."

"No." Samuel sounded like he was speaking with a tightly clenched jaw. "I do not see that it's necessary, and I will not take Jack's place in Hannah's heart. Good lord, don't you see that I can't? No one can. It's too late, Langley. Much too late."

Sylvia appeared by my side. I hadn't seen her approach. She took my arm and walked with me down the corridor. It wasn't until we were almost to my room that she spoke.

"You've had a turn," she said. "Lie down."

"No. I don't need to." But I let her take me inside and sit me on the bed.

"There," she soothed. "Do you want me to tell Jack you're here?"

I shook my head. "You're right. I do need to rest."

She left me alone, and I lay on my back on the bed. The tears soon followed, trickling past my ears onto the pillow. Why was Langley being so cruel to us? Why couldn't he see that Jack made me happy, and I him? I know he wanted Jack to do better, but why couldn't he see we *belonged* together?

Why would he force me to choose between the person I loved and a cure to save my life?

***

It was dark when I awoke. It would seem I'd needed the rest after all. I sat up, but giddiness forced me to lie down again. My stomach still felt unsettled, my limbs leaden and achy.

I lay there and listened to my own breathing. The ever-present heat within me swirled but didn't surge. I was definitely hotter than before.

How much longer did I have left?

Had Tate already died?

I tried not to think about it, or what Langley had said to Samuel, but it was no use. It was *all* I could think about. Had Samuel told Jack?

My stomach eventually settled then growled from hunger. I got up slowly and lit the lamp beside the bed. Six o'clock according to the clock on the mantelpiece. I frowned, not quite believing it was that early. We'd arrived home late in the afternoon, at dusk. I peeked through the curtains and was surprised to see the glow in the east. Dawn. It was six AM not PM. I'd slept all night.

One of the maids must have brought in a basin of fresh water. I undressed and washed. Slivers of cold water slipped across my skin, easing the aches and heat a little. It was bliss, but all too temporary. I dried off and dressed in a light day dress before heading out the door.

I stopped in my tracks. Jack sat slumped in a chair in the corridor. His eyes opened, and he stood when he saw me. "Hannah! You're awake." Enough light filtered through the window at the end of the corridor for me to see that his hair stuck out and the top two buttons of his shirt were undone. He wore no tie or waistcoat either. The stubble on his jaw made him look older, rougher. If I'd met him in a dark London alley, I wouldn't have thought him a gentleman.

"Have you been outside my door all night?"

He shrugged one shoulder. "I came in to check on you twice."

I wondered if Langley knew about his vigil. "You fool." It was supposed to be a scold, but it came out too sympathetic for that. "It must have been terribly uncomfortable."

"Sylvia said you'd taken a turn." He searched my face, no doubt looking for signs that I was going to faint or throw up. Or worse. "How do you feel now?"

"The same."

He didn't seem to detect my lie, thank goodness. "Care for an early morning swim?"

My heart thudded in my chest. I wanted to be with him in every way, wanted to kiss him and hold him and be held by him. But if Langley or Bollard saw...

"We shouldn't," I said. "Not after what happened the last time."

"We won't allow that to happen again, Hannah."

"It's too much of a risk."

He frowned. "You should go in by yourself then. It'll make you feel better. I'll watch from the side if it makes you feel safer."

"I'm not sure that's a good idea either."

He took a step toward me, his brows drawn together in a frown. "Hannah, is everything all right?"

"Of course," I said, more brightly than I felt. "Let's go down for breakfast." I turned my back on him and led the way. I didn't want to see the confusion in his eyes, or the worry. I didn't have the strength for it.

I stopped in the doorway to the dining room. August Langley was already there eating breakfast, Bollard attending him. I hadn't wanted to face him yet. My emotions were too raw, and I tended to do rash things when I was emotional.

He set his toast down and regarded me as if he were trying to determine if my health had worsened. When Jack looked at me like that, I could see the worry imprinted in every line of his furrowed brow, but with Langley, it was difficult to tell whether he was curious from a professional viewpoint or personal one.

"Good morning," he said. "How do you feel?"

"The same," I said, giving him the answer I'd given Jack.

"Sit down, Hannah," Jack said. "I'll get your breakfast." He pulled out a chair for me, but I didn't sit.

"I'm not an invalid." I bit my lip. If Langley was offended by my off-handed comment, he didn't show it.

It was Jack who flinched as if my words had stung him. "Hannah? What's wrong?"

"Nothing. I just don't want to be treated like a child. I'm perfectly capable of getting my own breakfast." I sounded so callous. I peered into a tureen on the sideboard so that I didn't have to look at him. Seeing his turmoil made my heart sore. If I watched him any longer, I would be in danger of telling him why I was dismissing him.

He shouldn't know about Langley's ultimatum. He couldn't. A confrontation between them would be a disaster and might inadvertently force Langley's hand.

"Did you speak to Samuel?" I asked Langley, innocently. "What do you think of him going to London to study with Myer?"

"I think he's a fool. Myer isn't to be trusted."

I placed toast and a boiled egg on my plate and carried it to the table, setting it down harder than I intended. "You know him well?"

He shook his head. "Only from what Jack told me last night and Wade the last time he was here. When he told us that Myer hypnotized you, it took me a while to place the name. Then I remembered him. He was an acquaintance from the Society, nothing more. I met him years ago, but don't recall him very well."

Jack poured a cup of tea for me, despite me not having asked. I thanked him and he nodded in acknowledgement, but his frown didn't disappear.

"What about Tate?" I asked. "Did he know Myer better than you?"

Langley stopped chewing for a moment, then resumed, slower. It seemed like an age until he swallowed. "It's possible. As you well know, I didn't watch Tate's every move in those days. That was a mistake."

His uncharacteristic admission surprised not only me, but his assistant. Out of the corner of my eye I saw Bollard's gaze shift to the back of Langley's head. He blinked twice, which on most people meant nothing, but on the usually immobile Bollard, was tantamount to a full conversation.

"Who was Grand Master of the Society in the years you were a member?" I asked.

"You're full of questions this morning, Hannah," Langley said.

"I wish to get to the bottom of things. You may not have noticed, but I have a wide inquisitive streak running through me."

Jack chuckled and even Langley smirked. Behind him, Bollard's eyes twinkled.

"Do these questions also mean you're feeling better?" Langley asked.

"The long sleep has refreshed me, yes." The journey had tired me more than I'd thought, however, I would never admit it. Jack would have me stay indoors, and I did not want to argue with him over whether I was going to the Beauforts' ball or not. I might be nervous about attending it, but I knew I'd regret not going. I wasn't one to shy away from new and sometimes terrifying experiences.

"Well?" I prompted Langley. "Who was in charge?"

"A gentleman named Price. He's dead."

"Did Price know about baby Jack and his abilities?"

"No."

I believed him. I don't know why, but I did and left the conversation at that.

Jack did not. He sat next to me, his plate filled with bacon, toast and eggs, all of which went untouched. He focused his full attention on his uncle. "So my being with you had nothing to do with the Society's wishes?" he asked.

"Of course not. It was a private arrangement between your father and me."

"Who was he?"

"I've told you, Jack, I cannot say."

Jack shook his head and set his knife and fork down, very deliberately. When he looked up again, the tiny scar above his top lip had gone stark white. "No. I don't accept that. Not anymore. Who I am—*what* I am—is linked to my parents. I *need* to know more about them."

Langley dabbed his mouth with his napkin. "I cannot betray a man's trust."

Jack's fist slammed down on the table. Cutlery and teacups rattled and my knife slipped off the side of my plate. "Enough games, August!" Fire danced along Jack's fingertips until he balled his hand, smothering them. "You may think it admirable to protect your friend, but I am your family. Why do you not want to do the right thing by me?"

Langley slowly lowered the napkin to the table. He scrunched it up, then let it go. He did not speak for an interminable length of time. I worried that Jack would explode again and set something alight, but he did not. The two men glared at one another across the table.

Bollard came to stand behind Langley. He rested his hand on the handle of the wheelchair. To quickly wheel him out of the way if necessary? To reassure him? Or for some other purpose?

When Langley did finally speak, it was not the words I expected. "You think of yourself as...my nephew?"

Jack sat back in his chair and unclenched his fists. The fingers were red but no longer alight. "I belong here at Frakingham," he said. "This is my home, and yours and Sylvia's too. It seems that we are a family, albeit an irregular one."

I smiled, but nobody else did. Langley breathed deeply and let it out slowly. "Then you should have no need to belong to another one."

"What are you talking about?" Jack snapped.

"This drive to learn who your parents are is dangerous."

Jack stood so fast, his chair crashed back to the floor. "*Why* is it dangerous? To whom?"

"To this family!"

Jack rounded the table, but Bollard stepped between him and his master. "Move aside, Bollard."

Bollard crossed his arms.

Jack swore then strode out of the dining room. Langley sighed and rubbed his forehead.

"I'd better go after him," I said rising.

"You'll do no such thing, Hannah." Langley sounded as tired as I felt, but his steely voice invited no disagreement.

I sat back down and swallowed heavily. I ached to go after Jack, but I dared not defy Langley anymore. His mood had darkened considerably, and I could not afford to anger him further. Not if stopping his research was the result.

Sylvia sailed into the dining room, humming. Her cheerfulness was a welcome relief, but quite out of place. She seemed oblivious to the tension in the room. "Good morning." She kissed the top of Langley's head. "Hannah, you look better today."

I attempted a smile. "The sleep did me some good."

She poured herself a cup of tea and sat near her uncle. He watched her with a worried expression, as if he half expected her to storm out of the dining room too, like Jack.

"Not eating?" I asked.

"I'm trying to keep my figure trim for the ball."

"Sylvia, your waist is tiny enough. You ought to eat something."

"She's right," Langley said. "This fashion for thinness is unhealthy."

"Since when have you noticed fashion, Uncle?"

"Since you stopped eating properly. That *Young Ladies Journal* you like to read should not encourage it."

Her eyes danced merrily as she peered at him over her teacup. "You read my periodical?"

"Bollard does. I don't have time to read."

Sylvia and I both giggled at the ridiculous image of the stiff Bollard reading a ladies journal. I wondered what articles he liked best.

Bollard didn't flicker an eyelash, though his Adam's apple bobbed noticeably.

"If you're going to stop eating because of a frivolous ball, then I'll have to forbid you to go," Langley said.

Sylvia sobered. "You wouldn't."

Langley finished his tea and did not respond.

Sylvia made a miffed sound through her nose and stood abruptly. Langley watched her as she filled a plate with food. And I do mean filled. The stack of bacon was in danger of toppling over and there was no room for toast. She brought three slices over on a second plate.

Langley made no comment as she sat back down with a flounce that made her skirts puff up.

"There." She sniffed. "Satisfied? I shall be hugely fat for the ball. My dress will need refitting."

Langley ignored her. "Where's Samuel?"

"I just saw him," she said. "He told me he's going for a walk."

"A walk? Why would he do that?"

She threw up her hands. "How should I know? For fresh air? For exercise? To get away from—" She looked down at her plate and sighed. "To get away from here?"

"He should be here," Langley said.

"Why?" I asked.

"That's not your concern."

It most certainly was, particularly if I was the reason he wanted Samuel in the house.

"When you see him, tell him I wish to speak to him," Langley said. "Bollard, my room please."

"Is it wise to interrupt you now?" Sylvia asked. "Aren't you busy enough?"

"Just do as I ask."

Sylvia and I watched Bollard steer him away. We both sighed once he was gone and I, for one, relaxed. "He seems quite angry lately," I said.

"It's just the way he gets when he's been working too hard. Pay him no mind."

I bit my lip. He was working too much because of me. Sylvia didn't seem to notice how her words affected me. She pushed her plate away just as Tommy entered carrying a teapot. She watched him beneath half-closed lids as he placed the fresh pot on the sideboard and picked up the old one.

"Tommy, fill my cup, please," she said.

He exchanged old for new again and poured tea into her cup. When he finished, he pushed her full plate of food closer to her. She scowled at it and pushed it away again. He hesitated before picking it up and returning it to the sideboard.

"What are you doing?" she snapped.

"Tidying up, ma'am. You appeared to be finished."

"I wasn't. Give me back my plate."

He gave me a triumphant smile over the top of her head when she wasn't looking. I grinned back. He must have heard the exchange with Langley and agreed that she ought to eat. It was a stroke of genius to use her contrariness against her. Only someone who knew her very well would have thought of it.

I supposed they had known each other a long time. It was surprising then that she treated him so formally considering he was Jack's friend. On the other hand, Sylvia was a stickler for propriety.

"Have you seen Jack?" I asked him. "He left just a few moments ago in a terrible temper."

Tommy shook his head. "I've been talking to Miss Langley here and didn't see anyone leave."

Sylvia stiffened. "Tommy and I were discussing...whether he ought to come to London with us or stay with Uncle."

Tommy frowned. "We weren't—"

"I think he should stay here," Sylvia said, speaking over the top of him. "But he said Jack needs a valet to attend him, and there ought to be a footman for the coach. I do see the point of that, I admit. Arriving at the Beauforts' house without a footman in attendance would make us seem rather base. However, I don't think we should leave Tommy with the other footmen and drivers. I've heard about the things they get up to while waiting to pick up their masters."

"Are you worried about me, Miss Langley?" Tommy's handsome face flushed to the roots of his hair, and a bashful smile appeared briefly before he banished it.

She scoffed. "Only in that you may be led astray, back to your old ways again. We can't have that. It would reflect poorly on us."

Tommy set the teapot down on the table with a thud. "What is it you're afraid I'll do?" he asked tightly.

"I have an imagination. I can guess what deplorable things you and Jack got up to as orphans. You both ran wild about the streets of London, I'm sure."

Tommy looked like he'd reply, but instead he picked the teapot up and returned to the sideboard. He fussed with the plates and dishes, making far more noise than usual by clanking them against one another. Sylvia appeared not to notice.

"That was a long time ago," I said. "Circumstances were vastly different. I'm sure the footmen and drivers won't do anything too silly. They have to pick up their masters and mistresses after all."

"Hannah, I don't expect you to have heard of the things they get up to, but I have."

"Oh? And what is that?"

She leaned closer. "They drink and gamble the night away," she said, her voice low, but not low enough that Tommy wouldn't have heard. "They cavort with loose women too." She clicked her tongue. "Disgusting."

"I'm sure Tommy won't do anything like that." I felt compelled to defend him since his position meant he was unable to defend himself.

I was wrong. He turned around, eyes flashing, chest heaving. "You fink not, Miss Smiff?" He spoke in his broad slum accent. He only ever did that when he forgot himself in anger or worry. Or perhaps he was using it to deliberately rile Sylvia.

She gasped in shock. "Tommy!"

"Never fear, Miss Langley. I'll be sure an' drink to yer healf. Many, many times. I'm goin' to cavort wiv every bit o' skirt that come my way too. I want to bloody enjoy meself." He was almost shouting by the time he finished. His face had gone quite pink, his eyes dark and fierce. He stalked out the door.

I watched him go, unsure whether to follow him or not.

"Well," Sylvia said on a huff. "Sometimes it's good to remember what he is and where he's from. He'll never be one of us."

I shook my head. "Sylvia…" I sighed. "You ought to apologize to him."

"Whatever for? *He* should apologize to *me*. Honestly, Hannah, you still have so much to learn about how the world works."

"If the world separates people based on where they were born and who they were born to, then I'm not sure I want to learn any more, thank you." I strode past her and out the door. Whether she stayed or left, I didn't care. I was quite sure she wouldn't apologize to Tommy though.

I went in search of Jack. I was worried that he might be down by the lake. It would be easier for Langley to spy us there through his window, but fortunately Jack was in our old training room on the top floor. He used to try to teach me to control my fire and my temper in that room, but we'd given up about the time we'd learned what Tate had done to me. We still used the room sometimes, just to sit together quietly and watch the world through the window. It had a wonderful view of the lake and the abbey ruins beyond.

Jack sat on the window seat, his knees drawn up. He turned as I entered and smiled. "I was hoping you'd look for me here."

"Are you all right?" I asked, sitting on one of the chairs.

He nodded and swung his legs down, facing me. "Langley will never tell me about my parents. I don't know why I bother trying to convince him. It's a waste of breath."

"You have every right to know. I don't understand why he doesn't tell you."

He shrugged. "He made a promise. I shouldn't expect him to break it, not even for me. If Tommy asked me to keep a secret for him, I'd do it."

"Yes, but Langley doesn't care about anyone as much as you care for Tommy. I'm quite convinced he has no friends."

"Except Bollard."

"Bollard's not a friend. He's a machine. I made a very funny joke, and he didn't even smile a little bit." I laughed and so did Jack.

"It's nice to see you laugh again," he said, turning wistful. "You don't seem yourself today. What's wrong?"

"I'm just…coming to grips with my situation."

He crouched beside me. He fingered the cotton of my skirt below my knee. It was as close as we could get without touching and risking combustion. "I understand, Hannah, but don't push me away. Not now." He closed his eyes and heaved in a breath. When he opened them again, the raw emotion was plain to see. He didn't try to hide it. "August will find a cure. He *will*."

"And if he doesn't?"

He pressed a finger to his lips. "Don't say it. Don't think it." He resumed touching my dress again, but his gaze was focused fully on me. Being the center of his world was a heady, intoxicating drug. I would never tire of it. "I want to be with you as much as possible," he went on. "I know you're trying to protect me, but pretending you don't care will not alter my feelings. What I feel for you is here to stay, forever. Nothing will make it go away. Not you trying to distance yourself from me and not your..." His voice came to a shuddery halt. He closed his eyes again and this time it was much longer before they reopened. "Not your death."

It took all my strength not to circle him in my arms. I desperately wanted to. "It will be all right, Jack," I said, echoing his earlier conviction. "You'll see. For now, we mustn't let him see us together."

"Why? I don't care if he does. He can't keep me away from you."

"No. He can't. But he doesn't like us being together and that distracts him from his purpose. That battle must be fought and won *after* he finds a cure. Understand?"

He sighed heavily. "You're right."

I blew out a breath, relived beyond measure. "The most important thing is not to distract Langley."

"Ah."

"Ah?" I narrowed my eyes. "What are you planning?"

"I'm going to lure him out of his room via a distraction."

"Why?"

"So I can break into his room and look for evidence linking me to my parents."

"And when do you plan on doing this?"

"Tonight."

"What sort of distraction do you propose will get him out of his room?"

He smiled wickedly. "That's where you'll play a role."

CHAPTER 6

"I'd like you to pretend to faint or do something equally dramatic," Jack said.

I gaped at him. "I'm not sure that will lure Langley out of his rooms. Or Bollard."

"Bollard will wheel August out in a hurry. Faint in the parlor and make sure Sylvia is present. Tell her to fetch August immediately."

"How can I do that if I've fainted?"

"Improvise. You can do this, Hannah. Make it convincing. I'd like him out of there for at least ten minutes."

"Surely you'll need more time than that to search his room."

"I know where he keeps his important papers. All I need is the key and I have a few guesses as to where that might be."

"This is important to you, isn't it?"

His eyes clouded. He blinked slowly. "Yes. Yes it is."

"Then I'll help. Tonight then?"

He grinned suddenly. "We make quite a team."

"Don't get ahead of yourself. We haven't accomplished anything yet."

Footsteps along the corridor signaled someone's approach. Jack stepped away from me, but it was only Tommy.

"Mrs. Mott's here," he announced. "She wishes to see you both."

"I wonder what she wants," I said. "I do hope she's all right."

We went down to the parlor. Mrs. Mott stood near the fire, warming her hands. She wore no gloves, and the backs of her hands were red and raw.

"Mrs. Mott," Jack said, taking one of her hands and guiding her to a chair. "Please take a seat. Did you walk all the way here?"

"I rode part of the way in the back of Mr. Trantor's cart. He was on his way back to the farm."

"It's a pleasure to see you again," I said, eyeing her carefully. She didn't seem upset or troubled, so that was a relief. Indeed, the shadows we'd seen on her face the last time we'd met had disappeared. "You look well."

"I am well, thank you, Miss Smith." She sat on the chair by the fire, her hands clasped in her lap and her knees pressed together. Her gaze traveled over me, taking in my outfit perhaps. I felt a little conspicuous dressed in pale blue cotton while she wore gray wool. Wool, *ugh*. It seemed an age since I'd been forced to endure a world filled with woolen hangings, rugs and clothing.

"Is everything all right?" I asked.

"Things is gettin' easier thanks to Mr. Langley's generosity. I want you to know that me and my children appreciate what you're doin' for us with the annuity. It's kind of you and your uncle, Mr. Langley. Very kind indeed. You didn't need to give us that extra, but I thank you for that too."

Jack lifted an eyebrow. "Extra?"

"The package what come yesterday."

"Hannah, did you organize a package?"

I shook my head. "Sylvia must have, or Mr. Langley," I said, knowing very well that it would never have occurred to him. "What was in the package?"

Mrs. Mott frowned. "Money of course."

Money? It probably wasn't Sylvia then. She might organize a basket of food or clothing, but she had very little money of her own. "Are you sure it came from this house?" I asked.

"Well, no, I suppose I ain't sure. It was on my doorstep when I got home yesterday from the market. I just assumed it were you and Mr. Langley here after everything else you done for us."

Jack smiled, but I could detect a hint of curiosity in his eyes. "Did any of your neighbors see who delivered it?"

She shrugged. "Don't think so."

"It would seem you have another benefactor, Mrs. Mott."

"How strange," she said. "I wonder who and why."

I glanced at Jack, but he stared silently at Mrs. Mott.

"Well, I better make hay while the sun shines, eh?" She chuckled. "I'll be down at the cobblers before the end of the day. My young 'uns need new shoes."

"I'm very pleased for you," I said. Indeed I was. Whoever had provided her with the unexpected windfall was kind indeed.

"You don't think it's from whoever employed Mr. Mott to do that new job, do you?" she said. "The one he was supposed to do after he finished here. Only...perhaps the mayor don't know he's dead, and this is pay in advance. Maybe he's goin' to want it back when he finds out."

"The mayor would know of your husband's unfortunate demise, surely," I said. "Anyway, why do you think it was he who employed Mr. Mott?"

"I found a letter from him in Mr. Mott's things, signed and all."

"What exactly did it say?"

She looked down at her tightly clasped hands. "Well, let's see if I remember it exact. It didn't say much. 'Do it at soon as possible.' That's all. It was signed 'Mayor.'"

Jack and I exchanged glances. Was Butterworth, the Harborough mayor, doing building works in the village? But what of the Society? Where did he fit in with that?

Jack thanked Mrs. Mott and she thanked him in return once again for taking care of her family in their time of need. "You and your uncle are so kind," she said. "Such gen'lemen as there ever was. If there's anything I can do for you, sir, be sure to let me know."

"I will," Jack said.

Mrs. Mott stood, Jack too, but I hadn't quite finished with the conversation. "Mrs. Mott," I said, "if I describe a man to you, will you tell me if you've ever seen him before?"

She shrugged one shoulder. "I'll try, Miss Smith. Is he a Harborough fellow?"

"No, he's a gentleman from London. He's quite tall and fine-boned, bald, but has thick eyebrows and whiskers. His voice is very…melodic. Does he sound familiar?"

"Aye, he does. It's not often we get London gen'lemen coming to the village, so they get noticed."

Jack and I exchanged another glance. Myer led us to believe he'd never been to Harborough.

"Do you know his name?" I asked.

She shook her head. "I've naught to do with him."

"Do you know who he sees when he's in the village?"

Another shake of her head. "Sorry, Miss Smith, I don't know nothin' about him."

I thanked her, and she bobbed an awkward curtsy that had me feeling just as awkward. Curtsies were for ladies and princesses. My only link to that sort was having lived in a gentleman's attic for most of my life.

Jack walked Mrs. Mott out then returned to me. "What do you make of that?" he asked, sitting down again.

"I think we need to speak to the Butterworths and ask them if they had any business with Mott."

"Agreed."

"The mayor belongs to a few societies in the area," Jack said. "His wife too. A building could have been commissioned for one of them."

It sounded reasonable enough, but after believing that the Society For Supernatural Activity was behind Mott's activities, I found it difficult to think of anyone else as having been involved. And the mayor, of all people! What did he have against August Langley, or us? Why would he go to great lengths to summon a demon here?

"Then there's Myer," he said. "It was clever of you to describe him to her."

I tried to think back to the conversation we'd had with Myer about Harborough and Frakingham. "He never told us he hadn't been here," I said. "So he hasn't lied."

"No, but someone with nothing to hide would simply acknowledge that he'd visited our area. He did mention that he'd heard about the Frakingham Abbey ruins. *Heard*, not seen."

"He makes me terribly anxious," I said. "I wish Samuel had not agreed to go to him."

It was just my luck that Samuel entered the room as I said it. "Stop worrying about me, Hannah," he scolded gently. "I'll be all right. His hypnosis is useless on me, and if he proves a physical threat, I'll box him."

"This isn't a joke, Samuel!"

"I wasn't joking." It was impossible to tell from his impish smile whether he was or not. "Hannah, it's sweet of you to worry about me, but you shouldn't. This is something I need to do. Surely you and Jack can understand that."

I sighed and appealed to Jack. He merely shrugged. "You know you're always welcome back here whenever you wish," he said.

Samuel clapped him on the shoulder. "Thank you, Friend. Now tell me what the Widow Mott wanted."

We told him about the letter to her husband, signed by the mayor, but he was more interested in where the extra money had come from.

"Do you think it was payment for successfully summoning the demon?" he asked.

"Or guilt money," Jack noted. "Whoever bought Mott's services sent him to his death and condemned his family to poverty."

***

Sylvia would not be left out of an excursion to the village, particularly when we had dresses to pick up. Mrs. Irwin the dressmaker had sent word that morning that our ball gowns were ready.

"Samuel and I will visit the Butterworths while you're at the dressmaker's," Jack said once we four were seated in the carriage.

"You will not," I told him. "I want to come too."

Sylvia groaned. "I should have suspected you'd say that."

We tried our gowns on one final time in Mrs. Irwin's house where she worked out of a back room. They fit perfectly, and she boxed them up for us. Jack, Samuel and the driver tied the packages to the roof of the carriage and we drove off to the Butterworths' house a short distance away.

Sylvia peered out of the window and searched the sky. "If it rains, our gowns will be ruined."

"There isn't a cloud in the sky, Syl," Jack said.

"There may be no clouds *now*, but you know very well it could be raining by the time we set off for home again."

"In that case, you can sit beside the driver and the boxes can ride in the cabin with us."

Her glare could have cut him it was so sharp. "Let's just get this conversation over with."

I'd met the Butterworths for the first time only recently. They were an oddly matched couple. She was taller than he and had a commanding manner, while he seemed more submissive in nature. They were both pleasant enough, however, and I had liked them on the whole. I wasn't sure what to make of the notion that one or both of them could have been involved in the summoning of the demon. It seemed unlikely.

As with our last visit, a face peered down at us from a high window upon our arrival. The girl watched us alight from the carriage, but she was too far away for me to see her expression. I waved at her and she hesitated before waving back. A woman wearing a white cap appeared and spoke to the girl, then both disappeared. The girl must have been the Butterworths' youngest daughter, and the woman her governess perhaps.

A maid ushered us through to the same parlor we'd sat in last time. I shed my hat, coat and gloves immediately and handed them to her before she departed. The fire in the grate was much too warm. Jack didn't appear nearly so uncomfortable, but then the heat never affected him as much as it did me.

We were not left alone for long. Two girls of about my own age were ushered in ahead of Mrs. Butterworth. They were identical twins, both with mid-brown hair and an abundance of curls artfully arranged to frame their long faces. They wore matching black and gold striped gowns with high collars and little bows down the front. The outfits weren't to my taste, but I noticed Sylvia admiring them.

Both girls bobbed curtsies at the same time then, eyes discreetly downcast, sat on the second sofa. They perched on the edge of the seat with rigid backs, hands clasped loosely in their laps and heads bowed forward in precisely the same way. I couldn't stop staring at them. Were they doing everything the same on purpose? Had they rehearsed this?

Mrs. Butterworth greeted us enthusiastically and introduced her daughters to Samuel and me. Jack and Sylvia had met them, of course, but we had not.

"This is Julia and Jennifer," she said. "My eldest daughters."

I wondered how she knew which was which. There wasn't a single thing to differentiate them, not even an extra freckle.

"It's a pleasure to meet you," I said.

Both girls looked up and smiled sweetly. "Thank you," one of them said. I don't know whether it was Julia or Jennifer.

"It's a pleasure to meet you too, Miss Smith," said the other. "And of course Mr. Gladstone."

Samuel gave them both a nod of greeting. "The pleasure is all mine."

He hadn't used his hypnotically deep voice to charm them, but charm them he did with those few words. Both girls giggled and blushed. Beside me, I heard Sylvia's huff of exasperation.

"Julia, ring for tea," Mrs. Butterworth said. The girl on the left rose.

"We're not staying," Jack assured her. Julia Butterworth sat again. "We actually wanted to speak to Mr. Butterworth. Is he here?"

"He's in his study. Julia, fetch your father."

Julia stood again and glanced at Samuel from beneath her lashes before she departed. I was quite sure that her walk had an extra sway to it compared to when she'd entered. If Samuel noticed, he gave no indication.

"Miss Langley, I was quite saddened to receive your note canceling the Christmas dinner." Mrs. Butterworth gave Sylvia a sympathetic smile. "Most disappointed. Mr. Butterworth and I were looking forward to it. It's been *such* a long time since we visited Frakingham House."

Sylvia sighed. "It is a disappointment to all of us, but with the renovations so far from completion, we simply had no choice but to postpone it."

"And in light of the recent deaths too," Jack added. He didn't glare at Sylvia, yet he somehow managed to scold her anyway. At least, she hurriedly agreed with him.

Everybody sympathized over the demise of Mott and Olsen until Julia returned with her father.

Mr. Butterworth beamed at us all. He reminded me of a snowman, all round and soft with small eyes and no eyelids. "Welcome, welcome! So good to see you young people again. What a pleasure, and with the girls home this time too. I've—"

"It *is* a pleasure," Mrs. Butterworth agreed, interrupting her husband. It would seem she hadn't broken her habit of cutting him off mid-sentence. "We've harbored hopes ever since your arrivals that you will all become friends. Haven't we, Mr. Butterworth?"

"I—"

"The girls asked me a thousand questions after your last visit. What did Miss Smith look like? What did she wear? Was Mr. Gladstone as handsome as Mr. Jack Langley?"

The Butterworth girls giggled again, neither looking up from their laps. I was beginning to see why Sylvia hadn't invited them to dine with us along with their parents. If they were always so silly, the conversation would be dull indeed. Besides, Sylvia was hoping the dinner would be a sophisticated affair similar to the dinners at the Beauforts' house, and there was nothing terribly sophisticated about the girls.

"We'll have to organize a picnic in the summer," Mrs. Butterworth went on. "You will both still be here in the summer, won't you?"

How should a dying person answer that? I blinked at her, my tongue suddenly too thick to form an answer. I dared not look at Jack to see his reaction, or Sylvia. Neither spoke, and it was left to Samuel.

"Of course," he said cheerfully. "Frakingham is our home now."

Mrs. Butterworth beamed. "Did you hear that, girls? Mr. Gladstone is staying. And Miss Smith too." The afterthought wasn't lost on me, although I didn't mind. I could see how a handsome gentleman would be more interesting to marriageable girls than a redhead of the same sex. "Just think, another gentleman and lady in our midst in little old Harborough."

I had the urge to giggle just like the Butterworth girls. If only they knew that I wasn't a lady. They'd turn up their prim noses at me.

"So what is it we can do for you today?" Mr. Butterworth asked, eyeing the clock on the mantel.

"This may seem a strange question," Jack said, "but I'm curious as to whether you've been planning any building works in the village recently. Perhaps for one of the societies you belong to?"

Mr. Butterworth exchanged a glance with his wife. "I can't think of any. Can—?"

"No, nothing," his wife said. "Why, Mr. Langley?"

Jack smiled and waved a hand, dismissive. "Ever since the renovations up at the house, I've become interested in architecture. I thought we could share plans and ideas."

"Oh. I see." Mrs. Butterworth seemed to accept his explanation, but her husband frowned at Jack. He said nothing. "There certainly haven't been any plans put forward through the council," she added.

I'd wondered if she had some influence in her husband's affairs, and her response confirmed it. Her domination of him was out of character for a man in a position of authority, and an elected official at that. I could imagine *her* taking charge of the campaigning on his behalf. She was quite a force.

A flash of something white by the door caught my eye. I seemed to be the only one who'd seen it. I kept watching and was rewarded with the sight of a little face peeking around the door jam. I smiled at the girl and she pulled back, out of sight.

"I'm sorry we couldn't help you, Mr. Langley," Mr. Butterworth said.

Jack held up his hand. "Another question, if you please. Do you know a man named Mott?"

Butterworth sucked on his lower lip. He shook his head. "Doesn't ring any bells."

"Why, Mr. Butterworth!" his wife cried. "Of course you know Mott. He was one of the men who died up at Frakingham. He's the reason the Langleys had to cancel Christmas dinner. Such a shame," she added with a shake of her head. Did she mean Mott's death or the canceled dinner?

"Ah, *Mott.*" Her husband gave an emphatic nod. "Yes, I remember now. Poor fellow."

"Were you in communication with him?" Jack asked.

"About what?"

Jack shrugged. "About anything."

"No, Mr. Langley, I was not. What are all these questions for?"

"Nothing," Samuel said quickly. Then, more soothingly, he said, "Nothing at all, Mr. Butterworth."

Both Sylvia and I glared at him. He was not going to hypnotize Mr. Butterworth, surely! Not when others were so close and in danger of falling under his spell too. It was bad enough having the girls blushing and giggling, we didn't need them throwing themselves at Samuel as well. It had been known to happen among the women he hypnotized.

Samuel blinked his wide blue eyes back at me, all innocence. The devil. His charming nature would be his undoing one day. I was convinced of it.

I smiled at Mr. Butterworth. "Do you know a Mr. Myer from London?"

Samuel cleared his throat. I ignored him. He may not think Myer was a danger, but no amount of charm from either man could convince me to agree.

Mr. Butterworth shook his head. "Never heard of him."

"Mrs. Butterworth?"

"No," she said, patting the curl of hair dangling near her ear. "Why?"

"He's a gentleman we met in London recently."

"Not very many London gentlemen make their way here."

I bit the inside of my lip. I would have to lie, and I wasn't sure I could make it convincing enough. Thankfully Jack took over.

"He said he was here recently, and we wondered if you'd met with him. That's all." He smiled benignly. If I hadn't known the truth, I would have believed him.

"We don't know anyone of that name." Mrs. Butterworth glanced at the gold carriage clock on the mantel, then at her husband. He was focused on Jack and didn't notice.

"Describe him," he said.

Jack did, but Mr. Butterworth shook his head again. "I've not seen him here. Tell him to visit next time he makes his way to our little village. Any friend of yours is our friend too, Mr. Langley."

We said our thanks and goodbyes. The Butterworth girls curtsied again and demurely thanked us for coming. They looked first to Samuel, then to Jack. Not once did they speak to Sylvia or me.

"I don't think much of those girls," Sylvia muttered, flattening her skirts as she sat in the coach cabin. "Empty-headed creatures, both of them. They couldn't take their eyes off you two."

"Can you blame them? Jack and Samuel are very handsome," I said with a wink at Jack. "I'm sure most girls can't take their eyes off them. I know I find it difficult."

Jack grinned at me.

Samuel sighed theatrically. "I for one am heartily tired of being admired for my beauty and not my accomplishments. Don't these girls see me for what I truly am?"

"Vain?" Jack offered. "Arrogant?"

Samuel laughed.

The coach rolled away, only to stop abruptly at the gate. I would have ended up in Sylvia's lap opposite if Samuel hadn't put his arm across me as a barrier.

"What's wrong?" Sylvia asked, straightening her hat.

Jack leaned his head out the window, only to be startled by the sudden appearance of a face. The same face that I'd seen in the Butterworth's window and at the parlor door. It belonged to a girl with her brown hair in ringlets and a smudge of dirt on her chin.

"Hello," I said. "Have you snuck out?"

"Shhh." She glanced toward the house. "I can't talk for long," she whispered. "Listen carefully."

"What a dear little thing you are," Sylvia cooed.

The girl dismissed Sylvia with a roll of her brown eyes. "I heard you asking about that London gentleman, and I heard my mother's reply."

"She said she's never met him," Jack said.

"She's lying."

My breath caught. "Why do you say that?"

"Because I've seen him here. No one else has. He's come here twice when no one is home except me and Mama. It's been Saturday afternoons, you see. My governess's day off."

Good lord. Why had Mrs. Butterworth lied? "What's your name?" I asked her.

"That's not important." Her big brown eyes shifted to the house again then returned to us. "I have to get back before they realize I'm gone. Are you going to make sure that man never comes back, sir?" she said to Jack.

"I'm not sure I can do that," he said. "Why don't you want him to come back?"

"Because he makes my head dizzy."

Oh my God. She wasn't spinning an extraordinary tale. Myer *had* been here, and he'd hypnotized someone, most likely Mrs. Butterworth? Whatever for?

"What about your mother?" I asked. "Does the gentleman make her head dizzy too?"

"I don't know. I don't think so. She wouldn't kiss him if she had a dizzy head, would she?"

CHAPTER 7

Sylvia's gasp filled the cabin. I pressed my hand over hers to silence her. The girl sounded brave, but I didn't want to upset her any more than necessary.

"She shouldn't be doing that with him," the girl said, baring her teeth. "If she does it again, I'm going to tell Papa." She stabbed a finger at Jack, stopping just short of poking him in the eye. "So if he's your friend, sir, you should tell him to stay away."

She ran off and hid behind a garden statue of a Greek goddess carrying an urn. She peered round it at the house, just as a woman wearing a white cap emerged from the front door.

"Jane? Jane?" the woman called.

The girl revealed herself and received a scolding from her governess for her disappearing act. The coach rolled off and I didn't hear Jane's response.

"What an extraordinary little girl," Sylvia said with a shake of her head.

"What an extraordinary accusation she made," I said. "Do you think Mrs. Butterworth was kissing Mr. Myer because she wanted to? Or…?"

Samuel held up his hand. "Don't accuse him of anything like that without proof."

"We have a witness who said the man makes her head dizzy," Jack said.

"That's proof that he has hypnotized, not proof that he, er, kissed Mrs. Butterworth without her consent."

"Samuel, I don't know whether your defending him is admirable or worrying," I said. "Why do you do it when you hardly know the man?"

He rested his elbow on the window frame and rubbed his finger along his top lip. "Just because he's hypnotized people, doesn't mean he does it all the time without their knowledge. I know what it's like to be accused of something you didn't do."

We all stared at him. He merely shrugged one shoulder and turned to look out the window.

Jack cleared his throat. "What it does prove is that Myer has been here. Mrs. Mott recognized him too. We can't dismiss him as a suspect in the demon summoning yet."

"Nor can we dismiss the Butterworths," I said.

Sylvia scoffed. "Surely you can't blame Mrs. Butterworth. If she contacted Mott, then it's likely she was doing Myer's bidding while under his hypnosis."

"Actually, I was referring more to *Mr.* Butterworth. He pretended not to know about Mott or his death, when clearly his wife knew."

"Perhaps he doesn't know everybody in the village."

"A man was mauled to death! That can't happen so frequently in such a small village that it goes unnoticed by the mayor."

She sighed. "Whether they're guilty along with Mott or not, there is one thing I can be certain about. The Butterworths are a very odd family."

Jack grunted a humorless laugh. "Almost as odd as us."

***

Langley had asked Sylvia to fetch him as soon as I awoke from my afternoon nap. I waited in the parlor. Jack, who'd joined me as soon as I emerged from my room, crouched next to me.

"This is as good a time as any," he whispered.

"To look through his things?" I whispered back. "Jack, are you sure you should do this?"

"No, but I have to try."

I didn't get the chance to protest further. Bollard wheeled Langley in. He had a tray in his lap, a neatly folded cloth on it. I pulled a face. "You want more blood."

Jack slipped out of the room as Langley unfolded the cloth. Neither he nor Bollard appeared to notice.

"Bollard," Langley said, passing the syringe to his servant.

"*He's* going to do it?" I shook my head. "No. He's not sticking that thing into me."

"Bollard is capable."

"I don't want someone who is merely capable. I want a professional!"

Bollard took a step toward me, and I shrank back. "Don't bring that thing near me."

Langley huffed out a breath. "You're being hysterical. He won't hurt you."

"He nearly beat me to death with a shovel in the woods. Do you remember that?"

Bollard's lips parted and a wheeze of air escaped. Was that his way of protesting? Apologizing? I'd since learned that he wouldn't harm me—most likely anyway—but at the time, I'd been terrified of the silent giant. I was still wary of him. My reluctance to have him poke me in the arm with a needle was genuine, although I was partly doing it to buy Jack time.

"He wasn't going to hit you with it," Langley said under his breath. "And you forget that you were trying to escape, something which was *not* in your best interests at the time. He was merely following my orders to keep you here."

"That makes me feel so much better," I said, snippy.

"I didn't expect these hysterics from *you*, Hannah." Langley wheeled himself closer and snatched the syringe from Bollard. "Roll up your sleeve."

I did as told, keeping an eye on the mute. He stepped back behind the wheelchair again, his expression once more vacant.

Langley prepared the needle and stabbed my arm with it. It stung, but I did not look away. I watched as the syringe filled with blood then Langley removed the needle. He handed me the cloth, and I pressed it against the drop marking the entry point. I was surprised that I didn't feel at all faint or nauseous. It was a small problem, one that needed rectifying—and considerable acting skills.

I groaned and fluttered my eyelids closed. "I feel strange," I murmured, then promptly fell sideways onto the sofa.

"Hannah!" Langley cried. "Hannah!"

Somebody helped me to sit up. I opened my eyes to see that it was Bollard. He tucked me into his side, my head beneath is chin. He flapped a copy of the *Young Ladies' Journal* in front of my face to cool me down.

"Thank goodness you're all right," Langley mumbled.

Bollard took my chin in his hand and gently forced me to look up. His narrowed gaze studied my face before letting me go. He stood and handed me the journal. I swallowed hard and continued to fan myself with it.

"Fetch some tea," Langley told his servant. "And perhaps something stronger."

My ruse had worked better than I'd hoped. Bollard would be gone for a few minutes, allowing Jack extra time. The only problem was, I'd not expected to feel so guilty. Both Langley and Bollard had been visibly shaken by my fainting spell.

Langley pressed the back of his hand to my forehead. "You feel hot."

"I'm all right," I tried to reassure him.

He asked me a series of questions about my health then felt my pulse at my wrist. We sat in silence as he counted, then continued to sit in silence until Bollard returned with Tommy. Bollard handed me a glass of sherry and Tommy poured me a cup of tea.

"I'm quite all right now," I said. "No need to fuss."

Samuel came into the parlor along with Sylvia and Jack. Sylvia gave a little gasp and plopped down beside me.

"Poor Hannah," she said, taking my hands in hers. "Are you all right?"

"I'm well." I gave her what I hoped was a reassuring smile. "Please stop fussing."

"This isn't fussing. It's us taking care of you."

"It doesn't require *all* of you."

Langley signaled to Bollard to wheel him away. "Take care of her, Samuel. I have to test this sample. Jack, those accounts need seeing to."

Jack nodded. "I'll do it now."

Bollard glanced back over his shoulder at me from the doorway. He still looked worried. I think I was more shocked by that than anything else that had happened all day.

"Hannah?" Jack said, handing me the teacup. He eyed me closely. "You are all right, aren't you?"

"Yes. Perfectly. Now stop fussing everybody." I was desperate to ask him what he'd discovered in Langley's rooms, but held my tongue. "What of the accounts? Shouldn't you be seeing to them?"

"I did last night. August is trying to get rid of me." He glanced at Samuel. "I'd rather stay here."

We all talked of other things until it was time to go in for dinner. Occasionally Sylvia would ask how I felt, but otherwise we passed the time as we usually did, in amiable conversation.

When Tommy announced dinner, Sylvia and Samuel went through to the dining room first while I hung back with Jack. "Well?" I asked him. "What did you discover?"

"A lot of old papers." He strode off.

"Any of them important?"

"No," he said without slowing down.

He was quiet through dinner, however, and afterward. I didn't get a chance to speak to him privately again before I retired for the night. By the time I rose late the following morning, Jack had gone into the village.

"He's hoping to find out more about Myer," Sylvia said when I joined her in the parlor.

"And to spy on the Butterworths," Samuel said. He folded the newspaper he'd been reading and tossed it onto the table beside him. "Sylvia, did you think he was acting strange this morning?"

She pulled hard on her sewing needle. "I don't know what you mean."

"Strange in what way?" I asked. "Quiet? Reflective?" That was how he'd been the previous night during and after dinner. I was beginning to think he'd discovered something in Langley's rooms after all. But why would he lie to me about it? He knew he could tell me anything.

"I'd say he was angry," Samuel said.

"Angry? That doesn't sound like Jack. Well, not most of the time and not without good reason."

"He was short with me over breakfast," Samuel said. "I only asked him what he planned on doing today and whether I could assist him."

"Perhaps he's frustrated that you still insist on going to London and Myer."

"That must be it," Sylvia said.

"No, I don't think so." He rubbed his finger over his lip. "He wasn't angry at me when we returned from Harborough yesterday, or last night. It's as if something has happened since then."

I bit the inside of my cheek. I couldn't tell him about Jack sneaking into Langley's rooms. Samuel might not approve and Sylvia certainly wouldn't. Besides, it was Jack's business. If he wanted anyone else to know, he'd tell them himself.

"Sylvia? You're very quiet," Samuel said. "Do you know something we don't?"

She lifted the fabric close to her face and inspected her stitching. "I'm often quiet."

He snorted. "No, you're not. Silence is not golden where you're concerned. It's worrying. Well then? What is it? You'd better tell us, or I'll insist on quizzing the servants. Perhaps Tommy knows what troubles you."

She set the fabric down with a huff. "Don't be ridiculous. Very well, I'll tell you what I think. I think Jack received some news that has upset him."

My heart skipped. I pressed my hand to my chest and could feel the thud through my gown. "What do you mean? What news?"

"A letter came for him early this morning, before breakfast. I saw Tommy give it to him. Ever since then, Jack's been snapping at everybody. I tried to engage him in chatter about the ball, and he as good as bit my head off! Then he stormed away and I haven't seen him since."

"Who was the letter from?" Samuel asked.

Sylvia pierced the fabric with her needle. "I couldn't say." That was her code for 'I'm not going to tell you.'

"Sylvia, we should try to get to the bottom of this."

She turned her shoulder to him.

"Ah, here's Tommy," Samuel said.

The footman hesitated just within the door, looking somewhat startled to be noticed. "Sir?"

"Jack received a letter this morning. Who was it from?"

"Don't you dare say anything!" Sylvia warned.

Tommy swallowed and seemed to shrink beneath her glare. "Er…"

"Sylvia, why won't you say who it was from?" I said. "Did Jack ask you to keep it private?" I asked Tommy.

"No, Miss Smith. He gave me no instructions about it whatsoever."

"That's not the point," Sylvia snapped. "I don't think it's wise to divulge who it was from."

"Aha!" Samuel crossed his arms and fixed her with a glare. "So you *do* know."

"Yes," she said on a sigh. "I know who it's from, but not the contents. It's not my place to tell you, that's all."

"That's never stopped you before."

"Well!" she huffed. "Of all the things—"

"It's true," I told her.

She threw her sewing in the basket at her feet. "For goodness sakes, Hannah! I'm not telling you for your own good!"

My own good? Why was she worried the letter would upset me? It couldn't have been estate business then, or from the Beauforts or Culverts. Lord Wade would correspond with August, not Jack, and everybody else Jack and I both knew lived here. Except…

Charity Evans.

A pang pierced my ribs. Miss Charity was a teacher at a school for orphans in London, but before that, she'd lived in the slums with Jack and Tommy. She'd also been Jack's lover for years, and there was a turbulent but deep history between them. It connected her to Jack in a way that I could never be. After meeting her recently and speaking to her about Jack, I'd thought myself no longer jealous of their relationship. It would seem I still was after all.

"It's very sweet of you to worry, Sylvia," I said, trying my best to be nonchalant. "But there's no need. I only hope Miss Charity is all right."

"Oh." She pouted. "You worked it out."

Tommy came more fully into the room. "Jack would have told me if she was in trouble."

"He's Mr. Langley to you," Sylvia said with a thrust of her chin.

"Hush, Sylvia," Samuel scolded. "What kind of trouble could she be in?"

Tommy's gaze slid to his. "That's not for me to say, sir."

Samuel nodded. "Good man. I understand perfectly. Perhaps I can look in on her from time to time at the school where she teaches."

I swallowed the lump in my throat. I was being silly. If Jack was receiving letters from Charity, they were entirely innocent. I was sure of it. Absolutely, positively, quite, almost sure.

"We'll be in London in a few days ourselves," I said. "Jack can check on her then if need be. Or we all can."

"Let's not worry about it until we know the contents of the letter." Sylvia picked up her sewing once more. "Tommy, I'd like some tea."

Tommy bowed and left. The rest of the morning dragged until Jack returned just before luncheon. As soon as he walked in I could see what Samuel meant. His shoulders were stiff, his eyes dark and piercing. It put us all on edge.

"Is everything all right?" I asked him.

He nodded and came to sit by me. "How do you feel today, Hannah?"

"The same." In truth, I felt like I was boiling inside. Sweat pooled in my armpits and behind the backs of my knees, even though I wore a light summer dress. "I'm going for a swim this afternoon."

"Will you be all right on your own? I'd better not come although I'll watch from a window if that makes you feel safer."

"I'll be fine. I won't go in too deep." I smiled, but he turned away as if he didn't want to look at me. Or didn't want me seeing him.

"Did you learn anything in the village?" Samuel asked.

Jack leaned his elbows on his knees and rummaged a hand through his hair. "No. It was a waste of time."

"Did you ask around the Red Lion?"

"Of course I did." Jack's tone was as hard as his glare. "I told you, Gladstone, I learned nothing that we didn't already know."

Samuel held up his hands in surrender and arched a brow at me. He mouthed, "*See?*" To Jack, he said, "Have you received any worrying news lately?"

Jack glanced at me then Samuel then back at me. "What's happened?"

"Nothing! At least, nothing that I know of. Well, have you?"

"Christ, Gladstone. If I had and it concerned you, then I would tell you. Otherwise, mind your own business." He stood and stalked off to the door. "I'm going for a swim."

"But it's lunch time!" Sylvia cried.

"Eat without me."

I almost went after him, but decided against it. If he'd wanted my company, he would have invited me to join him. It was most disturbing. Not knowing what had upset him was upsetting me.

"Well," Sylvia said. "You're right, Samuel. He's in a foul temper this morning. Hannah, you must ask him what's wrong. If he's going to tell anybody, it will be you."

"Later," I said. "Give him a chance to calm down first."

***

Jack didn't calm down. Not that day, or the next. On the third day, I confronted him in the training room. He sat on the window seat, staring out at the frost-covered lawn and the misty lake beyond. I stood beside him and rested my forehead on the wall of the window embrasure.

"What's wrong, Jack?" I asked gently.

He took a few moments to answer, then he turned to me and smiled. "Nothing, Hannah. Sorry if I've been a bear lately, but…" He shrugged. "I'm worried about you."

I knew he was worried, but his anger was due to something else. Why lie? Why didn't he confide in me? "You can tell me anything, Jack. Anything at all."

His smile turned sad. "I know. I just miss you. I miss swimming with you and walking with you." We had tried not to be seen alone together too much, and it seemed we'd been successful. While Langley still urged Samuel to attend to my needs, he didn't berate Jack or me anymore for being together.

"One day I'm going to tell August exactly what I think," he said. "I won't stand being apart from you for a moment longer than necessary."

"Be sure to wait until after he finds a cure. He mustn't be distracted." I still hadn't told Jack what Langley had said to Samuel, and nor would I. He was troubled enough. Angry enough too. Telling him would only raise his ire further. "Until then, let him think we're friends, nothing more."

A crease connected his brows. The lines bracketing his mouth deepened. "I'll try, if that's what you want."

"It is." I rested my hand on the wall near where his shoulder leaned. My fingers warmed, but there were no sparks. "Are you sure there isn't something else troubling you? You've not been yourself these last few days."

He shifted away from me. "Quite sure. Stop worrying. It's not good for you. Focus all your energies inward, on healing."

"I'll try."

I just hoped that my curiosity could stand not knowing what bothered him. My jealousy too.

***

Despite Sylvia's protestations, Tommy ended up accompanying us to London. He rode most of the way with the driver, but it mustn't have been a pleasant journey for either of them out in the icy cold. I offered to swap, but nobody would let me. Jack did a few times, but Tommy wouldn't ride with us, preferring to sit at the back out of the freezing wind.

We arrived at Claridges the day before the ball. On the day of the ball, I rested while Jack took Sylvia shopping. Samuel left us to stay with Myer. It was strange without him. Even though we would see him again at the ball, I felt like I'd lost a friend. It was silly really. He was coming back to Frakingham one day, and I... Well, I hoped I would be there to see him.

In the afternoon, Sylvia and I helped each other dress and did our hair together with the aid of one of the hotel maids. It was a tiring exercise in itself, but I was immensely pleased with the results. My hair was piled in soft curls, with a string of Sylvia's pearls threaded through it. The color of the pearls matched the lace sleeves and the frill at my bust line. The rest of the gown was as blue as a summer sky with an elaborate pattern of twisted rose strands in a darker blue through it.

"Oh, Hannah," Sylvia said, her eyes growing misty. "You're breathtakingly beautiful. I am so pleased you're in love with my cousin, or I'd have a terrible time competing with you for the available gentlemen."

I giggled and complimented her on her dress too. She wore a daringly low-cut pale pink ensemble festooned with swathes of fabric. With her pretty looks and luscious figure, there was no way I would win the hand of any gentleman when in her presence. Being the belle of the ball was the least of my concerns, however. I was excited to be attending and somewhat worried about getting through the night without fainting.

"Now for our jewelry," Sylvia said, but she did not fetch the box with the earrings and necklaces that we'd packed. She left the room entirely and returned a moment later with Jack. He cut a very handsome figure in formalwear of tailcoat and waistcoat as densely black as midnight.

He stopped inside the door and stared at me. His mouth flopped open and his breath quickened.

"I told you so," Sylvia sang. "Isn't she lovely?"

"She's beyond lovely," he murmured. "She's the vision of my dreams."

"I'll leave you two alone, shall I?" She departed through the door that led to our small private parlor, a pleased smile on her face.

I raised my brows at Jack. "What have you two concocted?"

He shyly handed me a rectangular silver box. "I had these made for you. I picked them up yesterday. Sylvia advised me on the current fashion."

I opened the box and gasped. Lying on a bed of black velvet was a necklace with a large blue pendant surrounded by smaller, clear stones that sparkled in the light. A pair of matching drop earrings nestled beside it.

"Jack," I said, my voice barely a whisper. "Are these diamonds?"

"Yes. And the blue stones are sapphires."

"They match the roses on my dress."

"They match your eyes," he said softly. His own eyes glistened back at me, full of emotion.

"Oh," I murmured. "Thank you, Jack. They're exquisite. I'm almost too afraid to wear them. What if I lose them?"

He laughed. "Then I'll have others made."

I picked up the earrings and clipped one on. "I'm not sure I deserve to wear such fine things as these," I said to my reflection in the mirror.

"Hannah," he scolded. "You deserve those and much more. Besides, a lady cannot attend her first ball without diamonds and sapphires."

"Did Sylvia tell you that?"

He laughed again, and I could have kissed him, not for the gifts but just because it was wonderful to see his happiness.

It didn't last long. His smile slipped as I draped the necklace around my throat. "I wish I could put it on you myself, but I'm afraid I might accidentally brush you."

"One day," I said, fighting the tears that hovered on my eyelids. "Soon."

We called Sylvia back in, and she fixed the necklace in place. "There. Now we're ready."

Our coach was waiting for us downstairs. Tommy looked very formal and a little cold as he opened the door for us. He helped me up the step into the cabin then held his hand out for Sylvia. She hesitated before placing her gloved fingers inside his. He touched her elbow to steady her, although she appeared steady enough to me. She settled herself opposite me, pulling her fur-lined coat tighter at her throat. Her gaze drifted to Tommy then snapped back to focus straight ahead. It was curious behavior for them both, and had me wondering what it all meant.

"If the ladies would permit me to tell them how beautiful they look this evening," Tommy said. Although he spoke to us both, he couldn't take his eyes off Sylvia.

She continued to stare at nothing in particular.

"Thank you, Tommy," I said, since she didn't speak. "I hope you find somewhere warm to pass the time tonight."

Sylvia sniffed. Tommy bowed and stepped aside for Jack to climb in.

We drove to the Beauforts' house, the brightest star among a street of stars. Light streamed from every window and extra lamps lining the front steps welcomed guests. Sylvia and I shed our coats in the ladies' dressing room, then Jack escorted us up to Emily and Jacob Beaufort, and Cara Moreau. The three stood side by side, greeting a steady stream of ladies and gentlemen outside the ballroom.

"The house is a picture," Sylvia gushed. "Hannah, we *must* decorate Frakingham when we return."

The decorations were indeed marvelous. Holly and laurel wound up the balustrade of the grand staircase and around chandeliers. Ribbons, garlands and glass ornaments brightened the greenery in festive colors. A tall Christmas tree stood by the ballroom entrance like a guard. A little doll perched on top, her hat brushing the ceiling. Other small toys hung from the branches, and paper chains that looked to have been shaped and colored by children filled the gaps. It made the grand house so joyful and friendly.

"Your first ball," Mrs. Beaufort said to us on a sigh. She wore a grown of crimson and cream and looked positively radiant. "How thrilling. You both look lovely, don't they, Jacob?"

Mr. Beaufort bowed. "They do indeed. I hope you'll both reserve a dance for me later."

"You may be out of luck," his wife said, eyes shining. "Their cards will fill up very quickly."

Miss Moreau greeted us, then Jack moved a little ahead to speak to a gentleman he knew. Miss Moreau took my hand. "Are you excited?" she asked, looking rather excited herself. I'd almost forgotten that this was a new experience for her too. She'd spent the last few years at the bottom of the world in a place called Melbourne with her brother and his wife, Mrs. Beaufort's parents. London balls were as foreign to her as they were to me.

"Oh yes," Sylvia said on a breath. "Everything is perfect. Just perfect. And you look lovely, Miss Moreau. I adore that shade of peach." She did indeed look very pretty. The dress would have looked awful on me with my complexion, but it complimented her warm skin wonderfully.

"Call me Cara," she said. "May I call you by your first names?"

We nodded and couldn't help smiling. I'd been so worried about attending the ball, yet now I'd just acquired another female friend. My second. Or third if I counted Violet. I still wasn't sure whether I would ever see her again, or if I wanted to.

"Are there many eligible gentlemen here?" Sylvia asked, craning her neck to see into the ballroom.

"I believe so," Cara said. "Emily invited all the ones she and Jacob knew, but..." She sighed and surveyed the throng outside the ballroom. "I can't say that the ones I've met are particularly promising. Compared to the men I knew in the Colonies, they're rather dull."

I don't think Sylvia heard her. She was too busy standing on her tiptoes to see past the crowd into the ballroom itself. "Just *look* at all these people! Oh, Hannah, everybody is *so* elegant. I feel quite drab."

I rolled my eyes at Cara. She smiled then focused her attention on the couple coming up behind me. "I must fulfill my duties, but I'll search you out later," she whispered.

"This is my aunt, Miss Cara Moreau," I heard Mrs. Beaufort say to the newcomers. "Cara, meet Lord and Lady Wade and their daughter, Miss Violet Jamieson."

CHAPTER 8

My heart slammed against my ribs. Violet. Here. Lord Wade too.

I kept my back to them and tried to calm my nerves. How had this happened? Why did Mrs. Beaufort invite *them*? But of course she would. Lord Wade was a nobleman, and Mr. Beaufort was the heir to a viscountcy. They must have known each other, and I'd not told them my history of being kept in his attic.

I grabbed Sylvia's arm and dragged her away. We sailed past Jack and wended our way through the crowd and into the ballroom. Despite my anxiety, I was entranced by the room and the people in it. The jewels draped around the slender throats of the ladies sparkled beneath the glittering chandeliers. Tulle and muslin gowns floated like clouds as dancers met and parted, twirled and swirled to the music.

"Hannah!" Sylvia said, pulling herself free. "Hannah, why are you rushing off?"

I didn't stop until I reached the high arched window on the other side of the room. I kept my back to the double doors leading out to the landing where the Beauforts welcomed their guests. I concentrated on breathing and calming my nerves.

Jack joined us, frowning. "Hannah? Are you all right?"

I nodded.

"You left so suddenly. I grew worried."

"What is it, Hannah?" Sylvia asked, peering at my face. "You look paler than usual. Your freckles are standing out rather frightfully."

I pressed my fingers against my breast where my heart skipped at an alarming rate. "Lord Wade is here," I said, breathless.

"Oh my!" She pulled a face. "I dislike that man intensely."

Jack glanced back to the doors. A muscle tensed high in his jaw. "Bloody hell."

"It's not just him," I said. "Vi is here too."

"The other girl from the attic?" Sylvia said.

They had once thought I was Violet. Indeed, that's why Jack had abducted me from Windamere. Although I was glad of the mistake now, at the time I was both angry and terrified. I'd wanted desperately to see my friend Violet again...until I'd learned of her duplicity. She, along with our governess, had conspired to have Jack kidnap me. I had never learned why.

"She was introduced as his daughter," I said. Yet I still had my doubts. If she were his daughter, why had Lord Wade kept her locked in the attic when there was nothing wrong with her? Well, it would seem she too was out now, and openly acknowledged.

"They're coming this way." Sylvia touched her brow to hide her eyes as she spied them. "She's a very pretty girl. Such lovely dark hair and fair complexion. She's clinging to Lord Wade's arm as if he were saving her from drowning. What a nervous looking thing she is. Her gaze darts about the room, and every time someone gets too close she shrinks away."

"She's unused to so many people," I said. I knew how she felt. The crush of the ball wasn't a place for the faint of heart. Now that my initial instinct to flee had lessened, other nerves had taken their place. The ballroom was large, but it was already full and everybody seemed to know everybody else. Many watched us surreptitiously from behind fans or out of the corner of their eyes, while others openly stared. We were the oddities in the room. The freaks from Frakingham, unknown in London society. The guests would be ogling Vi with similar thoughts on their minds.

Two gentlemen approached and bowed to us. "It's Langley, isn't it?" the shorter one said to Jack.

Jack, still watching Vi and Wade, took a moment to acknowledge them. "Yes, I...uh." He shook his head as if shaking off a somber thought. "Mr. Graham and Mr. Riddle, meet my cousin Miss Langley and her friend, Miss Smith." Introductions completed, he once more watched Wade.

I eyed Jack while Sylvia gave all her attention to the newcomers. They exchanged pleasantries, and I joined in with the required smiles and nods. Jack did not.

"Now, which of you will dance with me first?" Sylvia asked in what I thought was a manner too forward for the ballroom.

"If you'll permit me," said Mr. Graham with a bow.

"Then perhaps Miss Smith will dance with me?" Mr. Riddle asked.

"I'm not much of a dancer." I shrugged an apology.

Mr. Riddle smiled. "Neither am I. Perhaps between the two of us, we can make a passable attempt."

"Thank you, but no. I'm content to watch."

His eyes narrowed in a wince, and I regretted my response. Sylvia had told me it was poor etiquette to refuse to dance with a gentleman, but I'd not taken her advice to heart. Perhaps I should have. Perhaps I should not have come at all.

"May I watch with you?" he asked as Sylvia stepped onto the dance floor with his friend.

Beside me, Jack cleared his throat. Mr. Riddle's gaze slid to him then back to me. "I, er..." He looked around the room and spotted someone he knew. Or pretended to. "Excuse me, Miss Smith. Perhaps we can not dance together later." He strode off, his chin thrust out and shoulders square.

I turned to Jack and arched my eyebrow at him. "That wasn't very nice."

"I didn't do anything."

"You scowled at him."

"I did not. I merely looked in his direction."

"And?"

"And made it clear that you're spoken for."

"Jack!" I shook my head but couldn't stop my smile from spreading. It felt wonderful to be adored by him. "You scared the poor man away."

"If a mere look can scare him away, then he's a coward."

"I saw the look you gave him. It would scare away most people. You have a forceful way about you sometimes."

"I know Riddle. His reputation where women are concerned is dubious."

I watched the receding back of Mr. Riddle and lowered my voice. "You mean he ruins them?"

"Let me put it this way. Riddle didn't want to dance with you. He wanted to *flirt* with you, and would hope for more. I'm the only one allowed to do that. Once I made it clear, he was no longer interested."

"That shouldn't make me happy, but it does," I said. "Anyway, I'd rather enjoy your company tonight and watch others dance."

"Hannah," he said heavily, "I want you to dance. I truly do. Preferably with a gentleman who is also spoken for and not someone like Riddle."

"It doesn't matter. I can't dance."

"Dance anyway, as long as you don't exhaust yourself."

"Perhaps one or two later. You must dance also, at least with Sylvia and Cara."

"I wish I could be your first partner." His sad smile made my heart crack and my stomach do little flips.

"So do I."

His eyes turned dark, smoky. He leaned closer, his lips near my ear. My cheek warmed, but I didn't pull away. "I may never be your first," he murmured, "but I *will* be your last."

My heart swelled to twice its size. It felt too full to be contained within my ribcage. I nodded, unable to speak and tell him that I knew it with every piece of me.

He straightened and glanced over my shoulder. His lips parted. His eyes widened.

I turned and met Violet's gaze.

She emitted a small yelp and covered her mouth. "Hannah? Hannah, oh dear lord, it *is* you." Her eyes filled with tears, and her bottom lip wobbled. She bit it.

I'd expected this meeting ever since spotting her, and I thought I was prepared. I was wrong. Seeing her again brought up so many emotions I thought buried. Anger, confusion, relief, and chief among them, sorrow.

"Good evening, Violet," I said and bobbed a curtsy. Good lord, I felt ridiculous. I'd known her my entire life. She'd been my constant companion, my only friend, yet I felt as awkward around her as if we were strangers.

"I can't believe that you're here. I just can't." She clasped me by my arms and peered into my face. "Thank goodness you're all right. You are all right, aren't you?"

I nodded. There was no point telling her my life was going to end shortly. That, at least, wasn't her fault.

"Where did you go? What have you been doing these last few weeks? Tell me everything before…" She glanced over her shoulder, catching Lord Wade's searching gaze.

His face darkened. He abandoned his wife and marched toward us. Most people parted for him, but those who didn't received a bump as he passed. He didn't pause to apologize.

"You know where I've been," I said quickly to Violet.

"I, uh…" She looked to Jack, and her pale face colored. She focused once more on the advancing Lord Wade. "So you know."

"I know everything you and Miss Levine did," I said. "And I want to thank you. I have a wonderful life with friends and family who care for me. It's more than I'd ever hoped for."

She bit her lip again. She didn't have a chance to say anything, however. Lord Wade descended on us like a raging bull.

Jack blocked his path. "Careful," he said quietly, ominously. "Do not force my hand. I like the Beauforts too much to bring disgrace to their home, but I will hit you if tempted."

I thought for one awful moment that Lord Wade would plow right past him, but he did not. He closed his fists at his sides and breathed deeply.

"*You*," he said to me. "I told you to stay away from Violet."

Violet gasped again. "You've seen her? Where? When?"

Lord Wade didn't answer. He simply continued to glare at me, although the anger in his eyes dissolved. I don't think he was unhappy to see me, merely concerned about the repercussions.

And the repercussions were heading our way in the form of Lady Wade. She was a tall woman with a straight back and pinched mouth. It was difficult to tell how old she was, but I'd guessed her to be younger than her husband by about ten years.

"Who are these people?" she said, taking his arm.

I swept a low curtsy. "I'm the girl who lived in your attic for fifteen years, Lady Wade. It's a pleasure to meet you."

Those tightly pursed lips parted, and her breath left her in a shuddery gasp. Her gaze flicked between Jack, Vi and I. She swooned, but her husband caught her. He directed her to sit on a chair nearby under the curious stares of the other guests. Vi flapped her fan in front of her face, but Lady Wade appeared to have recovered already if her fierce glare in my direction was any indication.

I studied her face. It was sharp, the chin pointed, the eyes cold. Not at all like Vi's. Lord Wade might be her father, but I doubted this woman was her mother. I wondered how much Vi knew of her own origins.

I felt much too taxed to ask all the questions swimming around my head. It simply didn't seem worth the effort as I'd only upset myself. Besides, I was at my first ball. I wanted to enjoy it. It could be my last.

I turned on my heel, but Vi caught my arm before I could leave. "Wait." She swallowed heavily and did not continue.

"Yes?" I prompted. "Do you wish to say something?"

"A great many things, but...not here. Is there somewhere we can talk?"

"No." I regretted it as soon as the word was out of my mouth. Vi looked as if she'd burst into tears.

"Violet," Lord Wade growled. He placed his big hand on her shoulder. "Hannah's time with us has ended. It's best to forget her as she has forgotten you."

My blood heated along my veins, shooting to my fingers. I closed them into a fist as I'd seen Jack do to stifle any flames. "I have not forgotten. I never will." It was out before I thought it through. I glanced at Vi, and her face was white, her eyes full.

"Then we must talk," she whispered.

"Not tonight."

"When?"

"Forget her," Lord Wade growled. "For your own sake and Lady Wade's!"

"And your own?" Jack cut in. His voice shook. His lips were bloodless. I'd not seen him look so furious since he'd lost his temper with August Langley over his early treatment of me. "What are you afraid they'll discover? What are you hiding?"

"What has any of this to do with you?" The fingers clamped on Vi's bare shoulder whitened. "How dare you. Get away from us."

Jack looked as if he'd thump Wade, or throw fire at him.

115

"Come, Jack," I said, quickly. "I have a ball to enjoy."

We headed away from the dancers and into the adjoining refreshment room. Bonbons, cakes and an array of sandwiches were set out on the table, untouched. It was too early for most guests to require a rest. Thoughts of refreshments would come later. I sat on one of the chairs arranged around the perimeter, but Jack stood at the table. He didn't collect a plate of the delicious confections, but pressed his hands on the surface and bowed his head. His ragged breaths took several moments to calm.

"Jack? Are you all right?"

He slowly turned and gave me a smile that didn't convince me in the least. His fingers were red, his lips tight. "Of course. It's just...that man..."

"I know. Sit with me."

A footman came up to us with a tray full of glasses containing a drink that sparkled in the light. On closer inspection, I noticed the sparkles were actually tiny bubbles rising up and fizzing on the surface. They tingled my tongue as I sipped.

"It's champagne," Jack said. "Don't drink it too fast, or it'll go to your head."

I took another sip. "I like it."

"I'll order a case to be sent to Frakingham. Can I get you something to eat?"

"No, thank you. I need to sit for a moment."

He sat beside me. "Do you feel hot? Tired?"

"A little of both, particularly after Lord Wade's pronouncement to Vi." I sighed. "Do you think I was too curt with her?"

"Not at all. Her betrayal upset you, and she ought to know."

"But it's not her fault," I said quietly. "Not really."

"No." His jaw became rigid. "It's Wade's."

"Do you think we'll ever learn the full story?"

He pressed his thumb and finger into his eyes. When he pulled them away, he seemed a little less angry. "Of course you will. Give her time. One day she'll come to you, and Lord Wade won't be able to stop her."

Time was one commodity I had in limited supply.

"There you both are!" Samuel said, entering the room. "I've been looking everywhere for you." He shook Jack's hand and bowed over mine. "Are you well, Hannah?"

I nodded. "And you, Samuel? Is Myer treating you fairly?" I glanced past him to the door, but Myer was nowhere to be seen.

"He is."

Jack scoffed. "It's only been two days."

"Are you implying his attitude will change?"

"I'm suggesting you keep your wits about you."

"Always, my friend," Samuel said quietly. "Always."

I wasn't as convinced by his assurance as Jack seemed to be, but I said nothing. "Samuel, will you dance with me?"

He glanced at Jack.

"Yes, he will," Jack said. "Go on, Gladstone."

"I'd be honored, Hannah." Samuel bowed. "Although I'm quite sure *I'm* supposed to ask *you* to dance, not the other way round."

I waved my hand. "You were never going to ask, just like all the other respectable gentlemen. You're as afraid of Jack as they are."

"That's only because I've seen the devastation his temper can wreak."

"My temper will wreak pure havoc if you don't treat her gently on the dance floor. Don't overdo it."

Samuel bowed and held out his hand to me. I took it and stood. "What about you, Jack? You must find somebody to dance with too."

"I'll seek out Sylvia."

Samuel snorted. "Good luck. She had an audience of young hopefuls surrounding her when I passed by. I went up to her, and she turned away as if she didn't know me."

"I'd better check on her."

"Don't stifle her," I chided. "Give her some freedom."

Jack placed his hand to his heart. "Would I do that to my dear cousin?" He left us before I could finish rolling my eyes.

"I do hope he doesn't hover too much," I said to Samuel. "She's the sort of girl who needs to flirt and enjoy herself."

Samuel led me back out to the ballroom. "I must admit I'm surprised."

"Why?"

"I thought she and Tommy had an affection for one another."

"Tommy? But he's the footman!" Good lord, I sounded just like her. "What I mean is, she wouldn't consider Tommy worthy of speaking to her as an equal let alone anything more."

"She's not royalty," he said with a shrug of his shoulder. "She's not even nobility. Upper middle class at best."

"Yes, but *she* thinks he's beneath her, and that's enough to suppress any feelings they may harbor for one another before they can blossom."

"Perhaps."

The musicians finished a tune and the dancers dispersed to make way for new couples. I spotted Sylvia swanning her way onto the floor with a red-cheeked, whiskery gentleman.

I searched the room and saw Violet accepting the hand of a man who then led her onto the dance floor. Lord Wade watched them like a mother bird. Men weren't supposed to chaperone young ladies. That task was reserved for married women or elderly spinsters, however, Lady Wade was nowhere to be seen.

I saw Jack not far away, speaking to a young girl who did not meet his gaze. She wore a lemon-colored gown that didn't suit her short, plump figure, and I noticed a slight limp as Jack led her onto the dance floor. Other, far prettier girls, stared at them and whispered, but his partner appeared too happy to notice.

"Jack to the rescue again," Samuel said. "Perhaps I ought to follow his technique. I might have more luck with…" His voice trailed off.

I followed his gaze and was surprised to see Miss Charity standing near the door, chatting to Cara Moreau. The Beauforts were kind indeed to invite the teacher from their orphan school to the ball.

"Did you ask her to dance?" I asked.

"I did. She refused me."

Well, well. She was quite a remarkable woman. I doubted Samuel was used to being refused any request he made of a lady.

I continued to watch her as Samuel and I dodged other dancing couples. Miss Charity and Cara proved quite popular with the gentlemen, but none of them remained to talk for long. She wrote their names on her dance card, they bowed and walked off. After every greeting, Miss Charity rubbed the back of her gloved hands, as if conscious of the scars underneath. They weren't visible of course, but she seemed all too aware of them. She looked remarkably beautiful in her white gown, although its styling was simple with few embellishments or adornments like the gowns of the other ladies. Not that it mattered. Indeed, she could wear a sack and still have men ogling.

I sought out Jack and found him dancing with the limping girl. She wasn't a good dancer, due to her impediment, but he led so well that most of her mistakes were smoothly covered up. He smiled at her and they chatted the entire time, although his gaze frequently searched the room. It would settle on me and he would smile or nod. It wandered to Lord Wade often too, and once, it settled on Miss Charity. She looked away quickly, but not before I saw that she'd been watching him with an odd expression that I couldn't decipher.

"Would you like to sit down?" Samuel asked when the music finished.

A gentleman approached before I could answer. "Is your c-c card full, m-madam?" he stuttered. "I'm sure it is," he added, blushing. "I j-just hoped…"

"I have this dance free," I said.

The fellow beamed and bowed over my hand. "Th-thank you, M-Miss…?"

"Smith," I said.

"Hannah?" Samuel prompted. "Are you sure you don't need to sit down?"

"Quite sure." I felt a little heavy in the limbs and a headache bloomed behind my eyes, but I was otherwise well enough for one more dance.

He departed, and the musicians struck up another waltz. My partner, Mr. Fuller, danced well and fortunately I didn't make a fool of myself. We didn't speak much, mostly because it seemed such an effort with his stutter.

At each turn, I sought out Jack, but couldn't find him. His partner was once more seated on her chair, talking and giggling with a friend who'd joined her. Yet Jack wasn't nearby or among the other groups at the edge of the dance floor. It wasn't until the end of the dance that I spotted him in the corner of the room near a large Greek urn. He was talking with Charity, their heads bent close to one another.

It wasn't this that shocked me, however. It was their touching. She'd removed one of her gloves, and Jack was holding her hand. His thumb caressed the burn scar I knew to be there, over and over.

She suddenly withdrew her hand and pressed it to the side of his face. He closed his eyes, and I saw his chest rise and fall with his heavy breathing. She let him go and touched his hand again before putting her glove back on and disappearing into the refreshment room. Jack slumped against the wall, his head bowed, his hair falling over his eyes. My heart ached to see him like that, but it ached even more for what I'd just witnessed.

If I wasn't mistaken, there was still some affection and understanding between he and Charity. Something that couldn't be ignored. Something tender, despite Jack's reassurances to me that all of those feelings were in the past. I knew he'd hurt Charity, perhaps even given her the scars on her hands, yet she hadn't flinched from his touch.

This meeting must have been pre-arranged via the letter she'd sent to Frakingham. The contents of that missive had disturbed Jack, angered him even, although he didn't seem angry now. Only distressed and a little sad.

Samuel approached, breaking my concentration. "Hannah, did you enjoy your dance?"

I nodded and smiled, but my gaze wandered back to Jack.

"What's wrong?" he asked.

"I don't know."

"Is he all right?"

"I haven't spoken to him. Samuel, what do you think Jack will do after...after I'm gone?"

"Hannah," he murmured. "Don't think like that."

"I must. I must stop thinking of my own worries and start thinking how my death will affect him."

He folded his arms and glared at me. "What are you talking about?"

I could see he wouldn't understand, and I wasn't sure I had the energy to explain it to him. Besides, what I had in mind involved Charity, and I suspected Samuel was beginning to develop some feelings toward her. He wouldn't like my suggestion that Jack forget me and pay court to her once more.

He would only ask why, and I would have to tell him that I thought them well suited. I would also have to tell him that I planned on pushing Jack away from me and into her arms. It was something I *had* to do, even though my chest hurt just thinking about him with another. It was time I started considering Jack and his future. He would mourn me when I was gone, but if he had Charity, losing me wouldn't devastate him.

CHAPTER 9

I refused the next three gentlemen who asked me to dance and headed away from Jack. I wasn't sure where I was going, but I needed cold, fresh air and that meant slipping out of the ballroom altogether. I parted from Samuel who went in search of Myer and found a small parlor blessedly empty of revelers. I opened the door leading out to the balcony and closed it behind me. The breeze rustled my hair and swept the heat from my skin, although not the deeper heat that swelled inside.

After a few minutes, I turned to go back. I spotted Jack through the glass door, scowling at me, although there was relief in his face too. I gave him a reassuring smile, despite my heavy heart. Somehow I had to convince him to spend more time with Charity tonight. It wasn't going to be easy.

I opened the door. "Have you been looking for me?"

"Everywhere." He rubbed his hand through his hair and down the back of his neck. "Don't disappear again, Hannah. You had me worried."

"I wish you wouldn't. I don't like to be smothered."

He flinched. "I'm sorry. I wouldn't usually, but considering your health…" He cleared his throat. "When I couldn't find you, I panicked."

Oh God, I couldn't do this. He didn't deserve to be treated so poorly. There had to be another way to push him into Charity's arms that didn't involve me acting cruelly. I just wasn't capable of it where he was concerned. "I'm sorry, Jack, I didn't mean to speak harshly."

"It's all right." He put his hand on the back of one of the leather armchairs. "Come and sit down. I'll fetch you a drink. I probably should go in search of Samuel too."

"Samuel?"

"I sent him off to look for you."

I sat down and he left, but not before glancing back at me, his eyes hidden by shadows.

The chair was comfortable and deep, my eyes heavy. I closed them and rested my head against the chair wing. Music and chatter combined in a melodic cadence that drifted through the house from the ballroom. It surrounded me, filled my head, and made me drowsy.

"Hannah?" Jack's voice nudged the sleepiness aside. "I've brought you a cup of tea and a glass of punch. I wasn't sure which you'd prefer."

I opened my eyes and accepted the tea. He placed the glass on the table beside my chair. "Thank you," I said. "I must have fallen asleep."

He crouched before me. "Would you like to return to the hotel?"

"No. It's much too early."

"You can rest in here for a while. I'll keep everybody out."

"Jack, I appreciate everything you're doing for me, but you should be in the ballroom enjoying yourself."

"How can I enjoy myself out there when you're in here?"

His words thrilled me and worried me at the same time. "Go and find Miss Charity and ask her to dance."

He sat on the chair opposite. "She won't dance with me. She doesn't want to."

"But you're friends. Good friends."

He looked down at his hands in his lap. "We were."

"You could be again. Those feelings couldn't have completely disappeared."

"Hannah, what are you talking about? If you're worried about Charity and me, you shouldn't be."

"Oh, I'm not." I shrugged and pretended indifference. "I just think you should keep trying to be a good friend to her. I'm sure she needs one."

"Perhaps, but—"

Samuel strolled in, cutting Jack off. "Are you all right, Hannah?"

"Perfectly," I lied. "Now stop fussing, both of you."

Myer entered the room too and bowed. I was taken aback to see him, even though I knew he was somewhere in the vast, crowded ballroom. He must have followed Samuel.

"Good evening, Miss Smith, Mr. Langley." His voice had the smooth quality that I associated with Samuel's but wasn't hypnotizing, merely resonant and pleasant to listen to.

"Myer," Jack said with a nod. The greeting may have sounded benign, but there was coldness in it. Knowing that Jack didn't trust him, I wasn't surprised. If Myer noticed, he gave nothing away.

I sipped my tea and watched him over the rim of the cup. He was not at all handsome, but he had a friendly manner and chatted easily. Jack engaged him in conversation about banking and finance. At least, he tried to. Myer dismissed his questions with a wave.

"I don't get involved in the day-to-day running of the bank," he said with a laugh. "Those things are best left to the experts, eh? My expertise and interests lie elsewhere."

"In the supernatural?" I asked.

"Yes, and hypnosis in particular. I'm thrilled to be working with Mr. Gladstone."

"What do you hope to achieve by studying him?" Jack asked.

"Perhaps I can find what links he and I, why are we both able to hypnotize with ease, that sort of thing."

"And if you find a link? What will you do then?"

Myer shrugged one shoulder. "We'll cross that bridge when we come to it."

"Perhaps you should cross it now, so that Samuel knows what to expect."

"Jack," Samuel said with a frosty glare.

Jack held up his hands. "I think Mr. Myer should know that if anything happens to you, I'll come after him."

Samuel rolled his eyes. "Have you mistaken me for Hannah?"

"Are you threatening me, Mr. Langley?" Myer asked mildly.

"I'm merely warning you," Jack said.

"And what will you do if I harm your friend?"

Jack appealed to Samuel. "Are you hearing this?"

"Gentlemen," I said. "Enough. This is supposed to be an enjoyable evening."

Myer held up his hands. "I apologize, Miss Smith. Of course, you're right. I do want to assure you both that no harm will come to Mr. Gladstone. My only weapon is my hypnosis and he's immune. As are you, Mr. Langley." The pointed accusation wasn't lost on any of us.

Jack grunted and said nothing. Samuel too remained quiet. It was left to me to fill the silence.

"Are you and Mrs. Myer enjoying the ball?" I asked.

"My wife couldn't attend," he said. "Regrettably, she was feeling unwell."

"Oh. I, uh, I see." I cleared my throat and couldn't look him in the eyes. Was his wife truly feeling unwell or had he hypnotized her into staying home? I couldn't believe anything he said anymore in regards to her motivations.

"She suffers from a nervous constitution in crowded spaces. In many other ways, she's a strong woman, but in that she's weak. Social events distress her."

"You should remove her concerns under hypnosis," Samuel said.

"Will that help her overcome her nervousness?" I asked.

"Yes," both Myer and Samuel said.

"Dr. Werner's practice focused on helping ladies suffering from nervous constitutions and hysteria," Samuel added. "There *are* good applications for our ability, Hannah."

"Yes, of course. I didn't mean to imply otherwise." I set my teacup on the table beside me, and accidentally knocked the glass full of punch. It wobbled precariously, but before I could steady it, Jack was there. He righted it without a drop having been spilled.

"Thank you," I said as he sat back down.

He wasn't looking at me, however, but at Myer. Myer stared back at him, his mouth agape. He scooted forward on his chair and pointed a finger at Jack.

"Mr. Langley..." he began. He shook his finger and smiled curiously. "Mr. Langley, you were fast. Indeed, you were so fast that you saved the punch in the time it took me to blink."

I bit my lip. Jack became still. Only the Frakingham residents and the Beauforts knew of his unnatural speed. Indeed, even Jack seemed to have been unaware of how fast he was until I'd pointed it out to him. It had been a godsend while fighting the demons, but it only deepened the mystery surrounding him.

Now Myer knew. A man we couldn't trust. A man with an interest in the supernatural.

"It was nothing," Jack said with a shrug. "Yes, I'm a little quicker than most—"

"A *little* quicker? Ha! Mr. Langley, I can assure you, no man is as fast as that." Myer slid forward even further on his seat so that he was in danger of sliding off. "Will you permit me to time you?"

Jack laughed. "Mr. Myer, there is nothing odd in my speed. It's within normal limits."

"I beg to differ." Myer continued to shake his finger at Jack. "The speed, coupled with your immunity to hypnosis...Mr. Langley, forgive me, but what *are* you?"

"He's a freak," Samuel said, smiling. "Like the rest of us."

"I'm just a man," Jack snapped. His eyes flashed like two hard gemstones in the light. "Gladstone, shut it. You're not helping."

"Mr. Gladstone may be onto something," Myer said. "Mr. Langley, is your uncle studying you?"

"Of course not."

"Have you ever thought about subjecting yourself to study, either by him or…another?"

Jack gave a bitter laugh. "Meaning you? You heard what I think of Samuel studying with you, and yet you have the gall to ask me to subject myself to your tests. I don't think so, Mr. Myer."

"Why not? We may discover something about you that you didn't know. Or we may be able to hone your ability, make you faster."

"Why would I want to be faster?" He set his icy gaze on Myer. His face darkened, and I grew worried that he might unintentionally reveal his fire starting. If Myer thought him odd already, imagine what he'd think of *that*. "Listen to me. I'm not interested in being studied, either by you or anyone else. Neither is Hannah. All we want is to find a cure for her. Unless you can help, leave us alone."

Myer glanced at me and sat back in his chair. He seemed unperturbed by Jack's temper, although he changed the subject. "You appear more fatigued tonight, Miss Smith. Hotter too."

"My health is the same as the last time we met," I said. "It neither declines nor improves."

"I see. So have you gained any new knowledge about the demon summoner?"

"As a matter of fact, yes," Jack said, idly. Dangerously. "We discovered that the mayor of Harborough is likely involved."

"The mayor?"

Jack nodded. "You know his wife, I believe. Mrs. Butterworth."

Myer's eyes narrowed. A muscle in the corner of his mouth twitched, forming what could either be a smile or a grimace. "I don't believe I do."

"Now, Mr. Myer, it wouldn't be in your best interests to lie to us."

"Agreed," Samuel said. "I won't be staying with you if you continue down that path, Myer. We know you and Mrs. Butterworth had...assignations."

Myer's face colored. He stretched his neck as if his collar were too tight. "The lady herself told you that?"

"We don't break confidences," Jack said.

"If she did, then she was lying."

"Stop it!" I slammed my hands down on the chair's arms. I was tired, irritated and so frustrated by this evasive man. "Stop it, Mr. Myer. Stop the lies. Stop it all. We know about you and Mrs. Butterworth. We know that you hypnotized her in her own home. I hope to God that she agreed to the assignations. If she did not, Jack and Samuel here will have to show you what it's like to feel vulnerable and at another's mercy." The heat rose within me, swirling and boiling and aching. *Stay calm, Hannah.*

"It wasn't against her will!" he cried. "I can assure you of that." Tiny beads of sweat popped out on his brow, and his hands twisted in his lap, over and over. "She wanted to be with me, but had reservations. I told her I could allay her fears, and she gave me permission to hypnotize her. That's all."

I wasn't sure if I believed him or not. It sounded plausible, yet I didn't trust him. He was too slippery. "We'll ask her ourselves. If her story confirms yours, you'll be spared. If not, you *will* regret it."

"And I'll return to Frakingham," Samuel said.

A footman entered, shattering the tension in the room. "I'm looking for a Mr. Myer," he said.

"I am he," Myer said, wiping his brow with his thumb.

The footman handed him a note and Myer unfolded it. "It's from my wife," he said, reading. "She's asking me to return home." He scrunched up the note and tossed it into the unlit fireplace.

I sat there in the armchair, shocked to my core. Not because of the note or its contents, but by what the footman had said. *Myer*. Yet he hadn't pronounced it the way I did, or Jack, or Samuel. His accent made the name sound like *mayor*.

Both Jack and Samuel had noticed too. They exchanged glances then stood as one. Samuel calmly closed the door and remained there, guarding the exit. Jack, much less calm, grabbed Myer's arm and jerked him to his feet.

"Mr. Langley! I protest."

"You're not allowed to protest," Jack snarled. "You lied to us."

Myer's eyes widened. He tried to pull free, but Jack held him. The physical difference between the two was marked. Jack was taller than Myer and broader across the shoulders. Everything about him screamed power and fury. Myer trembled, and he didn't even know Jack's full capabilities.

"You are the 'mayor' that the Widow Mott spoke of," I said.

"What are you talking about?" Myer asked, once more trying to pull free.

"Whether she couldn't read the signature on the letter you sent her husband, or whether we didn't understand her accent, it's clear to us now that you knew Mott. *You* employed him to summon the demon, not Mayor Butterworth." Hot blood pounded through my body in a raging torrent. Pain splintered inside my head and shot down my spine, along my limbs. Sparks burst from my fingertips onto the floor.

I stumbled backward and found the chair as my knees gave way. I sat and concentrated on my breathing, on calming myself and reducing the heat within me to bearable levels.

"Hannah?" Jack was at my side. His raw fear stared back at me.

"I'm all right." I managed to sound almost normal as the heat subsided. "I was angry." I checked the floor for evidence of burning, but there was none. Jack must have stamped out the sparks before they could catch the rug alight.

He passed me the glass of punch and helped me drink since my hands trembled too much to hold it.

"Continue with your questions," I said to Jack. "I'll be all right."

"Miss Smith," Myer began, but stopped. He stared at me, more curious than anything else.

"Yes?" I prompted.

"I...I'm sorry. It troubles me to see such a pretty, vital young woman this way."

"Thank you," I said, meaning it. "Now answer Jack's questions."

To my surprise, he nodded. "Very well. You're right. I paid that man Mott to summon the demon."

"You sent him to a horrible death," Samuel snarled.

Myer crossed his legs and smoothed his trouser leg. "That wasn't meant to happen. The entire thing didn't go too well."

"That is an understatement," Jack said, standing by my side. "You'd better start at the beginning. Why did you want to summon a demon? What have we ever done to you?"

Myer held up his hands and shook his head vigorously. "This has nothing to do with you, Mr. Langley! Or anyone else at the house. You see, the Frakingham Abbey ruins contain strong supernatural energy. Energy that can be harvested, studied and perhaps put to use here in this realm."

"Is this a joke?" Samuel scoffed.

"No! Of course not. I treat the supernatural very seriously."

"What has the demon got to do with the energy at the ruins?" Jack asked.

"Demons are attracted to strong energy like that rumored to be at the ruins. I summoned it to observe its behavior near the abbey." He swallowed heavily. "That's all."

"That's *all*!" I cried. "You summoned a creature you couldn't control into this realm for no reason other than to study it?"

He held up his hands. "I hadn't expected to not be able to control it. I know about demons, Miss Smith. I'm well able to handle one."

"Then why didn't you?" Jack snapped.

"Because it consumed the mad spirits in your house."

"You mean those spirits of the children in the Frakingham dungeon?"

Myer nodded. "Summoning is not an exact science. The demons don't always appear where you want them to. That one fell into this realm in your dungeon and consumed those spirits. It became mad itself, and as such, I wasn't able to control it."

"So you simply left it and returned to London!" Samuel bit off. "Bloody hell. I cannot believe someone would do such a thing!"

"I didn't dare approach the house and search for the amulet. It was too dangerous."

"We're quite aware of how dangerous, thank you," I muttered. "We were prisoners within the house for days. People were hurt, Mr. Myer. Mott and our driver died. You should be ashamed of yourself."

"I am." He nodded. "I am very sorry. I sent money to the Widow Mott for her family. Anonymously, of course. I'll do the same for your driver."

"You think that compensates for the loss? Mrs. Mott is without a husband. Her children no longer have a father."

He buried his face in his hands. "I know. I'm deeply troubled. The experiment was a terrible failure. From what I could see, the demon showed no interest in the ruins. You were all closer to it. Did you see it go to the abbey?"

I couldn't believe what I was hearing. This man had very little conscience. He may have given Mrs. Mott money, but he seemed oblivious to the sorrow he'd wreaked on that family as well as others. He was blinded by the power of the supernatural. He was greedy for it, consumed by it, the way some are consumed by their desire for money.

"Is that all you can think of? You disgust me."

He nodded slowly without meeting my gaze. "You're right. I'll be sure to give Mrs. Mott more, and your driver's family too."

I sighed. He still didn't understand. I doubted he ever would.

"May I leave now?" he asked. "I'd like to enjoy more of the evening before it ends."

Samuel stepped aside. "I won't be returning to your house," he said as Myer opened the door. "Send my things to Claridges in the morning."

Myer opened his mouth, but shut it again and nodded. He left without another word.

We three remained in the room. None of us spoke for some time. I think we were all too shocked.

"I'm glad you're not going with him, Samuel," I said, finally.

He squeezed the bridge of his nose. "You were both right. The man has no morals. Something inside him is warped. To have done what he's done..." He shook his head. "He sickens me."

"Do you think he learned his lesson? He seemed sorry for what happened to Mott and Olsen at least."

"Sorry, but not troubled," Jack said.

I blew out a measured breath. It was such a relief to have the puzzle solved, even though Myer's actions had been reprehensible. He'd learned his lesson, at least. "Thank goodness it's over. He won't try it again, I'm sure. He wouldn't dare."

"Let's hope not," Jack said.

I stood. I still felt warm and a little light-headed, but not dangerously so. I was well enough to venture out. "Shall we enjoy the rest of the ball too?"

"Do you feel up to it?" Jack asked.

I nodded. "I'm hot and tired, but I don't want to leave yet."

"Very well, but be careful. I won't have you overtaxed."

We returned to the ballroom, and I spent the remainder of the evening chatting with Mrs. Beaufort, Mrs. Culvert and their friends. Cara, Sylvia and Miss Charity danced most of the time with different gentlemen, and occasionally joined us to rest in between sets. Jack and Samuel danced on occasion too, but mostly fell into conversation with others.

Myer danced with different ladies. I observed him as best as I could from where I stood at the edge of the ballroom, but it was impossible to tell whether he'd hypnotized his partners. They certainly seemed happy, but I knew the man could be naturally charming if he chose to be. I doubted he would have risked using his hypnosis. There were too many bystanders who might be affected, and he knew we were watching. His gaze connected with mine often, to the point where I felt decidedly uncomfortable.

Why was he interested in me all of a sudden? He didn't show the same level of interest in Jack, Samuel or any of the others.

I parted from them toward the end of the night to attend the ladies' dressing room. On my way back to the ballroom, Myer intercepted me.

"Don't be alarmed, Miss Smith," he said, hands up in surrender. "I don't wish to frighten you."

"Then you should leave me alone."

"I will, after we've spoken." He glanced through the open doors leading to the ballroom. "May we go elsewhere to talk?"

"Anything you wish to say to me, you can say here." People wandered past us, heading into and out of the ballroom. Even so, Myer made me nervous. "Indeed, whatever you wish to say to me can be said in front of my friends."

"No!" He glanced into the ballroom again. "They won't like what I have to say."

"Indeed? And what makes you think *I* will like what you have to say?"

"Because it's about finding a cure for you, yet it's not without some risk. A risk that I think will concern your friends more than you."

My breath caught in my chest. "Why is that?"

"They still believe August Langley will find you a cure."

Bile rose to my throat, burning and foul. His choice of words was damning. "And you don't?"

He shook his head. "Nor, I think, do you."

"You're wrong. I do believe it. He's an excellent scientist."

"No, Miss Smith. He *was* an excellent scientist when he partnered with Reuben Tate. What has Langley achieved since that partnership ended? Hmmm?"

"I...I don't know." It was true. Nobody spoke of any cures Langley had found since he and Tate parted, yet they all believed he could cure me.

Were they being optimistic for my sake?

"Tell me what you have in mind, Mr. Myer. How will I be cured if not by August Langley?"

"Work with Tate."

I snorted. "Don't be absurd."

"Miss Smith, you told me yourself that Reuben Tate has been working on curing himself for years. Langley hasn't. Whom do you think would be closer to a solution?"

"Tate may be, but he wants to trial it on me first. I don't particularly wish to be his test case."

"Why not? It may very well work. What have you got to lose?"

I didn't know what to say to that. In an odd way, it made sense. I shivered. Tate frightened me.

"Listen to me, Miss Smith. You don't have much choice. Tate is a desperate man, yes, but his wish is the same as yours—to find a cure."

"Only I may die in the process."

"Or you may not. Besides, you're dying anyway."

It all sounded reasonable. Yet Tate was a madman. He couldn't be trusted. Just like Myer.

I pressed a hand to my forehead. It came away damp with my sweat. "It's an interesting plan, but it doesn't matter anyway. We haven't seen Tate for a week. He may already be dead."

"I can find out for sure if you like."

"What!" I blurted out. "You know where to find him?"

Two ladies gave us a wide berth. Myer hushed me and beckoned me away from the door. "I don't know where he is, but I know of one or two others from the Society who may."

"What makes you think they will tell you?"

He cocked his head to the side and smiled wickedly.

"Oh. Right. You'll hypnotize them."

"I prefer to think of it as convincing them of the right course of action to take."

Good lord, is that how he justified it to himself? "Mr. Myer, why not just tell me who it is? Samuel can hypnotize them for me."

He shook his head. "I don't think so. I'm not sure I want to unleash your friends on innocent parties." His gaze slid to the ballroom entrance then back to me. "Hence this subterfuge."

"I'm going to tell them. I won't keep them in the dark about something like this."

"Miss Smith, I must warn you against involving them. They'll probably want to come with you to meet Tate."

"Why is that a problem?"

"I'm assuming Tate won't want them there after everything that's transpired. He'll feel threatened without his demon to keep him safe."

"That's too bad."

"A threatened genius is one who may not be able to perform."

I bit the inside of my cheek. It made me terribly uneasy to keep Jack in the dark, yet I could see Myer's point. "I'll think about it."

"I suggest you do. I'll talk to Tate's friends tomorrow and travel to Harborough immediately I've discovered his location."

"You think he's still in the area?"

"Of course. You're there, and he needs you. If the man's still alive, I'm sure he'll come searching for you soon enough."

My gaze locked with his. I knew that Tate was desperate enough to try anything to abduct me, and I suspected Myer knew it too. If I didn't go to him voluntarily, that is.

"Come to me at the Red Lion in Harborough on the morning of the twenty-second. If I've found where he's living, I'll take you to him."

"And if not?"

"I'll send you home again." He clutched my shoulders. "I urge you to consider my proposal, Miss Smith."

"Why did you not offer to do this before? Why now?"

"Because I'd never seen your fire in action until tonight. I admit that I assumed you exaggerated your ability, but seeing it work in the parlor was most intriguing." His finger brushed the length of my jaw before I jerked away. He smiled, and the hairs on the back of my neck rose. "You are quite amazing. When this is over, I hope you will allow me to ask you questions for research purposes."

I shivered, although of course I didn't feel cold. "Good night, Mr. Myer." I headed back toward the ballroom and my friends, away from a man who made my stomach roll and my nerves jangle.

"Good night, Miss Smith," he called after me. "See you soon."

CHAPTER 10

We left London the following afternoon and broke our journey in a small village along the way. The coaching inn was ancient, the black beams warped from centuries of shouldering the upper levels. Jack and Samuel both had to duck to get through the doorways, yet the main hearth in the taproom appeared to be sized for giants. The meal served by a blank-faced girl looked hearty, but I wasn't hungry. I picked at my food, unable to swallow more than a morsel.

"Hannah?" Jack said, eyeing me from across the table in the dining room. "Do you need to rest?"

"Not yet. I have something to tell you all first." I'd waited to mention my conversation with Myer because I didn't want to darken our memories of the ball. We'd had a wonderful time on the whole, although Sylvia was less buoyant than I expected.

"Go on," Jack urged me. "What's wrong?"

I told them about Myer and his proposal, leaving none of it out, including his advice that I not tell them. They were my friends. They'd come down this awful path with me, putting their lives at risk. It didn't seem right not to keep them informed.

"Absolutely not!" Jack said when I finished. "You're not going to meet him."

"Samuel?" I asked. "What do you think?"

He eyed Jack carefully. "I think it's worth considering."

"Samuel!" Sylvia cried. "Do you forget that Tate tried to kill us?" She remembered too late that we sat in a public dining room. The other six patrons all gaped at us. Sylvia dabbed her mouth with her napkin and pretended not to notice.

Samuel picked up his glass of ale. "I said worth considering, not agreeing. Not until we've discussed it further."

"There's nothing to discuss." Jack gave another emphatic shake of his head. "Neither Tate nor Myer can be trusted. Hannah, I won't let you near them."

"In all fairness, Tate only tried to kill us because he was so desperate," Samuel said.

Sylvia pointed her rolled-up napkin at him. "That doesn't change the fact. Anyway, I absolutely disagree with Myer's assessment of Uncle's capabilities. If anyone can find you a cure, Hannah, it's him."

Jack cradled his glass between his hands and stared into the golden ale. "After what we've seen of Myer, I'll not let you near him again."

Samuel and I exchanged glances. He gave me a one-shouldered shrug then concentrated on his food, sawing at the thick slab of beef. I wondered if the reason he was the only one considering Myer's proposal was because he knew Langley was going to stop searching for a cure if I didn't give Jack up. I felt like I was walking on a knife's edge where Langley was concerned, constantly worried about talking to Jack in his presence. Being in London had given us freedom, but that freedom was about to be ripped away again.

I didn't pursue the matter further. There was still time to sway Jack's opinion. Still time to make up my own mind as to what to do.

Instead, I spoke of the ball with Sylvia. I wanted to get to the bottom of her lack of enthusiasm. "You seemed to enjoy yourself immensely last night," I said cheerfully. "Were there any gentlemen in particular you liked?"

She screwed up her pert nose. "Not really." She sighed. "I enjoyed myself well enough. The gentlemen were pleasant, some of them fun, and all wonderful dancers."

"But...?"

"Cara was right. None of them are *interesting*. There's a sameness about them. They lacked individuality. All conversation topics centered around horses, hunting and which illustrious family they'd dined with in recent weeks. I had nothing in common with any of them, and none tried to change the subject to something of more interest to me."

Jack grunted a laugh. "To be fair, sewing isn't a topic on which many men can easily converse."

"Exactly!"

He bit back a smile and rolled his eyes at me.

"I do understand," I said. "Most of the gentlemen I met seemed quite dull too, some of them outright silly. I recall Cara saying that the men in Melbourne were more real, and I do tend to agree that the ones I danced with last night were foppish."

"I hope you're not including me in that assessment," Samuel said, hand on his heart, his lips turned down in an exaggerated pout. "I've always been convinced that I'm vastly interesting."

I laughed and threw my napkin at him. He winked and kept it.

Sylvia sighed. "I suppose I expected something more."

"You've been spoiled living with Jack and Tommy all these years," I said.

"And me," Samuel added. "For the last few weeks, that is."

Sylvia made a miffed sound through her nose. "Jack and Samuel, yes, but not Tommy. He's not a gentleman."

"You must stop reminding him of that in his presence," Jack said. "I think he's growing heartily sick of it."

"Well, he *isn't* a gentleman!"

"There's no need to harp on it."

"I'm not harping. I'm being honest." She concentrated on her beef, daintily slicing it into small pieces. "Jack," she said, idly, "did Tommy tell you what he did last night while we were at the ball?"

Well, well. Did she harbor an affection for Tommy after all? Surely not. Both Samuel and Jack gave her curious stares too, but she was too busy with her food to notice.

"He had a marvelous time with the other drivers and footmen," Jack said with a wicked gleam in his eye. "I believe they had entertainments of their own arranged nearby."

Whether it was true or not, I had no idea, but Sylvia seemed to believe him. She pushed the pieces of beef around her plate, arranging them into a pile. "What sort of entertainments?"

"The sort that people enjoy."

"Yes, but was there food and drink, and…dancing?"

"If there was any drink, he didn't partake in it. You know Tommy wouldn't when he's on duty." Whether Jack deliberately left out the part about dancing, I couldn't be sure. He did seem to want to tease his cousin. Or perhaps it was a test to see if she showed further signs of jealousy.

Sylvia, however, suddenly became very interested in her food. In only a few minutes, she'd wolfed it all down and drained her wine glass. "I'm going to retire early," she announced, standing. "Hannah?"

I nodded and rose too. Despite sleeping in, I was still tired from the night's exertions.

***

I slept late again the next morning, but we managed to reach Frakingham before nightfall. Langley and Bollard met us in the entrance hall upon our arrival. Langley's gaze swept past the others and settled on me.

"How do you feel, Hannah?" he asked.

"The same," I said, using my standard reply.

Langley rubbed his jaw. "That's a relief."

I caught Jack scowling at me, his arms crossed over his chest. I gave him a reassuring smile, but it didn't work. He continued to scowl. I suspected he'd noticed that I gave the same response every time I was asked about my health. I suspected he also knew I was lying.

"Have there been any incidences with Tate in our absence?" Samuel asked.

Langley shook his head. "No sign of him. He must be dead."

My mouth went dry. Tate's life was closely linked to mine. If he'd died, I wouldn't be far behind.

"Go and refresh yourself, Hannah," Langley said, oblivious to how his comment had affected me. "Then come see me. I need more of your blood."

Sylvia made a gurgling sound and screwed up her face.

"Haven't you taken enough?" Jack asked.

"No." Langley signaled for Bollard to wheel him away. They left us standing in the entrance hall, staring after them.

"He didn't even ask how the ball was," Sylvia mumbled.

"He's preoccupied," Jack said.

"I know, but..." She sighed. "Never mind. Come on, Hannah, let's dress for dinner."

I washed myself with cold water in my room, then changed into a pretty black and white dress for the evening. It was an effort, but I managed it without lying down on the bed, and only yawning a dozen times.

I went to Langley's rooms as ordered and Bollard let me in. The place was a shambles. The bed was unmade, papers spewed out of the waste basket onto the floor, and scientific apparatuses covered the desk in a jumbled mess. Why hadn't Bollard tidied the room up? Of course it was a much smaller space than Langley was used to since the fire had destroyed his main rooms in the eastern wing, but that was no excuse for sloppiness.

I picked my way across the floor to where Langley sat in his wheelchair at the desk, bent over a microscope. He held up his hand for silence, even though I hadn't spoken. I sat in a nearby chair and waited for him to finish studying whatever was smeared between the rectangular panes of glass.

"Roll up your sleeve, Hannah." He suddenly pushed himself away from the desk. "Bollard, the syringe."

I rolled up my sleeve and watched Langley, who in turn watched Bollard. The skin beneath his eyes was darker than usual and sagged a little. Now that I was up close, he also seemed somewhat grayer in the face and gaunt around the cheeks. He looked as exhausted as I felt.

"I do appreciate what you're doing for me," I told him. "You have my undying gratitude." I laughed hollowly at my own choice of words. Langley did not.

"There's no need for thanks," he said. "Not yet."

I watched as he took the syringe from Bollard and pressed the needle into my arm. "Mr. Langley, are you close to finding a cure?"

He didn't say anything as the syringe sucked out my blood. Once the cylinder was full, he removed the needle and handed me the cloth to dab the spot. He gave the syringe to Bollard. "I'd rather not say," he said.

Such an odd answer! "Why not?"

"Because if I am, I don't want to give you hope when it may yet fail. And if I'm not, then I don't want to disappoint you."

"Surely false hope is better than no hope at all."

He considered that for a moment, then nodded. "In that case, I am close."

If we hadn't been discussing my death, I would have laughed. For a genius, it was a rather stupid thing to say after his admission. I appealed to Bollard and was surprised to see a sardonic smile on his lips. Not an obvious one, mind. It was barely a quirk of the corners of his mouth, but it was definitely there. So the mute had a sense of humor, yet his master did not.

"Thank you, Mr. Langley. I feel infinitely more satisfied now than when I came in."

It would seem Langley did understand sarcasm. He narrowed his eyes at me then swung his wheelchair around. "I have to return to work."

"Very well. You work, I'll talk."

"You may talk, but that doesn't mean I'll listen."

"I overheard you tell Samuel that you'll stop searching for a cure for me if Jack and I continue with our assignations."

He paused. Bollard stopped what he was doing too. They both turned and stared at me. "You and Jack are dangerous together, Hannah. You know that. You've seen what happens."

"Yes, but your measures are a little drastic, don't you think?"

"Are they?"

"Surely there's no need to involve others."

"What others?"

I sighed. "You've been pushing me toward Samuel, and Jack to Charity."

Bollard's gaze slid to Langley's. The lines around his mouth flattened. He set the syringe down on the desk and began signing with his hands. I couldn't follow the nimble movements of his fingers, but Langley seemed to. When Bollard finished, he shook his head, and turned to me.

"Not Charity," Langley said with a tilt of his chin. "She's not good enough for my nephew."

"He's not your nephew. I do see your point though. If she's not good enough for him, then nor am I. Am I? I'm the daughter of an ordinary, poor couple. You want better for him." It came out as an angry sneer, but I didn't realize it until my hands grew hot. The rest of me too. I sucked in deep breaths to cool my temper before I emitted any sparks.

"If you say so, Hannah."

I wanted to thump something. I wanted to scream and rage at him, but I didn't. For one thing, I was too tired, and for another, I knew what happened when I let my temper take the reins, and I couldn't afford to start another fire. It wasn't easy to quell the heat boiling inside me, but I managed it.

"I can't believe you can be so cruel," I whispered, fighting back tears. "I can't believe you would actually stop trying to cure me just because you don't want Jack and I to be together."

He didn't answer immediately. He stared at me for a long time until he finally looked down at his immobile legs. "If you know what's good for you, you won't tell Jack. He'll grow mad and that will set my research back further."

Bollard clicked his tongue and signed furiously, earning himself a glare from Langley. The servant's defiance surprised me. It surprised me even more that Langley didn't admonish him except for that brief glare. It was almost as if there was no barrier of class or position between them. Indeed, their relationship was beginning to remind me of Jack and Tommy's.

"Why are you doing this to us?" I cried.

"I don't expect you to see clearly, Hannah. Not now. Jack too." He wheeled himself to the desk and picked up the syringe full of blood. "You will in due course. Bollard, show Hannah the door. I'm very busy."

Bollard sighed loudly and opened the door for me. I wiped away the single errant tear on my cheek and walked past him. He caught my elbow and put his finger to his lips to silence me. Once, such an action would have frightened me, but not anymore. I frowned and mouthed *What?*

He pressed his hand over his heart then pointed at Langley. I shook my head. I didn't understand. He didn't repeat the action, simply shooed me out the door and shut it. I stared at the door and tried to think what he could have meant. That Langley cared?

Or that Langley had no heart.

***

I overslept again the following day, only to be awoken by Sylvia charging into my bedroom.

"You have a visitor," she announced, throwing open the curtains.

I shielded my eyes from the light pouring through the window, but they stung nevertheless. Miraculously, it appeared to be a sunny morning. "Who is it?"

"You'll never guess."

"That's why I'm asking."

She inspected the gowns in my wardrobe, most of which were altered ones of hers that she no longer liked. Compared to the woolen garments I'd had to wear in the attic at Windamere, they were beautiful. I was happy to have her castoffs.

"I think green today." She pulled out a forest green skirt and matching jacket. It was more of an outfit for spring, but Sylvia knew me well enough now to know that I couldn't wear the heavy winter fabrics. "It enhances your slender waist, and it's one of the few colors that look good on you."

"Are you avoiding answering the question?"

She chewed on her lip. "Is it that obvious?"

"Sylvia, you and subtlety are not friends. Tell me, who is here to see me? Not Tate, surely."

"No, thank goodness. I never want to see that man again. It's that Violet Jamieson person."

I slumped back against the head board. "Vi! What's she doing here?"

"She's come to speak to you. Now hurry up, I'm dying to know what she has to say too."

She helped me dress and fix my hair. I checked myself in the dressing table mirror and wished I hadn't. My eyes were underscored by dark smudges and my skin glistened, pale and sickly. No wonder everybody had been looking at me with sympathy lately.

Sylvia remained with me until we reached the parlor and I asked her to leave. She glanced at Vi, sitting primly on the edge of the sofa, turned up her nose and strode off.

"Hannah," Vi said, rising as I entered. She gave me a tentative smile. "How *are* you?"

"Quite well, thank you."

Her smiled faded and a frown crept across her forehead. Clearly she didn't believe me, but she didn't say so.

Tommy entered and set a tray of tea things on the table. "I'll serve, thank you, Tommy." He bowed and left.

Vi watched me as I poured the tea. I felt terribly conspicuous, like something under Langley's microscope. It rattled my nerves. "Are *you* well, Violet?" I asked, handing her a cup and saucer. Politeness dictated we exchange pleasantries, although it galled me to go through the motions when all I wanted to do was get to the point of her visit.

"Thank you, yes." She sipped.

"Did you come here unaccompanied?"

"No, my father is waiting for me in the carriage outside."

I looked to the window, but the carriage was out of my line of sight. "Why doesn't he come in? He must be cold."

"He has furs for warmth." It didn't answer my question, and I suspected she was avoiding it on purpose. I'm sure after Lord Wade's last visit to Frakingham, he was keen to avoid us.

"You called him your father. So...is he?" Damnation, I was tired and ill. I didn't have the patience for politeness and avoidance tactics. It was time to find out what Vi wanted, and ask her some questions of my own.

"Yes. He is. Hannah, he's not a bad man."

"He kept us locked in the attic for fifteen years!"

"We weren't *locked* in there. We were allowed out on occasion. Besides, it was for your own good."

"And yours?"

She studied the teacup. "I think he regrets it. He's never said as much, but his actions since your disappearance would suggest he's sorry. He agreed to accompany me here, for instance."

"Whose idea was that?"

"Mine. After I saw you at the ball, I begged him to let me come. I couldn't rest until I spoke to you again. I had no idea until that night that he'd even found you. No idea at all. It was quite shocking to learn of his visit."

"But *you* knew where I was. You could have come here at any time yourself, once he let you out of the attic."

"I may be out, but I can't go wandering about the country unaccompanied. Young ladies are restricted, Hannah."

"I know that," I said tightly. "Tell me, did he let you out of the attic the day I disappeared?"

"Yes."

"So it was worth it then."

"What was?"

"Your conspiracy with Miss Levine to have Jack abduct me."

Her teacup rattled in the saucer. She set them down on the table and smoothed her hands over her sleek mauve and black skirt. It was made of silk, not wool. It would seem she was free of more than just the attic.

"I'm glad it worked out well for you," she said, leveling her gaze on me. "I really am. You seem to have nice friends here. I can see they care for you. I know you probably don't believe me when I said I miss you, but I do." She reached for me, but curled her fingers into a fist at the last moment and drew it back to her lap. "I miss you every day, Hannah. My only companion now is my half-sister Eudora, and she's not nearly as much fun as you. She's rather a spoiled little miss."

"Half-sister? Your mother isn't Lady Wade?"

Her gaze shifted to the door then back to me. "No, but please don't spread that about," she said softly. "Only four people know the truth. Now five."

"Why *are* you telling me?"

"Because I owe you an explanation. Several. I won't shy away from what I did to you, Hannah. The years of deception and outright lies, and then being involved in your kidnapping." She shuddered. "This is the first explanation I'll give you. Lady Wade isn't my mother. Miss Levine is."

I gasped and stared at her with my mouth open for several beats before I realized and shut it.

"It's quite true," she went on, still speaking quietly. It was as if she was scandalized by merely voicing it. "She and my father had a tryst, and it resulted in me."

"While he was married to Lady Wade?"

She nodded. "Shocking, isn't it? I'm being passed off as her daughter in public now, but she dislikes me intensely. She couldn't have children, you see. They tried for years apparently, and nothing. My father's eye wandered, and eventually it wandered in Miss Levine's direction. She was a maid at the time. She bore me around the same time you came to Windamere as a baby. Lady Wade was happy to have us both there then. She thought she couldn't have children at all, you see. She was desperate for a little one to love, so pretended that I was her daughter."

"But not me?"

"No. Your hair was a problem. There's no red hair on either side of the family. Besides, some of the servants knew you'd been brought to the house by a friend of my father's."

"So why did Lady Wade stop wanting us? Why relegate us to the attic?"

"Eudora. Three years passed, and Lady Wade fell pregnant. With a child of her own to spoil, she no longer wanted us. My presence reminded her of her husband's infidelity and you were…well, you were difficult to control then. Apparently your fire had become a problem. She didn't want a…a…"

"Deformed child?"

She cleared her throat. "She didn't want a child with your curious nature to be associated with the family. Since you and I were inseparable, they made the decision to confine us to the attic together."

"Two birds, one stone." I slumped back in the chair. It wasn't an elegant way to sit, and it was somewhat awkward with the bustle in my dress, but I didn't care. I was too engrossed in her tale. Miss Levine was Vi's mother. Remarkable. And somewhat horrible too. I think I preferred my motherless state.

"Lord Wade bedded *her*?" I said. "But she's a withered, heartless dragon. Oh." I bit my lip. "Sorry. I probably shouldn't disparage your mother to you."

She pulled a face. "It's quite all right. I'm not overly fond of her. When I asked how she felt giving me up to Lady Wade when I was a baby, she told me she was glad. She said she didn't like motherhood."

"I don't think she enjoyed being a governess much more. So how long have you known? Did you always know?"

"Miss Levine—I still can't think of her as 'Mother'—told me one day when we were out walking last spring. You were a little ahead of us. She told me I was her daughter and that it had been her idea to keep us in the attic. She said that if she hadn't spoken up and offered to be our governess, we would have been sent to a school for girls, never to return to Windamere."

"Would that have been such a bad thing? We would have been given more freedom. We certainly would have met more people."

She gave a resigned shrug. "It's too late to speculate."

"Why didn't you tell me, Vi? Why keep it a secret all those months?"

"Miss Levine ordered me to. She said I'd never get out of the attic if I told you." Her face fell. Her eyes filled with tears. "Oh, Hannah, I wanted to tell you. I doubted the necessity for silence every day."

"But your desire to leave the attic was stronger than your friendship to me."

She pulled out a handkerchief from her reticule and dabbed her eyes. "Miss Levine said I'd never leave while you were there. That day she told me she was my mother, she also told me about her plan to have you abducted. She knew that a gentleman had brought you to the house, but she didn't know his name or anything else about him. It took her all this time to learn more and contact him to arrange the abduction. She said you'd never agree to leave me behind. That's why it had to be kept a secret, even from Lord Wade. He would never have let you just leave. He cared about you, you know. In his own way."

I'm sure he didn't like to lose me any more than he liked losing a cufflink. I was his possession, a part of the Windamere Hall estate. As was Vi. I didn't say it, but I could see in her listless hands and the way she wouldn't meet my gaze that she knew it.

"If you'd disobeyed Miss Levine, you could have come here with me," I said. "There would have been no need for the elaborate arrangement. But you wanted to be left behind."

"I'm not like you, Hannah. I'm not brave or adventurous. Windamere is my home," she whispered. "The thought of leaving it scared me to death."

"But the thought of leaving the attic did not? That in itself was an adventure. How could you be sure Lord and Lady Wade would accept you into their home as their daughter?"

"Miss Levine assured me they would, and I believed her. She said they'd never accept you, but I had a chance for a normal life with them." Her lower lip wobbled. "I'm so sorry, Hannah. I had to get out of that attic. I felt like I was living half a life."

"I felt that way too."

"Yes, but…*I'm* the daughter of an earl. Please don't take offense. It's simply the truth of the matter."

I almost couldn't believe what I was hearing. Our birthrights had never been an issue before. On the other hand, she'd only discovered who she was for certain last spring. Before that, I knew she'd had doubts. Still, I'd not seen any sign that she thought herself above me in all that time. Not until now.

"Can you understand why I did it?" she asked. "At least a little?"

"Are you asking for my forgiveness?"

"I...I suppose I am." She looked so earnest, so innocent, like the Vi I knew and had loved like a sister. She'd always needed reassuring from me, whether it was to go outside, or to stand up to Miss Levine, or even just meet the butler in the eye as we walked past him. She needed it again, and I saw no reason not to give it to her. I didn't have the energy to pile more guilt on her. Besides, her betrayal had led me to Frakingham and Jack, Sylvia, Tommy and Samuel. How could I blame her when her actions gave me such blessings?

"I forgive you, Vi."

A tear slid down her cheek. "Truly?"

I stood and put out my hand to her. She took it and I drew her into a hug. "Truly. Now." I pulled away and went to look out the window at the carriage. Jack stood by it, his back to me, speaking to Lord Wade through the window. "Tell me, Vi, what story are the Wades putting out about your sudden appearance in Society?"

"They're telling everybody I was a sickly child and have only recently been allowed out of my sick bed by the doctors."

"What was your illness?"

"Oh, everything! Fortunately nobody has asked for particulars." She laughed as she came up behind me. "I must say, your abductor is quite handsome. Father told me he's the nephew of the man who owns this house."

"Jack Langley." I wasn't going to tell her the truth about Jack or all the other things that I'd learned since coming to Freak House. Once I would have told her everything, but the connection between us simply wasn't there anymore. I had other people to fill that void.

Jack suddenly threw up his hands and slapped them down on the coach's window frame. The driver's head swung around, and the horses' ears twitched. We couldn't hear what Jack said or see his face, but from the rigidity of his shoulders, I knew he was furious.

"Is he violent?" Violet whispered, as if she were afraid Jack would overhear.

"Only when he's angry." It was perhaps cruel to let her think that Jack might hurt Lord Wade, but I had no true sympathy for either of them. "Let's go out, shall we?"

She hooked her arm through mine like we used to do when going for our walks at Windamere. I didn't pull away. I could feel her tremble and realized she really was terrified.

I led her outside, but she planted her feet on the top step and would not budge. I untangled my arm from hers and left her behind.

"Jack," I said, coming up behind him. "Is everything all right?"

His arms hung loosely at his sides, the fingers red and hot. He did not look at me, but instead into the cabin where Lord Wade huddled on the far side beneath fur coats.

"Lord Wade and I were just reminiscing about the past," Jack said, casual as can be.

"So I see." I smiled and waved at the earl, but he did not wave back.

"Violet!" he roared.

She hurried up to us, her strides short and neat, dainty. Jack opened the cabin door, and she edged in, careful not to get too close and always keeping her wide gaze on him. I should have told her she had nothing to fear, but I didn't.

Lord Wade banged the head of his cane on the cabin roof, and the driver urged the horses forward. I watched as the coach rolled away, flicking up mud and gravel beneath its wheels as it quickly gained momentum.

It was still on the drive when I turned to Jack. "What were you and Lord Wade really talking about?"

But Jack wasn't looking at me. His head was bowed and cocked to the side as if he were listening to something in the distance. Then he looked up sharply and focused on the drive.

"Jack? What is it?" I followed his gaze. The coach had departed and a horse approached with a rider slumped forward. It was impossible to see his face. The only thing I could discern was that he had something long and thin resting across his lap.

"Bloody hell," Jack growled. "Hannah, inside."

"Who is it?"

"Inside! Now!"

I did as he ordered, just as the rider lifted both his head and the thing on his lap with the same hand that held the reins. Just as a one-armed man would do.

It was Tate. He aimed a shotgun at us.

CHAPTER 11

If Jack could touch me without combusting either one of us, I suspected he would have thrown me over his shoulder and carried me inside. As it was, I ran as fast as my skirts would allow to the front door. He slammed it shut behind us as the *crack* of a gunshot blasted through the tranquility of the frosty winter's day.

"Keep away from the windows and doors," he ordered. "Find Sylvia and go to August's room."

"What about you? What are you going to do?"

"Kill Tate."

Another shot rang out. It sounded closer than the last, but like the first one, I couldn't hear any glass breaking or wood splintering. The slug must have lodged in the brickwork somewhere.

"Tommy!" Jack shouted. "Tommy, my gun!"

Tommy met us at the arched entrance to the corridor that led to the service area. He already held two shotguns, a box of ammunition tucked under his arm. Jack pushed him back along the corridor a few paces. It was one of the safest places in the house.

"What the blazes did you say to the toff, Jackie?" he asked in his slum accent, a sign that he too was panicked.

154

Jack took the box of bullets. "It's not Wade. It's Tate."

Tommy said a very colorful word that had me blushing, then he and Jack both concentrated on loading the weapons.

"There you are!" said Samuel, entering the corridor behind me. He must have been upstairs when the shots were fired. "Is everybody all right? Who's shooting at you?"

"Tate," I said. "Although it's not clear if he's shooting at anyone or just frightening us." If the latter, he was doing a very thorough job.

Samuel beckoned for a gun. "Give me one of those."

Tommy pulled back and shook his head. "Let us handle him, sir."

"But I can hypnotize him if I get close enough."

"There's the flaw in your plan," Jack said. "He'll shoot you before you have a chance."

"Only if he sees me."

"That is a rather precarious 'if' to stake your life upon," I said. "Since Tate is here for me, I forbid you to try, Samuel. It's too much of a risk. That goes for all of you. Jack, I wish you wouldn't—"

"Hannah?" Sylvia called.

"In here!" I called back.

She held her skirts up, revealing her ankles, something that would ordinarily have horrified her. "I heard gunshots. I went to Uncle, and he said to find you and report back."

I told her about Tate. Her reaction was to let go of her skirts to cover her gasp with her hands. "If only that man had died!"

Well, yes, except it would mean I had little time left too. It was actually a relief to see him up and about. "Jack and Tommy are going to intercept him, but I don't know if it's a wise idea."

"Well, I *do* know! It's a terrible idea. Nobody is going outside while that madman is armed."

"What would you have us do, Syl?" Jack said, pointing the loaded weapon at the ceiling.

"I don't know, but it's too dangerous to be out there. Wait until he runs out of ammunition and leaves of his own accord."

"I should have pursued him when I killed Ham. I won't let him get away again."

"Perhaps he's not trying to kill anyone," I said. "He wants me alive."

"He's not getting you," he growled.

"I'm sure he doesn't plan on shooting at *you*," Samuel said quietly. "Rather the people trying to protect you."

My stomach heaved. My chest tightened. I put a hand to the wall to steady myself, but the world still felt like it was rocking.

Sylvia put her arm around my shoulders, but the men didn't seem to notice my turn.

"Gladstone, there's a loaded pistol in the drawer beside my bed," Jack said. "Fetch it. The external doors are already locked except the front one. Guard it. Only let Tommy or me in."

Jack and Tommy headed one way down the corridor and Samuel the other before either Sylvia or I could stop them.

"Please be careful!" I tried to shout, but my voice was weak. It wouldn't have carried far.

"Are you all right, Hannah?" Sylvia asked.

I placed a hand to my stomach and nodded numbly. But the bilious feeling of foreboding never left me. My friends were out there with a violent, unconscionable man—because of me. Tate wanted me, and he didn't care how he got me. By refusing to go with him, I was putting my friends in danger.

I let Sylvia lead me to Langley's room where we waited with her uncle and Bollard for the men to return. It was a little tidier than the last time I was there, but not much.

"I had not thought he'd sink as low as this," Langley said. He tipped his head back and squeezed his eyes shut. "Is it my fault? Did I do this to him?"

Bollard placed his hand on his employer's shoulder briefly before drawing back. The mute's eyes became glassy, and he turned away.

"No, Uncle," Sylvia said, going to Langley. "It's the fire in Tate that's made him desperate. Nothing to do with you."

"The fire is in Hannah too, and she doesn't hold me at gunpoint until I find her a cure."

"I don't know where the guns are kept," I said, trying to lighten the mood although not expecting to succeed.

To my surprise, Langley smirked. "I'd better get back to work before you do." He swiveled his chair around and worked side-by-side with his assistant.

Sylvia and I sat away from the windows. I desperately wanted to look out to see if I could spot Jack and Tommy, but I remained where I was.

A horrible half hour passed. Sylvia puttered about the room, folding clothes and picking up discarded pieces of paper, but always keeping away from the windows. We didn't speak. I suspected she was as reluctant to disturb Langley as I was. He spoke a few words of instruction to Bollard once in a while, but mostly there was only a quiet hush in the room.

And out of it too. No more gunshots were fired, thank God. The sense of relief became more potent as the seconds and minutes ticked past. It wasn't easy sitting there, waiting and doing nothing, but I managed it with only the loss of the fingernails on one hand. I'd bitten them to the quick by the time Jack and Samuel collected us.

"Where's Tommy?" Sylvia asked, before either had spoken a word.

"Putting away the shotguns," Jack said. He held a pistol, probably the one that he'd ordered Samuel to retrieve.

"Tate?" Langley asked.

"Gone."

Sylvia mewled like a kitten. "You killed him?"

"No, I mean he's disappeared again. He must have ridden off as soon as he fired the second shot. We couldn't find him. Hannah?" he murmured, coming to crouch by me. "Are you all right?"

"Yes." I tried to give him a smile, but it fell flat. He didn't return it, but scanned my face as if he could see in it how long I had left to live.

"We cannot continue like this," Sylvia declared. "The man must be stopped. Somebody in the village must know where he is."

"We've already asked," Jack said. "Nobody saw him, and I suspect he hasn't been living nearby anyway, or we would have heard rumors in the village."

"We can ask again," Samuel suggested. "He may have made an appearance today."

Jack sighed and nodded. Clearly he didn't hold out much hope.

Nor did I. I sat very still as they spoke, trying to order my thoughts. In the end, the only conclusion I came to was in direct contrast to Jack's.

I didn't want Tate dead. I wanted him alive and working to find a cure.

"Tommy's bringing tea to the parlor," Jack said to me. "Come and rest in there."

"You can watch me while I decorate the room," Sylvia said. "We don't have a tree, but I collected some laurel and holly this morning before you woke." She clapped her hands. "It'll be such fun! Mrs. Beaufort's decorations were inspirational. I have so many ideas, and it's just the thing to take our minds off…other things."

She skipped out of the room. Her capacity to throw off troubling events amazed me. Samuel followed her, and Jack arched his eyebrow at me. "Hannah?"

"In a moment. I want to talk to Mr. Langley."

He hesitated then inclined his head and left. Langley stopped what he was doing. Bollard too. "Are you worse?" he asked, blunt as a hammer blow.

I thought about giving my stock answer, but decided he needed to know the truth. "I'm hotter and constantly tired.

Exhausted. I feel as if I could sleep all day and still not be refreshed." To my dismay, tears puddled in my eyes.

Bollard stepped forward and retrieved a handkerchief from his pocket. He handed it to me, grim-faced.

"Thank you, Bollard. You're very kind."

He blushed. Even the tips of his ears reddened. I liked the big mute more and more each day.

"I suppose you want to ask me again how close I am to finding a cure," Langley said.

"I know that interrupting you doesn't help, but...I can't stop myself. I need to know."

"Hannah." He wheeled himself closer and took my hand. It was not what I expected, and I was moved by his gentleness. His hands were strong, capable, and stained from the ink used to write his notes. "My answer is the same as last time. I'm doing my best."

"I know you are." I bit the inside of my cheek and tasted blood. I wasn't at all sure that I should ask my next question, but I did so anyway. I had nothing to lose after all. Not anymore. "Mr. Langley, will you consider working with Reuben Tate to—"

"No!" He withdrew his hand and rolled himself backward. "Absolutely not. I can't believe you would ask me that after everything you've learned about him."

I got to my feet and stalked him across the floor to where he'd stopped at his desk. "Could it hurt to speak to him? Perhaps find out where he is in the process. He may be further along than you, after all."

"I cannot work with Tate, but more importantly, you'll find that he won't work with me. He detests me, Hannah."

"Why?"

"It doesn't matter. The reasons are lost to the mists of time, and I no longer care to talk about it. Is that all?"

I ignored his dismissal. "Mr. Myer said you and Tate worked well together once. That you made a brilliant team. Couldn't you do that again? For my sake?"

"Myer! Ha! What does he know? You shouldn't believe everything he tells you. For one thing, I did the majority of the work in our so-called team, not Tate. Tate enjoyed the spoils of our work, but preferred to dabble in the more…commercially unsuccessful drugs."

"Is that how you describe the fire starting compound? As 'commercially unsuccessful'?"

"I'd hardly call it a success."

I heaved a sigh. "So you won't even consider meeting with him to discuss it?"

"I think he's beyond the point of discussion. He's unreasonable now, Hannah. The illness and subsequent search for a cure have affected his mind." He tapped the side of his temple. "You'd better rest and keep your mind at ease. Otherwise, it may happen to you."

A discomforting thought. "I will. I'll spend the remainder of the day watching Sylvia decorate the house and being served tea."

I said nothing about the following day.

I couldn't stay in the house any longer and allow others to risk their lives for me. Tate would not give up until he had me in his possession, and I had no doubts he would use every unscrupulous method to get me, including harming my friends. He'd already proven that he cared nothing for them.

If Langley wasn't willing to work with him to find a cure, then I had no other recourse. I would give myself to Tate for testing, but I would go to him alone. I had to. There was no way Jack or the others would sit by and watch me walk into Tate's laboratory and offer myself up for his tests.

The idea filled me with dread, but I was determined. No one else should be harmed because of me.

The following day was the twenty-second, the day I'd arranged with Myer to meet him and Tate at the Red Lion. It could also be my last day at Frakingham…or anywhere else.

***

It was easier to sneak out of the house than I expected. When I arose late in the morning, Jack and Samuel had already left to question the villagers about Tate. I hoped they hadn't bumped into him or Myer in the Red Lion.

After breakfast, I told Sylvia I needed to lie down again. She gave me a frown and a pouch of dried lavender to place under my pillow for a restful sleep, then ordered me back to bed. Instead, I headed out via one of the rear doors, through the woods, emerging from the trees near the estate's iron gates. I couldn't walk all the way into the village in my poor health, so I waited at the side of the thoroughfare. It was the main road into Harborough and as such, reasonably busy even in winter. As luck would have it, I only had to wait ten minutes before a farmer's cart rolled by. The driver let me sit beside him rather than in the back with the caged chickens. I told him I was visiting friends in the village and had been out walking only to grow too tired to walk back. Whether he believed me or not, he gave no indication. Indeed, he spoke only a few words for the entire journey, perhaps because he wouldn't have heard my answer above the squawking poultry.

I lifted my cloak's hood to cover my conspicuous hair as we arrived in the village. The farmer dropped me outside the Red Lion and I hurried inside, checking this way and that for Samuel and Jack.

I was still gathering my wits and my breath when Myer approached. "Miss Smith," he said, bowing. "I'm so pleased you could make it. We've been waiting for you."

"Let's move away from the door." I glanced about, conscious of all the eyes watching me. Fortunately none of them belonged to Jack or Samuel.

The Red Lion wasn't old, having been built a mere ten years earlier after a fire destroyed the previous inn that had stood there for centuries. The rooms were big, the ceilings high, and every wooden surface was polished to a gleaming shine. I'd only been inside once, but the taproom looked exactly the same. Even the same five men sat on stools, hunched over tankards. The proprietor nodded a greeting from behind the long bar. If he thought it strange that

August Langley's female guest was meeting with a much older gentleman in his inn, he didn't say. I took Myer's offered arm, and he led me up the stairs to a small parlor off the landing.

I paused in the doorway and stared at Reuben Tate. He sat slumped in an armchair, his eyes closed, his mouth open. He was cadaverously thin, hardly more than a collection of bones beneath clothes that were too large for his slender frame. One shirtsleeve hung limply at his side, empty and useless. He hadn't bothered to pin it up. His throat was as white as the shirt, his face too except for two spots of color on his cheeks. It was the only sign that he was alive.

"She's here," Myer announced. He gently pushed me forward into the room and shut the door.

Tate opened his eyes a fraction, then fully. It was an effort for him to sit upright, but he managed it without once taking his gaze off me. Those eyes made me shiver, although I was very far from cold. They were watery and almost colorless, as if the soul behind them was already half-dead and staring into the Afterlife.

He pressed his hand to the chair arm and heaved himself to his feet. It was an effort, but Myer didn't offer to help. He remained beside me, and I was grateful for the solidness of his presence. He should be able to overpower a one-armed, half-dead man.

As long as Tate didn't draw a weapon or burn him.

"Good morning, Miss Smith," Tate wheezed. "Forgive my appearance." He indicated his lack of vest and jacket, his crooked tie, the limp, unpinned sleeve. "My visit to Frakingham yesterday has rather exhausted me."

"I understand." It was a stupid response, but I could think of none other.

Those eyes studied my face, no doubt noticing my pallor and the shine, so much like his own. "I expect you do. I would not have made the journey if I'd known you were coming here today."

I wouldn't tell him that it was his visit that had finally convinced me to come. I didn't want to give him the satisfaction of knowing his tactic had worked.

"Come and sit down, Miss Smith," Myer said, indicating another armchair.

But I didn't get the chance to move. Tate stepped in front of us and grabbed my arm. Heat swelled within me, centering on that spot like a sunbeam. It wasn't as hot as when Jack touched me, but the burning sensation was unpleasant enough that I wanted him to let me go. He did not.

"There's no time for polite conversation." His voice was weak and thready, but no less threatening because of it. "We must go. Now."

I tried to wrench myself free, but he was stronger than he looked. Or perhaps I'd grown weaker. "Go where, Mr. Tate?"

"I have a temporary laboratory set up in…" His tongue darted out, licking dry lips before slithering back inside his mouth. "Never mind where. You have to come with me, Miss Smith."

I bared my teeth and gave an almighty wrench of my arm, dragging myself free. "I'm not going anywhere with you until you explain what it is you plan on doing to me."

"Let's all be calm," Mr. Myer said in that soothing voice of his. "Sit and talk. I'm sure we can come to an arrangement that suits both your needs."

He waited until Tate sat grudgingly then directed me to one of the other chairs. Myer sat too. We formed a triangle in the small parlor, far enough apart that we weren't touching knees, but near enough that I felt uncomfortable. The last time I'd been this close to Tate, he'd tried to abduct me.

The fireplace at my back wasn't lit and the window stood ajar. A fresh breeze rustled the rust-brown brocade curtains and cooled my face. Myer pulled his coat closed at his throat.

"Miss Smith…" Tate rubbed his hand down his trouser leg. It left behind a damp, sweaty smear. "Miss Smith, when can we get started? This matter is urgent as I'm sure you can appreciate. I don't think I have more than a few days left. You perhaps have longer, but not much."

He stated it so matter-of-factly, as if he were reading an item from a newspaper, that it took a moment for his words to sink in. "Days?" I whispered.

He withdrew his handkerchief and dabbed his glistening forehead. "It's difficult to be accurate, but that's my informed guess based on this insufferable heat." He plucked his shirt at his chest. "Some days it feels as if I'm suffocating. Is that how it feels for you?"

I swallowed and nodded. "It's like a fire has been lit inside me and nothing can extinguish it. Nothing."

"Jack Langley…he's all right?"

Myer leaned forward ever so slightly. He hadn't known about Jack's fire starting, only the speed. It would seem that secret of Jack's was out now too.

"He's unaffected," I said. "But of course he was born with the fire inside him. We weren't. We shouldn't have it at all. If it weren't for your mad desire for power, Mr. Tate, neither of us would be in this predicament." Passing judgment was a pointless exercise, but I couldn't help it. Besides, I think I had a right to vent.

"It wasn't a desire to be powerful, Miss Smith." He spat out my name as if it burned his tongue. "What I desired was knowledge. It's a scientist's curse, the same as any explorer who sets off across oceans. We want to chart uncharted lands. We want to know what exists beyond the known. Don't let that pathetic excuse for a man tell you otherwise."

"August Langley?"

"That unfaithful cripple is as useless between the ears as he is between the legs."

Myer cleared his throat and held up his hands. "I say, Mr. Tate, there's no call for—"

"Don't interrupt me!" Sparks burst from Tate's fingertips onto the carpet at Myer's feet.

"Bloody hell!" Myer shot out of his chair and danced on the smoldering patches of carpet. Fortunately the pile was thick and woolen. The damage was minimal, and the small scorch marks blended in with the busy pattern.

Myer did not return to his chair immediately. He stood in the center of our triangle and blinked at Tate, then at me, as if he were seeing us both for the first time. Now that he'd gotten over his initial shock, he seemed more curious than anything.

Tate wiped away the spittle in the corner of his mouth. "You may sit down now, Myer. It's quite safe."

Myer sat. "That was…illuminating. Miss Smith, you didn't seem frightened in the least by his outburst."

"I can't be burned," I said. "Besides, I had warning. His fingers turned red. The signs are obvious when you know what to look for."

"I'll keep that in mind for next time."

Tate snickered. "There won't be a next time, unless you make me angry. I would advise against it. That…" He waved a hand at the carpet. "…was nothing."

I shelved my next question based on his advice, but it refused to be forgotten entirely: why did Tate refer to Langley as unfaithful? It seemed an odd choice of words for laboratory partners, particularly when coupled with the crude reference to his manhood.

Did it have something to do with Tate's preference for the love of men over women? Had he been in love with Langley?

Had Langley once been in love with him?

Oh. Oh my. It suddenly made sense. Langley's refusal to tell anyone why they'd fallen out, the fierce resentment between them. I also recalled Tate having very few nice things to say about Bollard, the man who was Langley's valet, assistant, friend…and lover? The lover who'd replaced him perhaps?

It was all so extraordinary that I momentarily forgot why I was visiting Tate and merely stared at him. He must have said something because he prompted me with, "Well?"

"Er, pardon," I said. "I missed your question."

He rummaged through his damp, stringy white hair and huffed out a loud breath. "May we go now?"

"Not yet. First, tell me in detail what it is you wish to do to me."

"Have you learned nothing of the scientific process from Langley?"

"Mr. Tate, were you always this rude, or is it a new habit?'

"Christ," he muttered. "Save me from insufferable idiots."

"I'd rather be an idiot than mad."

"Mr. Tate, Miss Smith," Myer cut in. "Might I suggest that these barbs aren't helping to speed matters."

Tate blew out another breath and settled his limp gaze on me. "I'm going to inject you with various remedies I've prepared and study the results."

"These injections…could they kill me?"

He seemed to weigh up his next words carefully. "I hope not."

I dug my fingernails into the soft leather arms of the chair. His casual disregard for my life turned up the heat inside me. "Let's be clear. Do you have any idea how your remedies will perform? Any idea at all?"

"I've tested them on my own blood samples and have had some promising results, but that's not enough. I need a human study, and you, my dear, are it."

I pressed my lips together. They were cracked and rough. "Can you guarantee the remedies at least won't make me worse?"

Again the weighty silence before he answered. "I can."

Only a fool would have believed him. "Mr. Tate, have you considered sharing your findings with Lang—"

"Don't!" He slammed his hand down on the armchair. A single spark shot violently from his index finger and landed on my skirt. I batted it out before it could catch alight. "I won't go near that man."

"You're dying, and you won't even consider working with him? Is your jealousy that strong?"

He lifted his chin. "I'd rather die with my pride, Miss Smith. It's all I have left. That man destroyed everything else."

"Not your life. The compound you injected into yourself from Jack is doing that." I shook my head. "I don't understand you, Mr. Tate. You would choose death over a rivalry? A broken heart?"

"Sometimes you shouldn't give in to base-born bullies. It makes them stronger. That remedy that we sold for a vault full of money? It was mine." He stabbed a finger into his chest. "I was the one who discovered it. I put in countless hours of effort while he was dallying behind my back with that lumbering imbecile. But because of our agreement, August was able to sell it and keep most of the proceeds. I received a pittance. So yes, I would rather die than give him this remedy too. I won't let him take the glory a second time."

His claim was in contrast to Langley's own statements on the matter, but I wasn't about to argue. "What glory? It's not a commercially viable drug. You and I are the only market for it."

He had edged forward in his chair, and now he sat back, slumping a little, as if he could no longer hold himself upright. He stared into the fireplace and rubbed his palm along the chair arm.

Myer uncrossed his legs and re-crossed them. He didn't meet my gaze either.

"I understand now," I whispered. "The Society wants it, don't they?" I didn't know whether I was speaking to Myer or Tate or both. But I did know that I was right. The way they avoided looking at me was enough of a clue. "You're going to use the compound from Jack to give ordinary people this…this *curse* of a disease, then provide them with the antidote when it begins to consume them years later."

It was so diabolical that I almost couldn't fathom it. I should have run out of the room, but my limbs felt too heavy to move. I would have tripped over my leaden feet.

"Now, Miss Smith," Myer said, soothing. "Calm yourself. There's no call for such frenzied words." He did look me in the eyes then, and I felt the familiar dizzying sensation, the feeling of having my thoughts smothered by a thick blanket.

He was hypnotizing me.

CHAPTER 12

I tore my gaze away from Myer before he completely took over my mind. It wasn't an easy thing to do. His voice was like a beautiful song I wanted to listen to again and again. It was comforting, and made me feel special, desired, like I mattered. A very heady, powerful thing indeed.

I forced myself to stand, but it took a great deal of will and physical effort. I also kept my eyes lowered. "Do not hypnotize me, Mr. Myer." I pulled out a small knife from my reticule. I'd stolen it from the kitchen before I left.

Neither Myer nor Tate seemed particularly worried that I'd stab them, but neither approached me either.

"Miss Smith, I wasn't going to hypnotize you," Myer said. "I simply wanted to assure you that there is nothing nefarious in the Society's plan to purchase the compound or the cure. We wish to study it, that's all. We seek to understand the supernatural."

"And use it? That's far too dangerous, Mr. Myer. You know that. And you lied to us about not knowing Tate. Clearly you do."

"I concede that I haven't always told the truth. It's a long habit of mine, and difficult to break. Please, sit down again and be rational."

"No!" Tate shouted. "No more sitting. Let's go. I've work to do."

I tightened my grip on the knife. My hands were slick with sweat, and I worried that I wouldn't be able to keep hold of it if I had to stab one of them. "This meeting is over, Mr. Tate. I'll put my faith in Mr. Langley finding a cure in time."

He spluttered a laugh, sending spittle flying onto the floor much like the sparks. Then he realized I was serious and he sobered. "Miss Smith…what choice is there?" Panic made his voice high. "I told you Langley is useless. *I'm* offering you the potential to be cured!"

"I need more than potentials, Mr. Tate. I need certainties. I don't see any point in shortening my life further based on hope." I backed up to the door, away from both men. "It seems that hope has made me do too many foolish things already." Foolish to trust Myer, foolish to meet Tate, foolish not to tell Jack where I was going.

"Stop her," Tate ordered Myer.

"No," Myer said. "I won't hold her against her will."

"I'm doing this for you too!" Tate's face turned pink, but I didn't think it was rage that fueled him. His fingers weren't red, only his face. He was scared and desperate.

Myer turned on him. "We don't want anyone to lose their life over this. She must come with you willingly, or not at all. I, or any other member of the Society, will not stand by and let you destroy her. I'm sorry."

"You promised!"

"I promised to *bring* her, not that she'd comply."

How could he have promised such a thing when I wasn't even certain that I would come myself until yesterday? There was no time to consider it. I felt behind me for the door handle and turned it.

"Hypnotize her!" Tate cried. "*Make* her stay!"

Myer shook his head.

Tate looked as if he wanted to claw Myer's eyes out. While he was preoccupied with his building rage, I opened the door and ran out to the landing. I picked up my skirts and raced down the stairs to the relative safety of the taproom. The five men looked up from their ales and the proprietor set down the glass he'd been drying.

"Everything all right, miss?" he asked.

"Yes, thank you. Is there somebody who can drive me back to Frakingham?"

The proprietor's gaze shifted to the stairs behind me. I turned to see Myer descending them. I quickly looked away.

"It's all right, Miss Smith," he said softly when he was one step above me. "I won't hypnotize you or harm you."

"Where's Tate?"

"Sitting calmly, waiting for me to bring him out of his trance. He was too upset to have the good sense to look away in time. Unlike you."

"Stay away from me, Mr. Myer," I hissed.

"Miss Smith." He smiled gently, as if indulging a child. "I could easily hypnotize everyone in this room and abduct you. But I won't. As I said upstairs, we at the Society are keen to learn more about all sorts of supernatural phenomena, including Mr. Tate's compound, but not to the point of harming anyone. You're quite safe with me."

"Nevertheless, we'll part company here."

He took my hand and bowed over it. "As you wish. I'll give you fifteen minutes to leave safely, then I'll set Tate free of the trance. Be sure to be long gone by then. I can't control him forever."

He climbed back up the stairs, and I left the Red Lion with one of the men who offered to drive me to Frakingham in his rickety old cart. Unlike the farmer who'd driven me in, this one wanted to chat. I politely told him I had a headache and would he please mind urging his horse to go as fast as possible. He complied with a shrug, and we drove the rest of the way in blessed silence.

***

I'd hoped that Jack would still be out and that Sylvia would think me still napping. Neither was the case.

Jack met me half way down the drive, having either heard the cart's approach or seen it from one of the upper windows. His face was a riot of emotions, each one as raw as the next. He didn't try to hide them. Perhaps he couldn't.

Relief came first when he spotted me beside the driver. He ran toward us. His speed scared the horse. It shied and almost took us completely off the drive into the grass. The driver pulled on the reins and Jack grabbed the bridle, steadying the creature. It stopped, but the ears twitched frantically and the muscles in its shoulder quivered. Jack pressed his forehead to the glossy neck and murmured something in its ear. When the horse had calmed, and Jack had too, he let go. I hopped off the cart, landing just in front of him.

He kept his hands behind his back. The stance squared his broad shoulders even more, and somehow made him appear taller. He towered over me, but wasn't intimidating. He was shaking, just as the horse had been. I wanted to press my forehead to *his* neck and whisper calming words in his ear. It would have to remain a wish only.

"Thank you," I said to the driver and watched as he turned the cart around and drove off. I was acutely aware that Jack hadn't spoken. His silence was like a mountain range between us, formidable and near impossible to scale.

I tried anyway. "Jack…" I wasn't sure what to say so I chose the safest course. "When did you notice I was gone?"

"An hour ago."

"Oh. That long."

His eyes flared, their green orbs bright despite the dull day. "It was the longest hour of my life." He closed his eyes and sucked in air. The force of his breathing rocked him back on his heels. "Did Tate take you? Or…"

"I left of my own accord to meet with him."

He opened his eyes. Their color was like nothing I'd ever seen before, a blend of gray and green so dark as to be almost black. "You left. To meet with Tate." He spoke as if his jaw was wired shut. He may have been relieved before, but now he was furious. With me.

I swallowed. Nodded. I was saved from explaining myself by the arrival of both Samuel and Sylvia. They ran along the drive, calling my name. Sylvia's face was red and swollen from crying, and she was still crying as she folded me into a hug.

"Oh, Hannah. We've been frantic." She sobbed into my hair. I rubbed her back and murmured all the things I'd wanted to say to Jack.

"What happened?" Samuel asked, his hand on my shoulder. "Tate?"

I drew away from Sylvia and handed her a handkerchief from my reticule. "I went to meet Myer and Tate in Harborough."

Sylvia gasped and dropped the handkerchief.

"What?" Samuel roared. "Hannah, are you mad?"

"That's one explanation for it."

"Don't joke," he snapped. "Bloody hell. I can't believe you let us go through *that*..." He trailed off with a cautious glance in Jack's direction.

Jack stood there like a marble statue. Only the ends of his hair moved as the breeze whispered through it. His hands were still behind his back and his eyelids half-shuttered.

"We've been searching all over the house and estate for you," Sylvia said. "Jack was...*we* were in a panic. Even Uncle and Bollard took up the search, all of the servants too. We've been terrified. Absolutely terrified. And you went on *purpose*!"

"I'm sorry," I whispered. My heart felt like it was trying to squeeze through my ribs and get away. I wanted to rip it out.

"Why, Hannah?" Sylvia asked, her voice small. "Why didn't you tell us? Why did you go? Why...?"

Nothing I could say would make them any less angry with me, or help them to understand. How could they, when they all believed Langley could cure me? I'd thought perhaps Jack might, but he was a pillar of simmering fury. I'd thought he could never be angry with me. It would seem I'd been wrong.

"I had to," was all I said, offering a pathetic shrug.

He spun on his heel and stalked off, not in the direction of the house, but toward the lake. I went after him, but his long, determined strides were fast, and I was exhausted from the journey. Nevertheless, I picked up my skirts and ran as best as I could.

My chest hurt before I'd gone more than a few yards and my legs felt like logs, heavy and cumbersome. I wasn't really running at all, more dragging my body across the grass.

I stumbled over something—or perhaps it was only my own foot—and fell to the ground in an unladylike heap with my skirts up around my knees. Mud caked my dress, shoes, hands and even my hair. It had fallen out of its arrangement and tumbled around my face in a damp tangle, my hat nowhere to be seen.

I was a mess. A pathetic, horrible, cruel mess who should have kept her friends abreast of her plans. I wanted to sink into the earth and bury myself there until the wave of hopelessness had washed over me and all was forgiven.

But that wasn't going to happen. I'd done something unforgiveable.

I cried instead. I didn't want to. I didn't want to make a scene or have Jack hate me either, but I didn't have the power to make any of those things stop. All I wanted was to wrap my arms around him and tell him I loved him, that I did what I did because I wanted to be with him forever. But I couldn't. I sat there and sobbed, my tears dripping onto the already sodden ground.

I heard footsteps come up behind me—Samuel and Sylvia—then retreat as another approached. Jack. He'd come back.

I didn't want to look up at him, didn't want him to see my face.

He sat beside me despite the mud and scrunched a piece of my skirt in his fist, as if anchoring himself. He swept my hair off my shoulder, careful not to touch me. "Hannah." My name was a mere sigh from his lips. "Shhh, my sweet. Don't cry."

"I don't want you to be angry with me."

"Then I won't be." He wound a lock of my hair around his finger and gently tugged, urging me to look up at him.

I wiped my face with my skirt and blinked away the blurriness. Pain pulled at his mouth and drew deep lines across his forehead. It brought shadows to his eyes and made the muscles in his jaw tense. He swallowed. "I thought you knew that I'd do anything for you, Hannah. I would have taken you if it's what you wanted."

I swiped my cheeks as more tears spilled. I just couldn't seem to control the blasted things. "He wouldn't have seen me with you present."

"I would have found a way."

Perhaps, but I wasn't up to arguing the point, and I suspected he wasn't either. He looked down at my skirt where his hand grasped the silk near my thigh. He slowly uncurled his fingers and released it.

"I don't want to die, Jack," I whispered.

His head jerked up. "You're not going to die. You're *not*."

It was easier to stay silent. My tears had drained me, and I felt hotter than ever. I was no longer confident that either Tate or Langley would discover a cure, but I couldn't shatter his conviction. It would be too cruel.

"I won't let you," he murmured, lowering his head so that I couldn't see his face. "If you go... I can't..." It would seem that conviction was a mask, and a broken one at that.

It was hell not being able to touch him. I didn't want much, just to cup his cheek would have been sufficient.

"Come with me," I said, getting up. I didn't turn around to see if he followed. I slipped off my shoes at the edge of the lake and walked into the shallows.

The icy water bit into my skin, like the needle on Langley's syringe, but infinitely colder and more soothing. I sighed and gathered up my skirts then sat down on the stony bottom so that only my head was above the surface. Jack stood beside me, the water lapping at his knees. I reached up and took his hand. Heat flared, but there were no sparks. He sat and the heat dimmed a little, although it didn't fade altogether.

I was finally able to hold his face in my hands. I dared not kiss him. Not after the last time when our kiss had sparked something so intense it had almost killed us.

He turned his head slightly and pressed his lips to my wrist. I sighed and almost lost my nerve for what I needed to say. Almost.

"Jack, listen to me." I withdrew my hands, but he grabbed one and closed it tightly in both of his. "Jack, you *will* go on after I'm gone."

He jerked his head as if I'd slapped him. "Hannah, I don't want to discuss it."

"We're going to. We have to." I pulled my hand free and held it up when he began to protest. "I know everything is topsy turvy right now."

"That's putting it mildly."

"But you're twenty-two, Jack. Too young to give up on a happy future."

"If you're not here—"

"Don't. People move on from loss. They do, given time and good company."

"Good company!" he barked. "You think I'll stop mourning you if I find myself another girl who is 'good company'? Christ, Hannah, that's absurd. If you think what I feel for you is replaceable, you're wrong. It's not." He clutched his wet shirt at the water line, near his heart. "This feeling won't go away after you die. *If* you die," he corrected. "It's not temporary or breakable, it just is."

My hands began to shake, so I sat on them. I had to tell him how I felt. Otherwise, he might never be able to move on. And he must. I loved him too much to have him suffer endlessly, thinking he owed me something, or feeling guilty because he'd thought he would love me forever.

"Don't speak so hastily. Your thoughts on the matter may change. I've seen how you are with Charity, for instance, and—"

"Charity! Is that what this is about?" He threw his hands up, splashing water in two perfect arcs that plopped back into the lake.

"I saw you together at the ball. There are feelings between you. Don't deny it," I said when he opened his mouth. He shut it again and gave me an arched, impatient look. "She'll be good for you. She's lively and clever, and I can see that she cares for you just as much as you care for her. Don't push her away because of any loyalty you feel to me. Don't reject happiness, Jack."

"Are you quite finished?" His face was only inches from mine. I could feel his breath on my lips and see the different shades of green flecks in his eyes. "You are an infuriating woman, Hannah Smith. First of all, you're not going to die. Second of all, I don't love Charity, and she doesn't love me. I've told you that, but in your stubbornness, you seem to have forgotten."

"I haven't," I snapped. "But you do care for her and she for you. That friendship may bloom into something more again, as long as you allow it. That's what I'm trying to tell you. You must let it. If the feelings are there, let her into your heart. Don't lock her out. It won't be disloyal to me or anything like that."

"This is absurd. I'm not discussing this with you, because my last point is the same as my first: *you're not going to die.*"

If he could cure me out of sheer force of will, I had no doubt I would have been cured at that moment. His conviction was absolute. His determination palpable. I didn't bother to counter him. It seemed too unfair to take away his hope.

"I saw you two in conversation at the ball," I said. "It was very…intimate."

His lips twitched into a sudden, unexpected smile. "You're jealous."

"I am not."

The smile faded and he sighed. "I'll admit that I'm worried about her. Her life hasn't been easy, and she's troubled. I want to help her, but..." He shrugged and looked away.

"But what?"

"But she doesn't want my help. She doesn't quite trust me."

"Because you burned her."

He seemed surprised that I knew.

"I guessed," I said. "I saw the burn marks on the backs of her hands. What happened?"

"Charity was—is—popular with men. Sometimes she attracts the wrong sort of man. When we were younger I tried to extricate her from an encounter with one so-called gentleman after he beat her, but things didn't go as planned. I used my fire."

I sucked in air between my teeth. "Did he die?"

He inclined his head in a nod, and shadows passed across his eyes. "Her hands were burned in the process. She's never quite gotten over it. We were responsible for a man's death. He was evil, but still... She witnessed a man burn to death that day."

"So did you," I whispered.

"She blamed herself, and me too, although she never said so. She became a little afraid of me afterward. It wasn't immediately obvious, and still isn't, but it's there. It's the foundation of the wall she's built around herself."

"Is that why you don't want to use your fire on anyone who could suffer from it?"

He swallowed hard. "I still remember his screams, the smell of his flesh. They're not things that can be easily forgotten. I won't do that to another human being again unless I have to."

"Did the police ever find out?"

He shook his head. "The building also caught alight. We left his body there and escaped. It was reported that he died in the blaze. Nobody knew how it started."

"Jack." I touched his cheek again, but there was nothing I could do or say to banish the haunted look in his eyes.

"That incident bound Charity and me together forever, but it also drove a wedge between us. Our friendship hasn't been the same since. I tried talking to her about it at the ball for the hundredth time, but she wouldn't discuss it." He took my hand and linked his fingers in mine. "So don't try to push Charity and me together, Hannah. It won't work. I don't love her the way I love you. I never have."

My throat swelled. I couldn't swallow or speak, only nod. He loved me. I knew it, yet that was the first time he'd actually said it.

He closed his eyes and drew in a deep breath, then sank back into the lake. He disappeared underwater for a few moments. I took that time to compose myself and wipe away the fresh tears before he saw them. It would seem there was nothing I could do to assure he had a happy, full future. Except live.

When he sat up again, my voice was strong enough to use. "If she didn't want to discuss it at the ball, why did she write to you beforehand?"

He frowned. "That letter was about one of the boys in her care at the school. She was worried about his behavior and asked me for advice. That's all."

It was my turn to frown. "But you were so distracted after reading it. Angry even. Everybody noticed."

His face darkened. "That had nothing to do with the contents of Charity's letter. Indeed, it was another letter that troubled me. One I found in August's room."

"From when you sneaked in!" I remembered now. It was the night before Charity's letter arrived. I'd linked his distraction and later anger to her missive, not to what he may have discovered. "Who was it from? What did it say? And why didn't you tell me you found something important?"

"I didn't want to give you any more burdens than you already have to bear."

"Oh, Jack." I took his hands in mine and kissed the knuckles. "Stop being a hero and just tell me."

He grinned. "Yes, ma'am." The grin faded. "The letter was from Lord Wade, addressed to August. I found it in the safe he brought from his old rooms."

"You broke into it!"

"I have the combination. August gave it to me when I took over the running of the estate. It contains financial deeds and other documents, but he's always been present when I've opened it, and I'd never inspected everything inside. I found the letter from Wade at the back. It mentioned arrangements for the delivery of a baby. At first I thought it was discussing you, but soon realized it wasn't. The baby was being delivered *to* August and *from* Wade, not the other way round. It was also dated three years earlier."

"You," I murmured. "You were the baby."

"Yes, although I was not named. The baby was a boy and was able to start fires. Evidence enough."

"Why did Lord Wade have you in the first place?"

"It didn't say, but I think...I think I'm his son."

My stomach plunged to my toes. I stared at him, trying to see the resemblance. They were of a similar height, and Wade was powerfully built like Jack, but that's where the likeness ended. "Lady Wade's too?"

He shrugged. "I don't know for certain, but I doubt it. Do you remember when he told us he had a child by a mistress?"

"Yes. He said it died."

"It may have been a lie to cover his tracks."

"Do you think he knew who you were when he came here?" That would have been heartless indeed if Wade had known he was in the presence of his son and not acknowledged it.

"No. My guess is August told him he gave me away to the Cutlers as a baby and never mentioned that he'd taken me in again years later. I haven't spoken to him about it."

"It might be time to do just that."

"I tried to ask Wade when he was here that day with Violet, but he refused to give me any answers. In fact, I think he was too shocked when he saw the fire on my fingers."

"You showed him?"

"It seemed like the best way to prove that I was that baby in the letter. He questioned me about my age, my name, and how I came to be living with August. I told him and asked him about my mother. He wouldn't answer."

"Not at all?"

"He said she's gone and that's all there is to it."

"But she's your mother! You deserve to know."

"I'll speak to him about it again another time after all this—" He broke off, his voice cracking. Did he mean to say when all this was over? When I was gone?

I stretched out alongside Jack him the water. He placed his hands under my back and I floated on the surface like a reed, staring up at the gloomy sky. Lord Wade was Jack's father. It connected us in a strange way.

"You're an earl's son."

He smiled. "An illegitimate one. That's worthless."

I sat up again. The water streamed from my hair down my back. "You're not worthless, Jack. Wade is. He should have answered your questions about your mother."

He lifted one shoulder. "People of Lord Wade's ilk are a law unto themselves. They answer to nobody. If they don't want to do something, then very few people can force them. I learned that as a boy on the street."

"And I learned it in his attic."

He gathered my hair and squeezed the water out of it then set about untangling the knots. He kissed my earlobe and whispered, "Do you think if we stay here all day, anyone will notice?"

I laughed. "I would think so. Come on, let's go inside and speak to Langley. We can ask him about your mother."

"He won't tell us. He's refused all along."

"He's refused to tell you who your father was, but now you know, I don't see the point of keeping secrets. Come on, Jack, we can only try." I stood and tugged on his hand until he too rose.

"We shouldn't disturb him."

"Nonsense. He'll want to grill me over my disappearance anyway. We can cut him off before he gets started and ask him our questions instead."

He laughed. "You, Hannah Smith, are a force of nature."

"I blame my hair. It makes me do wild things."

I went to walk back to the bank, but he grabbed my hand and swung me round to face him. My body slammed into his, and his lips came crashing down on mine. The kiss was fierce and filled with longing, but he ended it before the heat rose too much. He let me go and I cooled off, but my blood still throbbed like thick honey through my veins.

Feeling slightly dizzy, I led the way to the bank.

"You haven't told me what happened with Tate," he said, picking up his shoes.

We walked back to the house and I told him how Myer had remained while I spoke with Tate, and how I ultimately decided to put my trust in Langley finding a cure. I didn't tell Jack that Tate claimed Langley wasn't good enough to do it alone. It would only give him doubts when he needed to have faith.

"Did you ask him why he won't work with August now?"

I chewed my lip then decided I should just tell him. "They were lovers and had a falling out, possibly over Bollard." It all came out in a rush. I knew if I hesitated, I might not say it at all.

He stopped. We were almost at the front steps leading up to the house. Samuel and Sylvia must have gone inside to leave Jack and me in peace. I wondered if Langley had seen us in the lake together from his rooms, and if he was angry with Samuel for not trying to keep us apart.

All those things went through my mind while Jack simply stared at me. "Well," he finally said. "I had wondered, ever since we found out about Tate from his housekeeper."

"You did?"

He nodded. "I began to think how it seemed odd that August had never shown an interest in marrying, and how his friendship with Bollard was different to any other I've witnessed between master and servant, or even between two friends." He looked up at the solid arched door and the carved stone lintel above it. "There's a great deal I don't know about August."

That was quite the understatement.

CHAPTER 13

If August Langley had my affliction, his entire room would have caught fire by the time Jack and I reached it. His anger slammed into me as we entered, forcing me to stop in the doorway.

Jack charged in. He angled himself between a seething Langley and me. "Don't," he said, his voice a low warning.

Langley wheeled himself forward, and Jack had to quickly step aside to get out of the way. Bollard, standing near a table with teapot and cups on it, crossed his arms and glared at me. It would seem he was just as furious.

Langley stopped at my feet and bared his teeth. "How *dare* you put us through that! Bollard and I have been out of our minds with worry!"

I was prepared for his anger, but not his concern. He'd been worried about me? Bollard too? I was speechless. Although it wasn't his intention, it made me feel like part of the family, equal to Sylvia and Jack.

"I'm sorry," I said, finding my voice. My apology sounded pathetic, but it was all I had to offer. "I...wasn't thinking clearly."

Langley merely grunted, but all the anger seemed to leave Bollard entirely. He poured tea from the pot into a cup and handed it to me, but didn't immediately let go. His fingers brushed mine, and he gave me a sympathetic smile. Then he did the most extraordinary thing. He kissed my forehead. It was just a peck, the sort of kiss a father would give his daughter, but it brought fresh tears to my eyes.

"Thank you," I whispered.

He stepped back, checking over his shoulder. Langley had turned away and wheeled himself to his desk. Whether he witnessed the kiss or not, I couldn't say.

Jack stood in the middle of the room, his lips parted in surprise, his gaze following Bollard as he joined his master. The conversation appeared to be over as far as they were concerned.

"Sylvia told you where I've been?" I asked.

"Yes," Langley shot back.

"Don't you want to know how the meeting went?"

"I assume he didn't kidnap you since you're here."

"Your scientific powers of observation are impressive."

Bollard shook his head in warning, and I bit my lip. He was right. Now wasn't the time for quips.

"Tate couldn't assure me that I wouldn't be harmed during his tests, so I declined to help him."

"I'm not sure why you needed to visit him to determine that," Langley said. "I've been telling you all along."

I came up behind his chair, but he still didn't turn around. He did put down his dropper, however, and appeared to be listening. Jack stood at my back. His reassuring presence gave me the strength to continue. "If you and Tate could combine your knowledge, Mr. Langley, just this once, perhaps the cure is closer than either of you realize."

"Did he say he would work with me?" Langley asked.

I thought about lying, but it was pointless. He would find out. "He refused to consider it. Something about pride and…jealousy."

Bollard flinched, and his gaze slid to his employer. His lover? Langley went very still. He said nothing, just stared straight ahead at the wall.

I forged on. I'd come this far and couldn't back away now. There was too much at stake. "Perhaps if you approached Tate, he would be more amenable. I think he doesn't want to be the one to eat humble pie."

"There's a little more to it than that," Langley said. "What else did he say?"

"That the Society wanted the compound and an antidote. That's why Myer has shown an interest. He has been aware of Tate all along."

"You trust him?"

I hesitated. "No, but I think I have to if I want to live."

Jack shifted his weight behind me. I couldn't see him, but I felt his breath on the back of my neck now that my hair was once more bundled up. It was ragged and unsteady, as if he was struggling to hold himself together.

"Is that all?" Langley said. "You may leave."

"But—"

Bollard put up a hand. He half shook his head, more as a warning than an order. I nodded and closed my mouth. Of everyone in that room, the servant knew best how to handle Langley.

Jack wasn't so concerned with upsetting anyone. "It's not all," he said. "You owe me an explanation, August. I know who my father is."

Langley turned his face into profile. Bollard suddenly sat down on the edge of the desk and blinked at Jack.

"This isn't a good time," Langley said.

"It won't take long. All you need to do is tell me who Wade's mistress was. The one who bore his child twenty-two years ago."

Langley sighed heavily, but didn't speak.

"It's unraveling, August. The time has long past to give up some of your secrets."

"They're not *my* secrets."

"Then why keep them at all?" I asked. "You don't seem to particularly like Lord Wade."

"I don't. Not anymore."

"Then why were you so determined to keep Jack in the dark about his parents? Who are you protecting?"

"No one." He turned his wheelchair around and indicated we should both sit. I didn't realize how tired I was until I flopped into the seat by the window. The coolness from the lake had worn off after changing into dry clothes, and I felt feverish again.

"You lied," Jack said. He sounded calm, as if he was resigned to hearing the truth, no matter how ugly it might be. "You told me it was my father's wish to keep the truth from me."

"Lord Wade did ask me not to tell you, but I...I admit that I was happy to keep that news from you anyway."

"Why?"

Bollard cleared his throat. Was he urging Langley? Reassuring him?

"Because he would not have been a good father to you," Langley said.

Jack seemed to accept it, but I wasn't so sure. Why did he care what sort of father Wade would make? I had the feeling Langley was holding something back. Bollard also frowned at the explanation.

"Who was my mother?" Jack asked. "*What* was she?"

"Her name was Hannah Smith, the woman Wade later named you after," Langley said to me. "I don't know where she came from. One day she simply appeared on the Windamere estate, homeless, penniless and confused. Wade took her in and put her into household service. I know very little of her background. Perhaps he knows more. I do remember she was a beauty. Black hair, green eyes and vivacious. She won everybody over, including me. The first instance I can recall of her is when she served me tea one afternoon. She was charming, if a little inept. She spilled the tea. Wade took it upon himself to guide her, even though it went against protocol. He seemed genuinely fond of her. They must have been lovers by then, although it's difficult to determine how deep their feelings ran."

"Could she start fires?" Jack asked. "Was she fast? A good swimmer?"

"You would have to ask Wade those things, but I think it's safe to say that you've gotten your talents from her. They're certainly not from Wade."

"What happened to her?" I asked.

"She died giving birth to Jack."

Jack pressed back into his chair as if someone had pushed him in the chest. It was the only sign he gave of disappointment at the news.

"Wade brought you to us soon afterward," he said to Jack. His voice sounded thick and heavy. He cleared his throat. "He didn't want you. He didn't want a child who set things alight. So Reuben told Wade we would take you in. I was against it at first. What did we know about babies? I soon learned that he wanted you for his experiments, and I admit that I didn't see the immediate harm. His experiments didn't seem to work, and you weren't injured. It wasn't until later, when you disappeared..." He paused. Swallowed. Bollard put his hand on Langley's shoulder, urging him to go on. "In hindsight, it was perhaps for the best that you went to a normal family. You know what happened after that."

We did indeed. Unbeknown to Langley, his housekeeper had taken Jack to an orphanage and from there he'd been adopted by a childless couple. They died when he was still very young, and he ended up on the streets of London, fighting for survival. If it hadn't been for his fire and quickness, he might have starved or frozen to death. Years later, when Langley heard reports of a child with fire in him, he went to investigate. He told Jack he was his uncle and offered him a home.

Why he'd taken Jack in again was still a mystery, although I was beginning to think that he felt some responsibility as a guardian. It made him seem more human, if only a little.

"You should know that Wade was wracked with guilt," Langley went on. "He never wanted you back, mind, but he did ask after you."

Jack gave a harsh laugh. "How noble of him."

I placed my hand on the arm of his chair as a small means of comfort. Jack's frown lessened, but didn't vanish.

"Wade couldn't take you back anyway," Langley went on. "He'd put out rumors that you'd died, to appease the servants who knew he'd fathered Hannah Smith's child. He was also trying to win the future Lady Wade's hand in marriage at that time. Any scandal would have destroyed his chances."

"How very inconvenient it would have been to have me around."

Langley studied his folded hands. He rubbed one ink-stained thumbnail with the pad of the other thumb. "You…wish you'd grown up knowing he was your father?"

Jack heaved a deep sigh and pressed his fingers into his eye sockets. "No. I'd rather be here than Windamere, but it would have been nice not to have lived in London all those years."

Langley's thumb stopped rubbing. His nostrils flared. He stared at Jack, but Jack wasn't looking at him. He was looking at me.

"Strange to think we may have grown up in the same house if things had turned out a little differently."

"I wouldn't have given him Hannah if he hadn't given me you," Langley said. "He only visited me then because he wanted to know how you fared. Three years too late," he sneered. "Not exactly the actions of a loving father."

"Why *did* Wade take me when he'd already given up his own son?" I asked.

"I had to get you away from Tate, and Wade offered to provide for you. His wife had not given him a child, and I suppose he felt guilt or loss after giving up Jack. I don't know. You would have to ask him. I do know that I regret it, Hannah. If I'd known you would end up a prisoner, I would have fetched you. I promise you that."

Bollard echoed the sentiment with a firm nod.

"Just as you've promised to do everything in your power to cure me?"

He gave me a curious look. "I *am* doing everything in my power."

"It's within your power to approach Tate and offer to work with him."

Langley closed his eyes, but Bollard gently nudged him and he opened them again. The mute signed with his hands. Langley shook his head. Bollard repeated the motion, but this time the downward strokes were violent chopping moves. His face grew darker, his thick brows plunged together.

Jack leaned forward, and I wondered if he'd understood any of it. If I survived my illness, I was going to ask Bollard to teach me to speak with my hands.

"All right!" Langley roared.

Bollard's hands became silent. He crossed his arms and glared at Langley. The reversal of their relationship stunned me. A stranger would not have known who was master and who the servant. I wondered if they were this candid with one another in private, or if this was something new.

"Hannah, do you know where Reuben is now?" Langley snapped.

"I, er, no. He wouldn't divulge his place of residence, but I think it's some way out of the village. Only Myer seems to know."

"Send word to Myer that I'll meet with Reuben in the morning." He lifted a finger, dismissing us.

I hurried out before he could change his mind. Jack followed. We both leaned back against the wall of the corridor. My knees felt too weak to walk, my head dizzy from Langley's whip-fast change of heart.

"Bollard is a miracle worker," Jack said.

"Do you know what he said to Langley?"

"Not all of it. I can read only some of his hand signals. He told August that you were right. He and Tate need to work together, and Tate's unlikely to make the approach."

He smirked. "I couldn't understand the rest, but I suspect there were some strong and not entirely proper words used."

"That's quite brave of Bollard."

"Perhaps. Or perhaps we're seeing a different aspect of their relationship now that the truth is out."

We headed down to the parlor together to tell the others about Langley's about-face and to write a note to Myer. I was halfway along the corridor when I realized Langley hadn't mentioned anything about Jack and I being in the lake together. Surely he'd seen us from his window. So why didn't he make good on his threat to stop searching for a cure? I hadn't misheard him when he issued that warning to Samuel, I was sure of it. Perhaps he'd had a change of heart in that regard too. Perhaps he'd come to realize how cruel such a thing would be to us.

Or perhaps he'd decided that I wasn't going to live anyway, and Jack would soon be free to find a more suitable paramour.

***

Jack rode to Harborough to deliver the note to Myer personally. He hadn't returned two hours later. The late afternoon shadows of the oak trees stretched across the grass. A veil of mist covered the lake's surface. Not a breath of wind disturbed it.

"Where is he?" I asked for the hundredth time. I sat by the parlor window where I had a good view of the drive and surrounds.

"Myer must have left the village," Samuel said. "Jack's probably chasing him all the way to London."

Of course it must be true, yet an uneasy feeling settled in my chest and wouldn't shake free, no matter how much I tried to remain positive.

Sylvia, standing beside me, suddenly moved away. "Samuel, you must ride into the village and see if Myer has left or not. Then we'll know for certain if Jack is all right."

"It's almost dark!" he said.

"Then take the carriage."

He set his newspaper on the table. He hadn't opened it, despite holding it for the last twenty minutes. "I'll be as fast as I can."

He left and Tommy entered the parlor. The footman hovered at the doorway, his hands behind his back.

"Is everything all right?" Sylvia asked him.

"Mr. Gladstone's orders are for me to watch over you, ma'am."

"Oh," she said, her gaze slipping to me. "Of course."

It would seem the threat of kidnap was still on everybody's minds. I wasn't so sure of the need for concern now that Langley had agreed to work with Tate, but I didn't comment. Tommy had been given a job to do, and knowing him, he wouldn't be swayed from it.

I watched as the pale winter sun kissed the horizon like a shy mistress. It must have enjoyed the kiss because it sank quickly and had disappeared altogether by the time Samuel drove off in the carriage. The light from the two lamps swung in arcs, cutting through the dusky evening.

There was nothing to do now except wait.

"Shall we play charades?" Sylvia said.

"I'd prefer to just—"

Somebody screamed. It sounded like it came from the depths of the house, perhaps the service area.

Tommy ran out of the room, and I went to follow.

"Tommy!" Sylvia cried and the footman returned. His fists opened and closed, a picture of barely controlled restraint. "Stay here. Hannah must be protected."

Poor Tommy looked as if he would explode from his conflicting need to both follow orders and investigate. I decided to put him out of his misery.

"We'll all go."

"No! Tommy! Hannah, stay here!"

There was no time to explain to Sylvia that I couldn't let one of the maids suffer because of me. Because I knew, without a doubt, that Tate was at the root of those screams, and Tate wanted me.

I hurried through the maze of corridors and archways, trying to keep up with Tommy. I did a fair job, despite my heavy limbs, only to catch up to him at the entrance to the kitchen where he stopped. He held up his hands, either stopping me or protecting me, I didn't know which.

Beyond him, I saw Tate holding a pistol to Maud's head. His empty sleeve hung loose at his side. If she'd had her wits about her, she could have ducked and slipped away, but she was too hysterical to think clearly or be fast enough. To be fair, I didn't think I could manage it either.

The cook and Mrs. Moore the housekeeper stood to Tommy's right, out of the way but within Tate's sights. They looked as terrified as the poor maid.

"I'm here," I said, stepping closer.

"Shut it, miss," Tommy hissed, in his London accent. "Get back. Let me handle this."

"No. He's here for me, and I will not allow anyone to be harmed on my account." I touched his shoulder. The ridged muscle tensed. "Please, Tommy. Let me go."

"Jack'll murder me."

"Come, Miss Smith." Tate beckoned me with a jerk of his head. "Come with me, and this woman won't be harmed." His focus shifted to Tommy, and his mouth split into a warped grin. "You think I care about anyone else in this room? It's Miss Smith I want, but if I have to kill to get her, I will."

Maud whimpered, and I was afraid she would faint. "It's all right," I said to her. "I won't let him hurt you."

Tommy swore softly under his breath. I felt sorry for him. He was in a terrible position, his choice an unbearable one.

I ducked under his arm. He could have stopped me, but didn't. He muttered another curse and thumped the doorframe with the flat of his hand.

I calmly approached Tate, my hands up in surrender. "This is unnecessary. Mr. Langley has agreed to work with you."

"I already told you I want nothing to do with him." Tate's fingers flexed around the pistol's handle.

The maid shook and tears streamed down her face. She looked as if she'd collapse at any moment. I had to get her away from him.

"Please, Mr. Tate, don't let past hurts stop you from taking this opportunity. You need Langley—"

"I bloody well do not! I have the drug. It's ready, and I know it works, Miss Smith. All I need is to test it on you, and we'll both be cured. Come with me."

His words were like a siren song, calling to the heat within me, luring me closer. I wanted to believe him. Wanted to trust him. My head knew that it was madness to let him inject his drug into me, but my heart ached with the need to be cool, to be cured. To live.

Footsteps pounded on the flagstones in the corridor. Whether they belonged to Sylvia or Bollard, Jack or Samuel, I couldn't tell.

Tate heard them too. Sweat dripped from his temples, down beside his ears. His face glowed with it, and I suspected mine did too. He cocked the gun.

"Come here, Miss Smith. Now!"

The sobbing maid pleaded wordlessly with me. I had no choice. I could reason with him once we were away, and he'd calmed down. I stepped closer and allowed him to switch the gun from Maud's temple to mine.

He pushed the cool barrel hard against my hot forehead. "Walk quickly to the door."

I did as ordered, without glancing back. I didn't want to see Tommy torturing himself over his decision to let me go with Tate or not.

Sylvia's startled cry announced her arrival. "Hannah! Hannah! Somebody, stop him!"

As I left with Tate, her sobs were the last thing I heard. They rang in my ears as I sat on the saddle in front of Tate, and it seemed as if they followed us along the drive and out of the Frakingham gate.

CHAPTER 14

I had thought myself relatively unscathed from my time as a prisoner in Lord Wade's attic. I'd never felt like the walls were closing in on me, or that the air was dwindling. I'd gotten through those fifteen years with my mind intact and my confidence unshaken.

Until now.

My sanity was all a lie, an illusion. The memory of those days came crashing back to me as I sat tied to a chair in a hut deep in the woods to the north of Harborough. I remembered all those times I'd stared out of the Windamere attic window, wishing I could fly away into the blue sky. I remembered too the feeling of being smothered in wool. Everywhere, wool.

The weight of those memories now held down my limbs and pressed against my chest, suffocating. I would rather be in that attic than here.

I'd allowed Tate to tie me to the chair, my hands behind my back, even though I told him it wasn't necessary. I wouldn't try to escape. I couldn't. Despite having only one arm, he was too strong for me and too desperate to allow his chance of curing himself escape. Besides, I could never have run far with my leaden legs and the painful wheezing in my chest.

I sat there and tried to control the heat raging inside me. It was stronger than ever, but not the same as when I grew angry. This felt more like I was being consumed, the flames cooking my insides. I thought about Jack's soothing voice, his gentle eyes, but had to force those things from my mind too. Thinking of Jack only made me sadder, and my chest tighter.

Instead, I watched Tate work at the table that served as his workbench in the kitchen of the disused hut. We'd ridden from Frakingham to his hideout without incident, despite the darkness. The horse seemed to know the route through the dense woods well and carefully picked its way over fallen logs and between thick bushes. Tate had spoken very little on the ride, only confirming that he'd been lucky when he saw Jack and Samuel leave.

I closed my eyes and sucked in air. It cooled me a little and soothed my fractured nerves. I wiped my damp cheeks on my shoulder and tried to focus on Tate and not my captivity. I could not escape, but I had a voice and a promise from Langley.

"You could have made things much easier on yourself if you'd simply accepted that Langley would work with you," I told him.

He opened a wooden box, but I couldn't see the contents. He didn't answer. Was he ignoring me, or lost in his own world now that he was among his instruments?

"Why won't you work with him?" I pressed. "Surely two minds are better than one."

"Not when one of those minds is slow."

I clicked my tongue. With my hands tied, it was the only way to show my frustration with his and Langley's squabbling. "He's not slow and you know that, Mr. Tate. He's clever, but he's cleverer when he's working with you. That's a fact."

"He betrayed me once. More than once. He'll have no scruples doing so again."

"Don't be absurd. Whatever happened between you in the past is irrelevant."

"You're as stupid as he is." He turned around, a glass syringe in hand. It was filled with a clear liquid. "August Langley is a liar and a thief. He has no morals."

"That's not true. He cares about Jack and Sylvia, and me too. He doesn't want me to die, Mr. Tate, and I doubt he wants you to either. He's not entirely heartless. Talk to him and you'll realize it too."

He came to stand in front of me and lowered the syringe to my jaw. One small move and he could jab it into my throat. "I tried talking to him years ago. He laughed in my face."

My resolve to calm him down and make him see sense was fading fast. His hatred of Langley ran deep, perhaps too deep for me to convince him to let it go. "I know you loved him," I ventured. There could be no gain without risk, and from the raw pain in Tate's eyes, I was taking a very big risk indeed. "I know he betrayed you with Bollard. But are past hurts enough of a reason to jeopardize your life?"

"It's *your* life I risk, not mine. Listen to me, Miss Smith. August's betrayal with Bollard is only part of the problem. It's the icing on the cake, or, if you prefer, the lesion symptomatic of an underlying cancer. The far greater betrayal was when he tricked me into receiving much less than I deserved for the drug we created together. I thought we were going to split everything in half, but found out too late that the papers he made me sign had certain caveats that locked me out of the greatest portion of funds. So you see," he said with a mocking smile, "I don't trust him. He'll come in here, pretending to work with me, and then he'll take my cure and sell it to the Society. I wouldn't even trust him to inject me with it beforehand."

"He would never do that."

"You don't know him like I do, Miss Smith."

"Clearly not. But I do know him *now*. He's changed. He'll be fair with you, I promise. Just put down the syringe."

"Miss Smith." He spoke my name as if it were a weight he wanted to shove off once and for all. "I'm hot and tired. My time is close. Without a cure I have only a day or two left."

He did indeed look hotter than the last time I'd seen him in the Red Lion. He wore neither waistcoat nor tie, and his shirt was soaked with sweat. "I don't have the energy or time for Langley's games." He primed the needle. A squirt of the liquid dropped onto the floor and soaked into the boards. "Besides, it's not necessary to include him. I have the cure. He doesn't. I don't need him anymore."

"How can you be sure that's the cure if you haven't tested it?"

"Would you like to see my calculations?" He jerked his head at the table where papers were spread out and notebooks lay open. He laughed.

"You know I won't understand it."

"Then I'm sorry for you and your small brain, Miss Smith. You'll just have to trust me."

My stomach heaved. I wanted to throw up. Perhaps that would make him stop pressing the needle to my exposed arm.

I searched for the anger inside, but it was buried too deeply beneath fear and hopelessness. "Please, Mr. Tate. Please, be reasonable. He's different now, I assure you. He won't betray you again." My voice was shrill. Hysterical.

I shook my arm as best as I could, and he pulled the needle away.

It was only a teasing delay. "Hold still," he growled. "Moving will only succeed in making it hurt more."

I began to cry. Great, gasping sobs sucked even more precious air from my lungs, and I coughed so hard it felt like my insides were being brought up. It made it impossible for Tate to inject me.

He set the syringe down on the table and slapped my face with the back of his hand. My head buzzed. My cheek hurt. But I quieted. In a sense, I woke up.

I watched Tate pick up the syringe again and press it to my arm. I felt the bite of the needle as it pierced my skin, the heavy weight of anticipation as he emptied the contents into my arm.

The liquid was cold. I'd never felt anything like it. It slithered along my veins, up my arm to my shoulder, numbing. If the cold meant I was cured, then the drug had worked.

He removed the needle, and the coldness went with it.

"Well?" I prompted, searching his face for any sign of what was supposed to happen next.

"Now we wait and observe."

Wait. God, how I hated that word.

Tate pulled up the only other chair in the hut and sat, the pistol in his lap. He watched me intently, peered into my eyes. "How do you feel?" He sounded remarkably clinical for someone whose life depended on the outcome of this test. Perhaps, like me, he was resigned to fate. It was too late to tweak the drug now.

"Still hot," I said. "The drug's coldness didn't last. It's as if my heat overpowered it."

"Fuck!"

Dread punched its fist through my chest. "You...expected more?"

"It should have worked." He shot to his feet and stabbed the pistol barrel onto the open notebook. "It should have bloody *worked*."

I tried to swallow, but couldn't. My throat was too tight. Something was happening. Heat rose from the pit of my stomach up to my chest like smoke. Searing. Stifling. It stole the air from my lungs, wrapped itself around my insides like a burning rope.

"Mr. Tate." I tried to shout, but it came out a whisper. "Mr. Tate...help. I'm burning up."

He took one look at my face, and I knew from the horror in his eyes that it must be dangerously red.

"It hasn't worked, has it?"

He plopped down on the chair and buried his head in his hand. "No, Miss Smith. It hasn't worked. You'll be dead very soon. I'm sorry."

Ordinarily I would be a puddle of pitiful tears hearing that, but I concentrated on fighting the heat. I focused all my energy inwards, tried to conjure cool things in my mind, like swimming in the lake with Jack.

My efforts were useless. My fingertips were hot, perhaps even on fire. I couldn't tell, bound as they were behind me.

My blood throbbed between my ears, so loud that I didn't hear the door opening. It wasn't until Tate's head jerked up that I realized someone had entered the hut.

I heard their shouts. I recognized Jack's voice and Samuel's. Accusing. Cursing. Demanding to know what had happened. Somebody untied me, but had to jump back as I burned him. Samuel, I realized, as his face came into focus. He blew on his hands and shook them out.

"She's on fire," he said. "Too hot for me."

I caught a glimpse of Jack's face as he came to my side. There was no sign of relief at finding me, no worry either. It was as if he wore a mask, his eyes shining like two hard gems within it.

He began to untie me. My heat couldn't combust him unless there was desire between us, and there was nothing like it in him now. He was all fierce determination and calculating anger. I did not envy Tate in the least once Jack directed that wrath at him.

He never got the chance. Tate stood, the pistol in his hand. He pointed it at Jack. Cocked it.

Jack's head whipped around at the *click*. Samuel swore, as did someone else. Myer, I think. Tate pulled the trigger, but Jack dove out of the way at the last moment. The bullet bit into the floor and lodged in the boards.

Tate pointed the gun at me. My hands were still tied to the chair although Jack had got my legs free. But it was useless. I couldn't move out of the way. I was as limp as a rag doll. And hot. So damnably hot.

A fireball shot past my ear, singing my hair. It slammed into Tate's shoulder. He dropped the gun and screamed in pain. He slapped frantically at his shirt and was able to put out the flames.

Too late. His skin had blistered and burned off in patches. He stared down at himself, as if he'd never seen anything like it. I stared too, riveted by horror and shock. He should not have burned. Neither he nor I nor Jack should have been affected by flames. Yet Jack's fireball had scorched him. The smell of seared flesh was unmistakable.

Jack stood at my side, still staring at Tate. His mask had fallen away. He looked as horrified as Tate. He'd burned someone, something he'd sworn never to do again. The guilt must have returned, and the memories of that time he'd killed a man by using his fire to save Charity.

He shuddered and covered his face with his hands. I wanted to hold him, tell him it was all right, but I could do nothing. I could not even find my voice.

Samuel edged closer to the gun lying at Tate's feet.

But Tate got it first. He directed it at Samuel. "Get back!"

Samuel stayed still, hands in the air. "Jack," he said.

Jack stood there, doing nothing, not looking at Tate or anyone else. He stared down at his hands, his shoulders stooped as if he'd given up.

"Bloody hell, Jack!" Samuel cried. "Fire another one!"

Tate shifted the gun to me. "I'll put her out of her misery," he said. "She's dying anyway. It'll be kinder than—"

Jack's fireball hit him square in the chest and blasted him across the room. He slammed into the wall and crumpled to the floor. Dead. There could be no doubt. His body and clothing were alight, the fire quickly consuming him. The putrid smell of burning flesh grew stronger, clogging my throat and nose.

Jack rubbed his hands down his face. When he drew them away, it was as if the horror had been wiped off. The normal Jack had returned.

He bent to untie me. "Hannah?" he whispered. "Hannah, please...fight it."

"I'm hot, Jack. So hot."

"There's a stream nearby, we'll take you there. You must live, Hannah. For me."

"We have to get her to August," Samuel barked out.

"No time," Jack said. "Myer, fetch August here. *Now*."

Myer hurried out, and I heard the pounding of a horse's hooves.

"I dare not carry her," Jack said to Samuel. "Can you?"

"No," I rasped. "I'll burn him."

Samuel ran through a door to an adjoining room and quickly returned carrying a blanket. He wrapped it around me. The familiar smell was a comfort. Wool. I laughed at the irony.

I closed my eyes. They were too heavy to keep open, and my head felt like it was going to explode if I used up even the small amount of energy needed to do that.

"Hannah, wake up," Jack shouted. Samuel picked me up, and Jack stood close. I could feel his breath on my face. It was cooler than my skin, which was odd. So odd.

"Hannah! No. No, don't go."

I had to. I was too hot, too weak to do anything but sleep. I wanted to tell him that I wanted to be with him, tell him I loved him, but my voice had been consumed by the fire. I had nothing left. Not even tears.

"Stay with me." Jack's plea clawed at my heart, his sobs wrenched a cry from my chest.

I tried to rally for him. I tried so hard. But in the end, it was too much effort. The heat blasted through me and the darkness came.

CHAPTER 15

I awoke in a stream, fully clothed. It was dark, but I could just make out the tall shapes of trees and people standing on the bank. Somebody held my head above the swiftly flowing water and the weeds. Somebody strong but gentle. Somebody who cradled me like I was the most precious thing in the world.

Jack.

I was alive. I was quite sure of it, but I wanted to be doubly certain. I tried to sit up, but lacked the energy to do it on my own.

"Hannah?" Jack sounded wondrous. He shifted and his face appeared in front of mine. He stared at me, unblinking. "Hannah. Thank God," he muttered. "Thank God, thank God." He raised me a little and pressed his lips to my forehead. I hadn't been surrounded by weeds, I realized, but by my own hair.

Jack pressed his hand to my cheek, his lips to my mouth. He was shaking and his face was wet, either from crying or the water, or both.

I tested my limbs and found I had some strength in my arms. I wrapped them around his neck and clung to him. Relief and happiness burst out of me. I sobbed against him, unable to stop myself. He held me fiercely, rocking me, as shudders wracked us both.

Water splashed, and I heard voices. Sylvia called out my name, and somebody stroked my hair. I looked over my shoulder and was greeted with kisses on my cheek, first from Sylvia then Tommy and finally Bollard. The mute's eyes shone in the moonlight. I looked past him and saw Langley sitting on the bank, his useless legs stretched out in front of him. Behind him stood Myer. He had his back to me, facing the smoking ruin of the hut beyond. His shoulders were slumped forward, his head bowed, like a defeated man.

"It's cold in here," Samuel muttered.

I laughed then stopped. Needles of pain shot along my limbs, through my veins, piercing my skin. It was back. The fire...

No, not the fire. It felt different. It wasn't heat, but something else. Something I'd never felt before.

"Samuel?" I said, my voice rough. "What does cold feel like?"

"Well, like...it's hard to describe."

Jack drew away to look at me properly. "Why? What do you feel, Hannah?"

"Like I need to get out of this water before I turn rigid."

He grinned. "You're shivering."

"Get her out!" Sylvia cried, charging back to the bank. "Dry her before she catches her...uh, before she catches a chill."

A chill. I'd never had a chill.

Jack lifted me in his arms. I expected to feel his heat warming me now that we were out of the water, but I felt nothing like that. I continued to shiver, perhaps even more than when I was sitting in the stream. Touching Jack felt like being touched by anybody else.

Normal.

"I'm cured," I said to him.

He looked down at me. It was dark, but I could see the brightness in his eyes, the curve of his mouth as he smiled. "It would seem so."

He set me gently on the bank beside Langley, but didn't let me go. He remained at my back, propping me up, his arms wrapped around me.

August's hand gripped mine. "Welcome back, Hannah."

"Did you save me?" I asked.

He didn't answer, but turned to Tommy. "Fetch the blanket. She's freezing."

What a funny thought. I laughed until a shiver coursed through me. Tommy handed the blanket to Jack and he folded me into it.

I felt their stares on me, wondrous, happy, relieved. All the same emotions that welled inside me where not long ago only excruciating heat had been.

"We ought to go now," Sylvia said. "Hannah needs dry clothes and rest."

Myer, Tommy and Samuel remained behind to ensure the fire in the hut was completely doused. We left the three horses with them. Bollard lifted Langley into his arms, and Jack picked me up in the same manner. We were carried through the woods to where the carriage awaited us on a track nearby. The driver sat huddled inside his coat, his chin on his chest. He sat up when he heard us coming. He rubbed his eyes and picked up the reins.

"Why did Myer look so sad?" I asked Jack as he set me on the seat in the cabin.

"The cure was in that hut," he said. "The original compound Tate took from me too. He wanted them both and now he has neither."

Jack sat beside me, Sylvia opposite. She fussed with the blanket, ensuring it was closed tightly at my throat. "Keep your chest warm," she directed. She sounded like a mother hen, clucking at her chicks. I didn't scold her. It was nice to be coddled.

Bollard put Langley down beside her then closed the door. The carriage dipped as he got up beside the driver. We drove out of the woods and made our way along the road back through Harborough and onto Frakingham. The sky in the east was lighter, the clouds edged with gold. Dawn was near.

"What happened after I fainted?" I asked.

"I carried you into the stream," Jack said simply.

"Keeping you cold saved your life," Langley said.

I tilted my face to look at Jack. He sat beside me, his hands on his knees, quite still. He was wet through, but as achingly handsome as ever. More so. I kissed him lightly on the lips. Saying thank you didn't seem adequate enough. There were no words to express my gratitude and love.

He grasped my hand and pressed the knuckles to his lips. He closed his eyes and drew in a deep, shuddery breath.

"We were so worried about you," Sylvia said. Her uncle held her hand between both of his own. He did not try to separate Jack and I. Not that I could be separated from him ever again.

"When Tate took you..." Sylvia bit her lip and shook her head, unable to go on. Her eyes glistened in the weak dawn light.

"By the time I arrived in Harborough, Myer had already left," Jack said, picking up the story. "I found him on the London road and brought him back to Frakingham. It was the middle of the night, but the entire household was awake. They told me what had happened." He cleared his throat, and I suspected it had been a tense time for them, far more so than his blunt retelling indicated. "Samuel, Myer and I set out for the hut immediately. Myer knew its location, thankfully."

They must have all been exhausted traveling hard and fast to return to the house and then the hut. And the night hadn't ended then.

"You sent Myer back to fetch Langley," I said. "I remember that."

He nodded. "It felt like forever before they returned."

"What happened then? How was I cured?"

"Uncle brought his notes and things with him," Sylvia said, shooting him a proud smile. "He mixed Tate's formula and his own, and voila! You were cured."

Jack laughed. "I'm sure it was a little more complicated than that, Syl."

"Somewhat," Langley admitted. "I found the ingredients of Reuben's formula in his notes. He'd come at it from a different angle to me, but our findings weren't all that far apart. I knew almost immediately where we both went wrong. I made some adjustments to my formula based on his calculations and tested it on your blood sample."

"Obviously the results were positive," Sylvia said.

"Actually, they were inconclusive. Testing on blood samples alone wasn't enough."

He needed to test it on a real human case. Me. He didn't say so, but he didn't need to. There'd been no time to conduct full tests, and he'd injected me anyway.

Tate had been right all along in that regard. He *did* need me. Myer had also been right—Langley and Tate worked better together, not alone.

Now Tate was gone, and all his knowledge with him.

***

I ate a good breakfast as Sylvia dried and brushed my hair. Then, wrapped up in blankets, I slept the entire day and the following night. It was Christmas Eve when I awoke. I felt refreshed, and cold. For the first time since my arrival at Frakingham House, I dressed in warm winter clothes, complete with woolen jacket, waistcoat and skirt. I even wore gloves inside the house.

I had hoped to find Jack alone, so I could thank him properly for saving my life, but he was with the others in the dining room.

"Hannah!" Sylvia leapt out of her chair and drew me into a hug. "You're awake! Let me look at you." She held my hands and surveyed me from head to toe. "You look wonderful. Just wonderful. Your skin is glowing, although I'm afraid you still have freckles."

I laughed. "I think those are permanent."

"Good," Jack said quietly, joining us. "Because I adore every one of them." He kissed me gently on the forehead.

"Come and eat," Samuel said.

Everyone was there. Even Langley sat in his wheelchair, eating eggs. Bollard and Tommy stood by the sideboard. Both nodded greetings at me and smiled.

To my utter dismay, tears filled my eyes. This was my family. This odd collection of people from vastly different backgrounds meant the world to me. I loved every one of them.

"What can I get you to eat, Miss Smith?" Tommy asked.

"Nothing. You don't serve breakfast."

"Today I do." He wouldn't hear of me filling my own plate, so I told him to pile it with whatever he thought looked good. I was starving.

He set the plate down in front of me, and Bollard passed me a cup of steaming tea. I sipped, scalding my lip.

"Too hot?" Samuel said, chuckling.

I ate while they chatted and finished up their breakfast. Jack spoke little. His attention hardly wavered from me. I felt self-conscious at first, but grew used to it. Indeed, I rather liked being the focus of his attention. It was a thrill to know he cared so much for me that he couldn't take his eyes off me. To my surprise, it didn't seem to bother Langley in the least.

I finished my breakfast and accepted a refill of tea from Tommy. "Mr. Langley," I said over the rim of the cup, "did you ever stop looking for a cure?"

"Never," he said. "Not since Jack has been living with me, but it only became urgent when you came here, Hannah. With your training a failure, you were never going to be able to control the fire."

"And then when we discovered Tate was dying…" I said. "Finding a cure became more urgent still."

"Fortunately I was already some way along the path to discovering it."

"Yes. Fortunate," I echoed, setting the teacup down. I swallowed and tried to smile my thanks. Once again I was aware how inadequate words were at such a time. How did you thank someone for saving your life?

Jack's hand covered mine. It was warm and I slipped off my glove so that I could feel his skin on mine. Again, Langley made no comment about our intimacy.

"Why did you try to keep Jack and I apart?" My question may have been blunt, but he seemed prepared for it. They all did. Indeed, nobody seemed surprised, and I wondered if they'd been discussing that very thing before my arrival.

"I was worried about Jack," Langley said. "And you. You saw what happened when you were together. It was disastrous. Dangerous. You had to be kept separate for your own good, or..." He wiped the back of his finger across his upper lip. "You know what would have happened."

"So you did it to protect us." It was rather ironic. What was the point of being protected when I couldn't be with Jack? "You shouldn't have tried so hard."

Jack's fingers tightened around my own. I didn't dare look at him, or I might have burst into tears.

"Love can be fleeting," Langley said, avoiding my gaze.

"Some love. Not all. Not ours."

"That may be, but you must understand that you were my responsibility. You both were. If I had to save you from yourselves, then I would try."

I frowned, not fully understanding. Bollard shifted behind his master, beckoning my attention with his hands. He pressed them both over his heart then pointed at Jack. His lips flattened and he looked to Langley then Jack with sympathy and love and I finally understood. Langley cared for Jack as his own son. He would do anything to keep him safe. Perhaps that also explained why he'd not told Jack that Wade was his father. He was worried that Jack would reject him and wish to get to know his real parent.

I sat, stunned. Langley might be selfish, but he had the capacity to love, even if he had a terrible way of showing it. To be fair, there had been small telltale signs. He'd given Jack enormous responsibility in managing the estate and worked furiously to find a cure for me. Because he cared for me, or because I was what Jack wanted?

Bollard touched his chest again. This time he didn't point at anyone in particular, but spread out his hands, encompassing Sylvia and me, Tommy and Samuel too. Was he implying that Langley loved us all?

"That's enough, Bollard," Langley said without turning around. There was no anger in his tone, no real admonishment. "I think what my valet is trying to tell you is that it's my duty to do what's best for you, and sometimes what's best is not what you want."

Bollard rolled his eyes and tapped his chest again. I smiled. I understood completely. His master was simply too proud to admit that he loved us.

"Hannah is best for me," Jack said. "You need to understand that, August, or I can't stay here."

"I do understand it, after…" He half-turned in his chair. To see Bollard? "After it was explained to me in no uncertain terms."

"You were never going to stop looking for a cure for me, were you?" I asked.

He stared down at his empty plate, his hands flat on the table on either side of it.

"What made you think he would?" Jack asked, his voice low and ominous. "August?"

"I overheard him tell Samuel. Mr. Langley, you told him if he couldn't drive Jack and me apart, then you were going to tell me you were stopping your research."

Langley settled back in his chair and folded his hands over his stomach. "You overheard that, did you?"

"I don't believe it," Jack growled.

"I wasn't going to stop," Langley said. "It was a threat only. One I would never have followed through, I might add."

"That doesn't make it right!"

"Jack, it doesn't matter now," I said. "He did it to keep us apart, something he thought was in our best interests. It's what any good uncle would do. Or father."

"I'm not so sure about that," Jack said, gruff. He did not take his eyes off Langley, and Langley did not meet his gaze in return.

He stretched his neck and cleared his throat. "Enough of this. We've notes to write up, Bollard. Hannah, rest today. Tonight is Christmas Eve, and I believe Sylvia has a feast in store." He beckoned Bollard to wheel him away.

"I'll rest in the carriage," I said.

"Where are you going?" Sylvia asked.

"To Windamere. Jack and I have some things to discuss with Lord Wade, and I prefer to do it today. I want to enjoy my first Christmas at Frakingham, and I can't do that when there are still things to be resolved."

"Very well," said Langley. "Be sure to take blankets for warmth, and borrow Sylvia's fur coat."

I laughed. It seemed absurd to be worried about the cold, but I needed to get used to it. I would have to suffer through winters just like everybody else now.

"Is that it?" Sylvia asked her uncle as he was wheeled from the dining room. "You're not going to send me or Samuel to keep an eye on them?"

"Sylvia, my dear, I won't be stopping them from being together ever again, and I suggest you do the same. Besides, I rather think propriety no longer matters." His eyes twinkled at Jack. Above him, Bollard smiled, then he wheeled Langley out of the dining room.

***

It was bliss to be alone with Jack finally. He sat opposite me in the cabin of the coach, our knees inches apart. As soon as the Frakingham estate gates were behind us, I closed the curtains and patted the seat beside me.

He arched an eyebrow and didn't move. "I'm quite sure it would be inappropriate for me to get any closer to you," he said, a teasing smile on his lips.

"And I'm quite sure that I don't care about doing what's appropriate."

He leaned forward and placed his hands flat on the seat on either side of my hips. Trapping me. His natural heat infused me with warmth, his power sent a thrill down my spine.

"Hannah." My name was a hum on the air, full of desire and promises of what was to come. "My Hannah." A vein throbbed in his throat above his collar, and his lips twitched.

I placed my hands on his face and caressed the curve of his mouth with my thumbs, trying to capture his perfection.

He groaned low in his chest, a plaintive, aching growl of need.

I kissed him. It was slow and tender, full of our relief at being able to kiss and touch without fear. Perfect. So utterly perfect. I didn't think it possible to feel so much happiness. We took our time, exploring one another, relishing the sheer sweetness and joy, the beauty of simply being together.

But I needed to taste more of him. Needed to feel and hold him, have him. I pushed him back and sat on his lap. He groaned and folded me into his arms. I placed my hand to his chest. The hard muscles shuddered and twitched, and beneath them, his heart beat a steady rhythm.

"Jack," I murmured against his lips. "I want you. Take me."

He groaned again and pulled away, breaking the kiss entirely. "No."

I frowned. "Why not?"

He pressed his forehead to mine and heaved a sigh. "Because I'll not let your first time be in a coach."

"But—"

He pressed his finger to my lips. His other arm tightened around my waist. "God knows, I want you with every piece of me. I ache for you, Hannah. I want to claim you in every way possible. And I will. But not here. We're going to do it properly." He removed his finger and kissed me lightly. "Be patient, my sweet. We have time."

I pouted. "I'm not sure I want to wait."

He set me back on the other seat. "Believe me when I tell you it's not easy for me either. Being alone with you, kissing you and not taking you completely, is damn near torture. Best if you stay over there and just talk to me."

"Talk?" I folded my arms and gave him an innocent smile. "Let's see. I know. How about I tell you all the things I want you to do to me?"

His gaze turned smoldering, smoky. "You don't play fair."

I kept smiling.

"On the other hand," he said, "we could talk about all the places I'm going to show you."

I gasped. "We're going to travel?"

His eyes twinkled. "Would you like to?"

"Oh yes. Yes, please." Of course, I had to kiss him again to show him how much I liked the idea.

***

Windamere was exactly the same as when I'd left it, a perfect, symmetrical house set in a perfect, symmetrical garden. Not an arch or turret in sight. I looked up at the attic windows. The curtains were shut, something only ever done at night when I lived there.

A face appeared at one of the second floor windows, but quickly disappeared. Eudora, Vi's half-sister. I wondered if she recognized me.

Pearson the butler opened the door. He fell back and gasped when he saw me.

"Hello, Pearson," I said. "Have you been well?"

"I, er, I…"

"Is Lord Wade home?" Of course he would be. It was Christmas Eve, the one day of the year he was always sure to spend with his wife and child. Children. He was spending it with Vi now too.

"Hannah!" Violet called from the staircase. Eudora must have told her of our arrival. She ran down the stairs, laughing. "Hannah, it's so good to see you."

I smiled and accepted her kiss on my cheek. My feelings where Vi was concerned were still conflicted. We would never return to our easy friendship from the attic, but that was understandable. I'd changed, and she probably had too.

Her gaze slid to Jack and she curtsied. He bowed and asked after Lord Wade.

"Pearson, fetch him," Vi said to the butler. She had indeed changed. She never used to speak to him directly. The very thought would wreck her nerves.

"Is Miss Levine here?" I asked as we waited. "I'd so like to see her. I'm sure she'd want to see how I'm getting along too, don't you think?"

"Oh, believe me, she knows. Father made sure to tell her how well you turned out, right before he severed her employment."

"He did?"

She chewed her bottom lip, but it didn't stop her smile. "I feel rather wicked, considering who she is to me," she whispered. "But I can't help it. I'm glad she's gone."

Pearson returned and bowed again. "His lordship will meet you in the library, Miss Smith."

"You'll have to show me where that is," I said. "I'm afraid I haven't a clue."

We left Vi and followed Pearson up the stairs and into a room smelling of leather and cigar smoke. The walls were lined with books, and a desk commanded a spectacular view over the lawn. Lord Wade sat in one of the deep armchairs gathered around the fire. He indicated we should sit as Pearson backed out of the room and shut the door.

Once, sitting so close to an open fire would have been too hot for me, but not anymore. It didn't bother Jack at all. The heat had never affected him to the same extent it had me.

"I thought we'd said everything we had to say to one another," Wade said. "What is it you want?"

"Is that any way to speak to your ward?" Jack said idly.

"I wasn't speaking to her. I was speaking to you."

"In that case," I cut in, "it's certainly no way to speak to your only son."

Wade's jowls wobbled, his face paled. "Who else have you told?"

"No one," Jack said. "Your secret is safe. I want as little to do with you as you do with me."

"I never said that."

"You didn't have to. Your actions have spoken far louder than your words." Jack seemed remarkably calm, almost amused at Lord Wade's discomfort. But if one looked closely enough, one could see that he was holding himself very still, as if he were keeping tight rein on his temper.

"I reiterate," Wade said. "What is it you want?"

"Answers. We're not leaving until we get them."

Wade rubbed his forehead and sighed. "Very well. I'm ready to tell you what I know. I think it's what your mother would want." He pressed his finger and thumb into his eyes. "Her name was Hannah Smith. She was happy when she fell pregnant with you. She wanted to have you very much."

He paused, perhaps waiting for Jack to say something, but Jack was silent. He stared at his father, hardly even breathing. It was left to me to ask the questions.

"Tell us about her," I said. "Where did she come from?"

"From another realm." He lifted his heavy-lidded gaze to Jack's. "She was a demon."

Jack's nostrils flared. His chest rose and fell with a sudden deep breath. "Who summoned her?"

"That's the thing. She wasn't summoned. She was sent by the authorities to our realm. One of their kind came here to escape their justice system. He was a criminal, sentenced to death there. She arrived, weakened and hungry, and consumed a gypsy girl whose people had squatted nearby on the land neighboring the estate. She took on the girl's appearance, then came here to the house, begging for work and food." She told me her name was Hannah Smith, but I found out much later that she'd chosen it on a whim.

"That doesn't sound like demon behavior," I said. "By all accounts they're rather mindless and need controlling by their summoner."

"She wasn't summoned. She was sent. The two modes of arrival cause a difference in behavior. She'd been trained to survive here and knew what to expect. Indeed, it was her third visit to our realm. She knew our ways, our language. Her kind didn't want to inflict harm on us, in general, and it was their policy to eat what we eat, do what we do, in order to survive and blend in on the occasions they had to come here. Summoned demons, on the other hand, have no control over themselves and cannot make the same decisions."

"So you fed and housed her," I said. "That's commendable of you."

"I...took a liking to her. She was very beautiful."

"Did you know what she was?"

"Not a clue then. Not for months. We became lovers. She stayed here, convinced her quarry was in the vicinity, but..." He studied his fingers, clasped loosely in his lap.

"But?" Jack prompted.

"I suspect she wasn't interested in leaving. She liked it here. She liked me. When she told me she was carrying my child, I made plans to install her as my permanent mistress."

"How noble of you," Jack sneered.

"Don't be a fool," Wade snapped. "I couldn't marry her. She was nobody. To all the world, she was just a gypsy girl."

Jack turned away and stared into the flickering flames in the grate.

"It was only then that she told me what she was and why she was here," Wade went on. "I was…stunned. I thought her mad until she showed me what she was capable of. She could set things on fire like you." He nodded at Jack. "She was fast and strong too. Not at all normal. I had no choice but to believe the evidence and accept her for what she was."

"Mr. Langley said she died giving birth to Jack," I said.

"She died of child-bed fever. She was still exhausted after the birth, and it took her swiftly." He cleared his throat and looked away, but not before I saw the sad twist of his mouth, the rapid blinking. This man, who cared for few people, had cared for Jack's mother.

I sighed and as the breath left my body, so did any lingering anger I felt toward Wade. He was a flawed man, but he wasn't bad. Blaming him for my time in the attic got me nothing except a heavy heart, and I wanted to start my new life light and free. My new life without fire, and with Jack.

"I own a knife," Jack said. "It was apparently given to me by my parents when I was a baby. Is it hers?"

Wade nodded. "She wanted you to have it. It was the only thing she brought from her realm. The only thing that was truly hers."

A blade forged in the Otherworld. It was only a small thing, but lethal to her kind. Jack's mother had saved us.

"What happened to the demon she was supposed to be chasing?" I asked.

"I assume another of her kind was sent to capture it and return it. Otherwise, we would have heard of it in the newspapers. That sort of creature can't go about unnoticed for long."

It did seem the most likely scenario. He was right in that a demon would attract attention, even if it were able to blend in for a while.

Wade's fidgeting grew faster, and he didn't meet Jack's or my gaze. He took great interest in the fire crackling in the grate. "Mr. Langley…I cannot give you my name."

The declaration seemed to take Jack by surprise. "I neither want it nor need it. The Langley name is good enough for me. Indeed, I don't want anything from you, sir."

Wade looked up sharply. "Not even money?"

Jack laughed. "No."

Wade's jowls wobbled as he grumbled, searching for words. "I'm sorry I couldn't have been a proper father to you. I would have liked a son. But circumstances didn't allow it, and now...now I have a full family. Besides, you're a grown man. You don't need me. You understand, don't you?"

Jack leaned forward. "Sir...I have never considered you my father, nor will I. I have no interest in being part of your family either. You can rest easy on that score."

"Well then, we have nothing more to say to one another."

It was such an odd way to end their conversation, yet I wasn't sure what I'd expected. Too much time had passed for Wade to accept Jack as his son, and I suspect Jack was telling the truth. He simply didn't care.

"Thank you for your honesty, my lord," I said. "We have to leave now. There's a family feast tonight at Frakingham, and we don't want to be late."

Was it just my imagination, or did he flinch when I said 'family'?

Jack took my hand. "Hannah, I want to speak to Lord Wade alone for moment."

"Oh. Of course." What did he want to say to him that I couldn't hear? I admit to being put out, and I would certainly tell him so when we were alone in the coach.

"Wait, Hannah," Lord Wade called after me as I walked off. He hefted himself out of his chair and came up to me. "I'm pleased to see you looking well."

"I am. I no longer have any fire in me."

"That's good news."

I smiled. "Yes. I'm finally normal."

His jaw tightened. He leaned forward and took my hands in his big ones. "You'll always be special to me." And then he did the most remarkable thing. He kissed my forehead. When he drew back, his eyes were damp. "Goodbye, Hannah. I wish you well."

I left him alone with Jack and shut the door to the library. I stood there for some time, thinking about Wade and my life in his attic, about the first Hannah Smith, and Jack. How different our lives may have been if she'd lived. Or if she'd never been sent here at all.

It was silly to think of what-ifs. I shook off the thoughts and made my way back to the top of the stairs. I stopped when I heard feminine voices coming from a room across the landing. I peeped inside and saw Violet, Eudora and Lady Wade sitting in the drawing room, surrounded by hats and ribbons. It was a contented, domestic scene, one that I knew would have made Vi happy. Her life was so different now too.

"Hannah!" She set aside the hat she'd been redecorating. "Come in."

I shook my head. I didn't want to endure polite conversation with Lady Wade and her daughter. What on earth would I say to them? "Jack won't be long and we have to be going."

"Oh. I see." Vi stood, but did not come to me in the doorway. Lady Wade and Eudora stood too. They held hands and kept a little apart from Vi, excluding her. Vi pretended not to notice, but I saw the downturn of her mouth, the slight wobble of her chin. She wasn't a part of their family, no matter what Lord Wade said or how it had appeared at first. She might never be. Poor, sweet Vi. She deserved better.

I ran to her and hugged her. "My dear friend," I whispered in her ear. "I miss you."

She held me fiercely, her slender body shaking as she cried. We stayed like that for a few minutes until Jack appeared at the door. He'd not made a sound, but I knew he was there as surely as I knew that I was sorry for Vi.

"I forgot to tell you," I said, drawing away from her. "I'm cured."

She smiled, but Lady Wade gasped. I watched her over Vi's shoulder, and she quickly looked away, holding Eudora close as if I might harm her.

"I'm so happy for you," Vi said, wiping her cheeks. "So terribly pleased. Your life has changed remarkably since you left here." She peeked at Jack from beneath her damp lashes and colored. "You're very lucky."

"I know." I squeezed her hands. "I'll write to you."

"You must," she said, smiling sadly. "And be sure to visit too."

Lady Wade cleared her throat, perhaps annoyed at being excluded from the arrangements made for visits to *her* house.

"Perhaps you should visit me instead," I said to Vi.

We said our final farewells at the front door. Jack helped me into the carriage then settled beside me. I waved at Vi through the window until she was no more than a speck on the steps.

"Well?" I asked Jack. "What did you need to talk to Lord Wade about?" I stifled a yawn and arched my brows at him.

He arched his own right back at me. "I'll tell you later. You need to rest now." He moved to sit beside me and wrapped the blanket tighter around me. "Come here and close your eyes."

I rested against his warm body and tucked my head beneath his chin. The steady thump of his heartbeat and the gentle rocking of the coach soon sent me into a peaceful, contented sleep.

EPILOGUE

I didn't wake up until we reached Frakingham. Jack still held me in his arms, and gently woke me as the horses slowed to a stop.

"We're home," he murmured.

Home. Yes. Frakingham was my home. The house loomed ahead, a majestic building with unnecessary turrets and crenellations, an abundance of arches and no two pitched roofs exactly the same. It wasn't symmetrical and it certainly wasn't ordinary, but it had a beauty all its own. It was where I belonged.

Tommy greeted us and opened the coach door. He bowed to me. "Safe journey?"

"Yes, thank you, Tommy." Then, just because I felt like it, I pecked his cheek.

Jack cleared his throat. "Tommy, inform the others we'll be inside in a moment. Hannah and I are going for a short walk."

"We are?" I said as Tommy walked off and the coach drove around to the stables.

He placed my hand on his arm and we walked together across the lawn.

It had been a sunny afternoon, although the shadows grew long and the air crisp. We walked past the lake where we'd spent so many hours touching and kissing, dousing the heat within us. Its surface shimmered in the waning light and the first mists had already settled in the middle.

We reached the abbey and Jack laid his jacket over a low, ruined wall. "Sit," he ordered.

I did and shivered, despite my resolve not to let him see that I was cold. He sat beside me and angled me so that I was sitting with my back to him, his arms around me. His heat soaked through all the layers of fabric between us, and I sighed with pure pleasure.

"Better?" he murmured.

"Mmmm. Much."

We sat like that, watching the sun dip behind the ruins together. It sank quickly until it gave a final gasp and shot rays through a jagged arch like a beacon. But they too slipped away and dusk rolled in, turning everything shades of bronze. The old stones seemed to sigh, weary of the day and content to give themselves over to the evening.

"There's something magical about this place," I whispered. I didn't want to speak any louder and disturb the peace.

"That's why I wanted to bring you here."

"What do you mean?"

He reached into the pocket of his jacket and handed me a small velvet box.

"Oh, Jack. I haven't got you a present yet. There hasn't been time." Nor did I have any money of my own. I would have to borrow some from Sylvia. I wanted to get Jack something special.

"It's not a Christmas present," he said. "Go on. Open it."

I lifted the lid. My fingers shook so much that I almost couldn't manage it. Inside sat a ring set with a sapphire and surrounded by diamonds. I gasped. "Jack, it's so beautiful. But you shouldn't have. The necklace and earrings were more than enough."

He took the ring from the bed of velvet and took my hand. "You have to wear a ring," he said. "That way everybody knows you're going to marry me."

The breath left my body. I stared at him and he grinned back. "Is that a proposal?"

"No. This is." He got down on one knee and held both my hands in his. "Hannah Smith, will you do me the honor of marrying me?"

I threw my arms around his neck and kissed him hard on the lips. When we came up for air, I said, "Yes."

He kissed me again, more tender this time, until I drew away to stare at my beautiful ring. I could feel him watching me, his gaze hot and intense. I would never grow tired of the way he looked at me.

"We ought to go inside," he said after a moment. "We should tell them our news."

"Soon. I want to be alone with you a little longer."

He grinned and kissed me again.

"Is that why you spoke to Lord Wade alone?"

He nodded. "He's still your guardian. I needed his permission."

"I take it he gave it."

"Yes, albeit reluctantly. Hannah," he started then stopped.

I touched his lips. "What is it, Jack? What's wrong?"

"By marrying me, you're not taking on a normal husband. I'm a half-demon."

"I don't want normal. I want you." I traced his lips with my thumb. "And you're not half-anything."

"If my mother was a demon, then that makes me half of one. There's no dressing it up in pretty clothes and calling it something else."

"By that reasoning, you're also half a pompous, selfish toad."

He laughed. "Your point?"

"What I'm trying to say is that you are what you are. You're not half of one parent, and half of the other. Yes, you have some of their characteristics, but they're put together in a way that is unique to you. I love you just the way you are."

"And I love you, Hannah Smith." He traced his finger down my cheek to my chin then let it fall to my waist. "With all my heart and soul."

He kissed me thoroughly, possessively, greedily until I was weightless and, believe it or not, hot. I burned for him, but not in the way I had when the fire boiled inside me. It was all from the pent-up desire and need.

And from love.

LOOK OUT FOR

The 2nd Freak House Trilogy

Samuel Gladstone gets his own story in the 2nd Freak House Trilogy.

To be notified when C.J. has a new release, sign up to her newsletter. Send an email to cjarcher.writes@gmail.com

ABOUT THE AUTHOR

C.J. Archer has loved history and books for as long as she can remember. She worked as a librarian and technical writer until she was able to channel her twin loves by writing historical fiction. She has won and placed in numerous romance writing contests, including taking home RWAustralia's Emerald Award in 2008 for the manuscript that would become her novel *Honor Bound*. Under the name Carolyn Scott, she has published contemporary romantic mysteries, including *Finders Keepers Losers Die*, and *The Diamond Affair*. After spending her childhood surrounded by the dramatic beauty of outback Queensland, she lives today in suburban Melbourne, Australia, with her husband and their two children.

She loves to hear from readers. You can contact her in one of these ways:
Website: www.cjarcher.com
Email: cjarcher.writes@gmail.com
Facebook: www.facebook.com/CJArcherAuthorPage